A TALE ᴏꜰ NINE LANDS

J. K. F. SANDHAM

ELDERWORLD

Published by Elderworld Studios

www.elderworld.io

For more information, contact: books@elderworld.io

First paperback edition March 2024

Book cover by Ashley Crossland
Map of Nine Lands by Joshua Jay Christie

ISBN 978-1-7385387-0-6

Published by Elderworld Studios
books@elderworld.io

www.elderworld.io

For Boncott. I hope you're reading this from the aether.

P.S. I stole your initials and added them to my pen name.

The Nine Lands

The Silent Desert

The forest of Darpirich

Urwald

Palace of Ul Nirin

Palace of Ter Noris

Palace of Izmoran

Barrier

Blackhill

Lord Sully's Manor

Stone Circle

Midvale Castle

Unknown

Palace of Okuden

Mindwatcher Tower

City of Eliniar

City of Garaduk

Barrier

Garaduk Eastport

Giant Stone Circle

Eastport Crabdockside

The Greeneye

The Nine Lands

The Silent Desert

URWALD

UL NIRIN

TER NORIS

The Forest of Daapiaich

AVENIA

IZMORAN

ELINIAR

OKUDEN

Barrier

GARADUK

CRADDOCK

CHAPTER 1

THEO

The giant cracked the massive whip and it roared harsher than thunder. Human and dwarven slaves scurried to clear the ground and build the wedding site faster. What was often a beautiful and tranquil lake in the woods was a site of chaos, transformation, and exhaustion: the felling of perfectly good trees and the massacre of healthy undergrowth, dozens of slaves at the brink of collapse. The calm lake reflected the grey and pink sky and the thick green trees surrounding it.

Theodore eyed the blunt, rusting scythe he held and imagined jamming it into the taskmaster's leg and running.

Crack! The monstrous whip so close to his ears they hurt, ringing. He hacked at the greenery, breaking and slicing it low—attacking, hack hack hack at the thick stalks—with satisfaction in watching them fall. He was so fed up and exhausted and angry and hacking was the only place his anger could go.

Piles of undergrowth and trees scattered the area and were being collected and removed. As the greenery was removed, the ethereal glow vibrant with luminescence, butterflies, bugs, and birds, and all manner of wonderful nature also left. An eerie, quiet glumness remained. Theo wondered if others noticed it.

The taskmaster, Kirakai, roared, "Get on with it you damned slime, it will be dark soon. This is going to be the finest wedding in history. You rats could never understand, so do as you're told and do it faster."

We could hack him to death. He couldn't stop us all. Blunt tools or not. Theo imagined all the servants swarming the giant, jumping on him and hacking and grabbing and dragging him down and hacking some more. Every scenario he imagined ended up with humans and dwarves eventually being thrown about and broken like twigs. He couldn't understand why he couldn't imagine a victory. Even his imagination was weak. He hated that.

"Theo, you're asking for the whip. Stop daydreaming," Pika said. He was strong, as most dwarves were, and he broke the undergrowth with ease. Theo was human, and he wished he had the strength of a dwarf. "Whatever you're thinking, forget it and work."

He's right, Theo thought. *I need to stop thinking like that.* All his life he had been told to stop thinking like that. The mindwatchers might hear his thoughts, and even if they didn't, thoughts like that were a waste because they never led to anything. The thoughts kept coming back though, no matter how useless or dangerous they were.

Theo continued hacking beside Pika, while Tico collected and disposed of the waste left in their wake. The air smelt earthy and fresh, and Theo tasted a drop of stale salty sweatiness as he licked his lips involuntarily. He was desperately thirsty. His muscles ached. *What's the point in thinking like that when I never do anything? I'm a coward, and I always will be.*

The setting sun reddened as it sank behind the trees beyond the lake, and everything softened. The lake rippled gently, refreshingly, and Theo yearned for cold, fresh water. His clothes were thick with dirt and sweat.

"Better get some lanterns out here and forget your evening slop," Kirakai said. The whip thundered once more, so loud everyone ducked.

"Great. More work. No food," someone moaned.

It had been like that ever since the wedding had been announced. The grounds were being razed so that they could plant seeds and regrow the site to suit a wedding, with colourful flowers and rich shrubbery.

Everything else was also already in full flow. They would

accommodate many important guests from all of the Nine Lands, including royalty. They had been clearing and laying paths, running errands to the city, constructing arches and platforms, fashioning canopies, building the altar, adjusting seating heights for witches, rearranging stores, polishing furniture, preparing food, crafting, crafting, and more crafting. Everyone was at the brink.

The thought of Toarer getting married and living elsewhere with that demon of a wife made Theo feel heavy with fear and defeat. The fear squeezed his insides, slowly, firmly. That squeezing of his stomach reminded him of how starved he was. He wondered whether Toarer would sneak some food into the servants' quarters that night. The thought of food, real food, made his dry mouth attempt to salivate, but it just ended up in a thick, messy movement of his tongue against his mouth.

The whip cracked and Avira shrieked. Blood dripped from her arm.

Theo fought hard to stop himself shouting at Kirakai. It would only make things worse. *You never do anything,* he told himself, as he watched Avira weep and force herself to continue working. He felt as much hate for himself as he did the giants and witches that enslaved them all.

CRACK! Avira shrieked and curled her back awkwardly.

"You, Blondie," Kirakai said. "Do your damned work."

Theo was known as Blondie to Kirakai. He had unusual platinum blonde hair and pale skin. Terror and disgust flooded over him. Anger. No. Rage. He hacked and hacked. "I'm sorry," he said to Avira. She was trying not to cry.

Kirakai knew the best way to get to Theo. The taskmaster's perverse and savage attraction to Avira plagued Theo more than anything else. She was only fifteen. It disgusted him. It ate at him in his sleep and made his blood boil like a rancid infection. It made him want to kill everything in sight, including himself. Yet he was too much of a coward to do that. Too much of a coward to do anything.

He hacked and hacked, tearing everything green down, roared

and hacked and screamed trying to fend off a wild insanity that crept over him, and he hacked and hacked, and his head went weird and everything went blurry.

"Theo?" Concerned, muffled voices.

The giant laughed, "Worked himself into another fit. Hah." His words sounded as if they came from a distance.

Everything was black and relaxed. A woman sang words and sounds he didn't understand. Pleasant sounds. Harmonic, tranquil, powerful. An orange light swirled with the rhythm of the words. Theo wanted to remain there forever.

∽∾∽

He woke to darkness and the sounds of servants stirring in their sleep. He was on the floor on a thin mat. A thin mat and blanket were all the servants had for bedding. The hard wood beneath the mat pressed into his side.

Avira was close to him. She must have sensed him stirring for she opened her eyes and whispered, "You had one of those fits and then you wouldn't wake. I was worried."

"I'm fine," he said, remembering the orange glow and the woman singing in his dream. He wished he could remember or understand what she had said. It seemed significant, but he couldn't grasp much more than that.

"Shh," someone hissed. It was frowned upon to talk after lights out.

He turned onto his back and relaxed. Avira put her hand on his arm, and he found himself smiling and relaxing even more.

Sometime later, almost inaudibly, the door crept open and closed again. Pika tiptoed to his mat and lay down. *What's he doing?* Theo thought. *If he gets caught out and about at night, we'll all get the whip. What's worth that risk? I'll have to confront him tomorrow. Pika wouldn't do anything like that without good reason though.* Pika was the smartest dwarf Theo knew. *Smarter than all the humans, dwarves, witches, and giants, despite witches and giants saying humans and dwarves could never be as smart as them. Maybe I should leave him to it. I wouldn't have confronted him anyway.* Theo felt an anxious knot in his stomach. *I never confront anyone.*

"Food." Avira's voice. Her hand on his shoulder, waking him gently. The sounds of wooden spoons scraping wooden bowls, everyone desperately trying to get more food out of their portion. The smell of slop. Servants scurrying into action. Groans of exhaustion.

Avira came back from housemistress Mildred and the gigantic slop pot with two bowls and handed one to Theo. She moved awkwardly, the lashes evidently still causing her pain. Theo felt terrible.

"Mistress said we'd better hurry, Toarer's summoned us," Avira said, hiding a smile.

The slop was made from the giants' leftovers, which was much better than plain crop slop, so Theo was grateful, yet it was thick and fatty and barely warm. A horrible, heavy, sloppy texture. Theo really hoped Toarer had a treat for them. He often did. They finished their meagre portion quickly, rinsed their hands in the washbowl that was already mucky, and joined the queue of servants waiting their turn at the single hatch entrance to the servants' quarters.

They climbed through the hatch and down the ladder that led to the servants' entrance to the top-floor hallway. At the foot of the ladder, rough wooden flooring and a door. Through the door, the top-floor hallway. It wasn't the grandest floor of the manor because it was seldom used. Old and dusty, elaborately framed landscape paintings decorated the walls.

Avira led the way and Theo noticed black and blue and yellow bruising at the bottom of her skinny neck where it met her shoulder, mostly hidden by her clothes.

"Avira," he said.

"Yes?"

His heart beat hard and flooded him with anxiety and shame. "Nothing," he said. *She wouldn't want to talk about it with me anyway.*

They descended a flight of stairs to the second floor, which, along with the first and ground floors, oozed excessive grandeur. Toarer had deliberately chosen a room that offered distance from the rest of his family, whilst avoiding the dilapidated third floor so as not to cause offence. The second floor halls were lined with intricate wall carvings, tapestries, and ornaments. The floor was soft-pink marble veined with subtle black swirls.

Toarer's room was enormous like all the other giants' rooms, yet much simpler. He had a big, comfortable bed and valuable paintings on the walls, but the elaborateness ended there. No ornaments, no jewels, no exotic rugs. There were many books scattered around the room, half read, half waiting to be read. There was a tray of uneaten breakfast and juice on a table. It smelt delicious. Meaty, buttery, fruity. Theo's mouth watered.

"Come on, sit," Toarer said, once he had closed the door. They climbed onto his giant bed and lay back. Theo took a deep breath and sighed. It felt like he was floating on clouds. He yearned to sleep on a bed like that for one night, to recover.

"Don't marry her," Avira said, taking the words out of Theo's mouth. She wrapped a bit of the silky, puffy cover over herself.

"If I could get out of it..." Toarer said. "I have a duty to my family and the Land, and she's the minister's daughter..."

"She's wretched," Avira said.

"It's a good job you don't have to marry her then, isn't it?" Toarer laughed. "Make sure you are careful with what you say and think beyond these walls though, the watchers might catch you."

Theo felt a pang of guilt. He had been indulging in his thoughts too much beyond the manor. The manor had protection from the mindwatchers, but outside of the manor, he was vulnerable. He imagined hacking Kirakai with his scythe again, remembering many of the indulgent and defiant fantasies he often had around Kirakai. *Even the mindwatchers don't believe in me,* he thought.

"Looks like the wedding stress has taken away my appetite," Toarer said, putting the beautifully carved and gilded tray of food on the bed. "I couldn't even eat my breakfast," he grinned.

A sausage had been half eaten but the rest was untouched. Sausages, bread, juicy fruits, jam, butter, orange juice. It all smelt and looked too good to be true.

"Go on," he said, pushing the tray closer to them.

Theo waited for Avira, and as soon as she grabbed a piece of fruit, he dived in. It was indescribably good, and they ate until they might burst. Toarer watched them affectionately, letting them eat in peace.

"Life's going to be unbearable when you go," Avira said.

Theo couldn't bear to think about it.

"I will be here as much as I can. It will always be my family house. I will not abandon you."

"Do you have anything to do with Pika's disappearances at night?" Avira said, picking at a piece of bread with rich purple jam on it. They were full now, but it was hard to leave such delicious food uneaten.

Toarer grinned mischievously. His big face was endearing. "I have not mentioned it because I don't want to get anyone's hopes up." He appeared to deliberate for a bit. "We are close now, though, and I know I can trust you both."

Theo perked up with curiosity, but he felt worried because he couldn't control his thoughts. He didn't want to get caught by the mindwatchers.

"Pika has been working on something with me. For a long time, I just knew things didn't add up. When I got access to the ministry's restricted literature, all my suspicions started unravelling. We have been researching and exploring an alternative history, and we have found some scriptures that could change everything. The only problem is that there are parts missing, we haven't patched it all together yet."

"What do you mean, change everything? An alternative history to what?" Avira said.

"Everything. The whole lore of the Nine Lands, for witches, giants, dwarves, and humans. We have got a lead, a quest that can prove our suspicions. So, we are going to visit the royalty of Okuden, and make a discrete detour."

It was so much to take in that Theo almost blanked. "What?" he said.

"Everything? Everything!" Avira was excited. "You have to tell us everything then."

"I can't until I am sure. It would be dangerous for you to know, anyway. The mindwatchers might find your thoughts."

"Ugh, Toarer, this is going to torment me. Please, tell us."

"No. It's for your own good. When I return, when the time is right, that's when you will be told."

"Take us with you, please," Avira said. "I would love to change history."

No way. This is treason. It's got a death sentence written all over it, Theo thought. He didn't want to seem a coward in front of Avira, so he kept his mouth shut.

"You know I would if I could, but it would raise too many suspicions to take all three of you. We will be back as soon as we can." The giant grinned a warm and comforting grin, with just a little cheekiness seeping through his lips. "Don't you worry, you will get your chance to change history with me if we have the luck that I think we will."

Is that supposed to be a good thing? Theo thought. He worried intensely. It was so much to take in.

The work bell rang and Kirakai's voice raged through the manor. "To work, vermin. To work. Get that wedding ready like your life depends on it." He chuckled with a deep, dumb voice. "It does depend on it."

Theo's heart sank as he slipped off the bed onto the floor.

"Tell us," Avira said. The bells rang louder, and the servants could be heard springing into action.

"I need more time," Toarer said. "You don't want to be late. You know what the taskmaster is like." Toarer was right. Lateness meant lashes.

CHAPTER 2

EXILUK

Exiluk and Captain Greavis stood on the forecastle deck of the Greeneye. The figurehead of gold serpents with green eyes led the way.

"That's the land where giants and witches rule," Captain Greavis said. He looked towards a faint outline of black cliffs and a sky wisped with clouds. White-whipped patches of brown dotted the choppy surface of the vast navy blue and grey ocean surrounding them. The captain was tall for a goblin. The top of his head almost reached the height of Exiluk's cheeks. He was lanky and lean, though his muscles appeared dense through his yellowish-brown, tough, leathery skin.

"What do you know of it?" Exiluk said, gently running his finger along one of his thick, ribbed horns. His hairy, blue-skinned and stocky body felt vigorous as he looked towards the cliffs.

"They say there're riches and resources beyond a goblin's dreams in that land, but the giants would tear us apart before they'd share it, and the witches'd turn us to toads. I'd rather trade goblin steel with the Disians, and so I do," Greavis said. "They've got lavish palaces and grand cities built by human and dwarven slaves. They don't like strangers. It's said to be a cruel, old land, and I'm glad they keep themselves to themselves."

Exiluk stared at the cliffs, imagining a giant standing in a palace of gold that reached into the clouds. He ran his finger from the top of his head, around his ear, to a sharp point behind him, the ribbed ridges creating a sensual rhythm between finger and horn. The sharpness of the point satisfied his fingertip as he pressed it. As he revelled in the satisfaction he also cringed at the thought of his other horn, mangled at the end. He curtailed the thought so he didn't have to relive it in his mind. "I have heard that to the west of that land is a barrier cast by witches. My village, Si'hantikup, is in the swamps that line the northwest of the forest beyond that land. It is a forest so vast and mysterious that rarely will a creature cross it."

The goblin captain nodded. "Ten years you said you've travelled, what does it feel to be almost home after so long?"

A yearning for more panged inside of Exiluk. The thought of home agitated him. He was no longer keradin, no longer a lifelong student of the mind. His abilities to see into other minds had diminished to the basic instincts he had as a child. His daily practices had almost all reduced to nothing. His hunger for the material world had grown beyond recognition. And he felt good; the hunger was infused with intense excitement. "I feel," he paused, "conflicted."

The goblin captain peered through his looking glass at the land where giants and witches rule. "If I heard of goblin slaves in some cruel land, I wouldn't sleep so well. I don't know how the free ones can." He shook his head. "If we don't look after our own kind, what will we look after?"

"You don't see many dwarves around, not enough to take down a land as powerful as you say that one is. Humans, though, I wonder why they do nothing. Yet in other lands, humans also take humans as slaves. What a strange creature!" As Exiluk spoke, he felt a deep urge to visit the land of witches and giants. He had to see it for himself, the power of giants, the magic of cruel witches. *What a place it must be.* "Keradins practise the philosophy that everything is connected on different planes and when we harm one thing, it harms us too, in one way or another."

"It's a nice philosophy, but I wouldn't want to live my life in perpetual fear of my actions," the goblin captain said.

"Yet there is enormous power to be had in accepting the fact.

There is an indescribable satisfaction in living the way of the keradin, a serenity, a peace, a depth of mind and awareness that only rigorous practice can unlock. Yet the way of the world outside of our swamps is more..." he paused. "It is difficult to describe." He looked around the ship. "It is more exciting. More addictive. More intense. I feel... opportunity."

A rogue swell rolled underneath them, lifting and jerking the ship. The goblin crew whispered to each other and gave Exiluk worried looks, their unease growing palpable. They had been sailing together for many days and yet they couldn't let go of their superstitions. Taking a horned being they had never seen before on their ship would bring them bad fortune.

"I understand you. It's that sense that made me the most respected steel trader in the world. In your swamps, the keradin may have their peace and serenity, and it may be nice, but they'll never know the feeling of being world-renowned."

Old wisdom battled with Exiluk's new mind. He knew that something in what they were saying was wrong, but he couldn't quite grasp it or put it into words. Ten years of travel had changed him many times over. The feeling of being world-renowned tingled inside of him. "When we left Anhera, I was ready to go home. I thought my adventure was over. Yet now I know, I must visit the land where giants and witches rule."

Captain Greavis laughed. "Those treasures've called me too, yet we've always got temptations, don't we, keradin?"

"My kind spends all our lives learning to master the mind. We learn how to tell the difference between temptation and intuition, and we learn to catch on to that path that drives us towards our fate. I think I can tell the difference, goblin. This will be a fitting end to my adventure," Exiluk hissed. Something inside of him knew he was lying. He wasn't sure if he could tell the difference anymore. So subtle were the strands of the fabric of the universe.

"We can't dock in their ports without the right permissions and that coastline's too treacherous. See that over there?" Captain Greavis pointed to a patch of grey haze on the horizon that Exiluk could barely see. "That means a storm's coming. You can already feel the wind's about to pick up. We'll not get close enough to shore for you to row in before the storm hits, and I can't wait it out. I've got three days to get to Portwood and deliver this steel or my contract's void. No, keradin, I'm afraid this is not your destiny. We must continue full sail."

The ship rose and fell upon another rogue swell. "Must I swim?"

The goblin laughed. "If you wish to die."

"Destiny does not fear death," Exiluk said. He felt compelled by the thought of one last adventure before settling in the swamps again. He remembered he had once seen the swamps as brilliant and full of life and energy. Now, he pictured mediocrity and glum brown sludge. "I have treasures from my travels worth more than this ship and its cargo."

The goblin looked at the incoming storm, looked at the land, and at Exiluk. "No treasure's worth my reputation, keradin." He looked towards the storm again and pondered. "You know, us goblins love a good gamble. You've got to take risks in life. How about this, then?" He grinned. "The ultimate bet, a bet of destiny." He grinned and laughed, revealing sharp teeth and yellowish saliva. "We'll sail closer to the shore and I'll give you a boat. If we beat the storm, you might just crash that boat into the reefs and survive, if you're lucky. That swell looks like it'd take the best of seacraft to manage. If the storm beats us, well, I wouldn't fancy anyone's chances."

Another swell rolled under the ship, rocking it violently from side to side. The wood creaked and yawned, settling as the swell moved on. The wind picked up and a gust howled through the ship's sails. Dense, low and sodden clouds surged towards them, swallowing the blue sky in their path.

"The wager?" Exiluk said.

"I'm not interested in what you've got now, I'm interested in our destiny. When we meet again, I'll be entitled to one thing you've acquired, no matter what it is, and no matter its value to you."

"What if I have nothing?"

"What if you've got the whole world?" the goblin laughed.

"Fine, we will roll the dice of fate."

The goblin's big, black pupils grew bigger, and he bellowed laughter. Rain began to fall gently and Exiluk noticed the sky above had thickened and was becoming darker, fast. In the distance, lightning flashed. "Change her course ten degrees starboard," the goblin shouted. "We're dropping our guest off early."

The goblins darted around the ship with impressive agility and strength, eager to finally get rid of the horned being.

"A storm's a sea goblin's greatest enemy and we're about to toy with one in a dance of destiny, all for a keradin stranger. What a tale this'll be. I hope you can row, keradin, 'coz the waves'll swallow you whole and chew you up on the reefs."

The wind caught the sails and the ship picked up speed towards the land. The ship lifted and rocked upon the swells, the wood groaning as it flexed. The rain gathered in Exiluk's hair and beard and soaked his robe, and he couldn't take his eyes off the land ahead.

Close to the shore, waves rolled, lifted, and crashed against the rock. Exiluk couldn't tell how big the waves truly were. They seemed monstrous. Yet, they coaxed him, lured him. *This way*, they said. *To destiny*. There was only a small alcove of sand between sharp, jagged rocks and a cliff face that loomed perilously.

"Your rower's ready," Greavis called from the deck. "You'd best go now before the storm gets any worse. We need to get out of here."

A small rowing boat hung from a frame. It swung from side to side, pushed by the wind and the rocking of the ship. A vivid flash of light ripped the sky. A pause. Explosive thunder. The clouds burst.

The boat lowered to the side of the ship and Exiluk climbed in as it rocked. His bag was packed and in the boat already.

"Good luck, keradin," the goblin captain winked, and the boat lowered quickly towards the sea. "I'll be seeing you for my half of the bargain," he shouted, laughing so loud it overpowered the sounds of the storm. "Faster," the goblin shouted.

The boat dropped as if it was in freefall. It hit the side of the ship and jerked and lowered again. There was no fear in Exiluk. Only determination. *Get to the land where giants and witches rule.*

Water met wood and Exiluk's boat rocked in the turbulence as he detached the ropes that lowered him in. He grabbed the oars and began rowing towards the land. The goblin captain shouted something, but the storm drowned his words.

The swells jerked the boat about mercilessly. The closer to land he got the more violent they became, until waves surrounded him and crashed into him and tossed him, and he felt exhilaration as they slung him towards the shore. The ocean was the true master of his destiny. The storm scorned Exiluk's efforts at rowing but the currents were in his favour. "Give me all you've got," he roared, and laughed hysterically. Thunder exploded and rain bombarded down. Icy water flooded the boat, and he soared upwards as a swell lifted him higher than a watch tower. He laughed like a madman dancing with death as the wave dropped him into freefall. The boat flipped. He soared into the water. The cold bit him hard as the ocean swallowed him, gripping him, turning him, dragging him. Rock. Thud. More dragging.

He held his breath. Calm and determined. Not fearful. He surfaced and gasped for air. Another wave landed on top of him and slammed him into rock.

He woke on a bed of wet, slimy rock, the storm relentlessly battering him with rain. He was cold and had no idea how long he had been there. No sight of his pack or the boat. He was drenched and his muscles were stiff. The wind gusted, dragging stinging sand with it. He wiped his face and bolted towards shelter in the cliffs. Wind howled like an angry ghoul as it wrapped into the entrance of a cave. Patches of crystals glimmered on the cave walls.

He sat on a rock and took a deep breath. His pack was lost. All the trinkets from his travels gone. Panic. Rushed his hand into his pocket and felt for the three items he kept with him always. The black gold coin, still there. Relief. The aerie jewel, still there. More relief. The golden dragon's tooth, also there, and he breathed a deep sigh of relief and relaxed.

He removed his robe and spun it tight, wringing as much water from it as he could. He was cold, but not as cold as he could be. He was fortunate that his body retained heat much better than many other beings he had encountered. He wrapped his robe back around himself, huddled in between some rocks, and lay on his back. Damp, but warming up. Tired, and becoming more comfortable. Drifting off, happily, satisfied. The semi-sleep state made him aware of passing thoughts and dreams, and a slight, niggling guilt.

As he had travelled, his ego had grown. He had learnt what it was to feel important, selfish, and powerful. That was not the keradin way. He didn't mind too much, that guilt was a remnant of his old self, and it was becoming easier and easier to push away. The thought of an exciting future overpowered the guilt of becoming egotistical, and he could recognise his ego, which meant he was not that bad. Only creatures with big egos, and those who were blind to their egos, were dangerous. He smiled at that thought, that he wasn't that bad, or that lost, and he drifted into a mesh of dreams.

Metal plunging into flesh. Life leaving body. Exiluk snapped awake, heaving and sweating, his mind full of the nightmare. He tried to block it out, but it was hard to remove the image from his mind. The gasping, the helplessness. Once the blade had bound with her body, her soul had been helpless. And that helplessness haunted him.

He focused on the sounds of the water. He pictured the waves crashing outside. The moonlight. Anything but the blood. Just the waves. The coaxing, relaxing waves. He drifted back into the dream state. This time his dreams were calmer, more pleasant.

Exiluk woke to the sound of water licking the rocks in the cave. The high tide must have engulfed the beach. Alert, he rolled his robe up around his waist and walked outside. It was light, and the storm had passed. The sky was white and grey with clouds, and the sea a dark grey. Whitish brown patches formed where the waves broke on the shore and upheaved sand and rock with their force. The air was crisp and fresh. He smiled.

A large wave broke in the distance, surged up the beach until it lost all speed and power, and gently wrapped around his ankles and into the cave. It pulled back, gathering speed as it flowed into the ocean again. Another wave surged up the beach, this time, just as it pulled back, he left the cave and followed the edge of the cliff, found a path that had been shaped by water erosion, and made his way to the top.

From the vantage point of the cliffs, he searched the beach for his boat. He didn't expect to find it, as it had likely been swept away with the storm and his belongings with it. That didn't matter. He had his three precious trinkets and his damp robe. Steam came from his mouth as he breathed, and from his robe because of his body heat.

He headed for what looked like a settlement of tents or huts in the distance. He could just about make out the flickering of a fire, and two figures. Giants, he hoped. It was hard to tell with the distance.

The cliff tops were covered in soft, greenish-grey grass, stiff with frost, leaving clear footprints as Exiluk headed towards the settlement. The land was mostly flat, forming large open plains that led, far in the distance, to wild, black and deeply fissured snow-capped mountains that climbed majestically into the clouds. The air was crisp and still, and Exiluk's footsteps rhythmic. As he walked, he paid attention to the still landscape and the changing clouds, and the quiet beauty of his surroundings made for a pleasant journey.

He reached the settlement. A giant caught sight of Exiluk and froze. His expression, slightly gaumless, was one of confusion and intrigue. He wore grey furs and was two or three times the size of Exiluk and bulging with muscle. He tapped the giant sitting next to him and pointed at Exilluk, saying, "Oi... What the bloody 'ell is that? It looks like a goat man."

The other giant was wrapped in a brown robe. His hair was thick and messy and it reached all the way to his waist. He said, "What the bloody 'ell are you? I've never seen a goat man before." He said to his friend in a different tone, "Look at his eyes, they're glowing like a magicker's."

"And one of his horns is mangled," his friend replied. "You, are you a magicker?"

"I am a keradin, not a witch, nor a goat man. I come from the other side of the forest of Darpirith, from the swamplands. I have been travelling around the world, and I am on my way home. Please, could I have some water, and perhaps sit by your fire? My boat capsized. I am cold."

"Well, you look like a goat man and a magicker, how do I know you're not trying to trick me? And what happened to your mangled horn?"

"Has a goat ever done you any harm? Or a witch, for that matter?" Exiluk ignored the question about his horn. He hated thinking about it.

The muscular giant said, "No, I like goats, that's true. Not such a fan of witches, though, and you've definitely got magicker's eyes."

"Well, I am much more of a goat than a witch, I can't even cast magic," he said. "My name is Exiluk. It is nice to meet you."

"You talk a lot for a goat," the long-haired giant said. "And you talk clever, like the witches and the giants past the mountain are said to."

"I am not quite a goat, you see." Exiluk smiled. He could sense the pleasant and simple nature of these giants and he felt comfortable, despite their size and strength.

"Oi, wife, come and look at our new friend the goat man," the muscular giant called loudly.

From inside the round building, a softer voice said, "What've I told you about smoking wisptree in the morning?"

"No, he's bloody real, come look," he said. "Oi, Exiluk, tell her you're real, and come take a seat by the fire."

"I assure you, I am real," Exiluk said to the wooden door in the round building. "I am a keradin."

The wife giant poked her head out of the door and said, "Bloody 'ell, you weren't joking. Good morning mister. Let's get you some food." She went back inside and closed the door behind her. The structures seemed to be made of a flexible lattice, furs, and a sturdy canvas outer.

Tall orange flames of various hues wrapped around thick, chunky firewood. Big black stones surrounded the fire. The warmth was almost harsh, yet it was most welcome.

The muscular giant gave Exiluk a wooden cup the size of a jug. Exiluk dived in, gulping the water down. It was cold and crisp, so refreshing. He ran some through his hands and his face and beard, and it made him feel less salty and clogged.

"There's plenty water, help yourself," the giant said.

The wife giant came out of her home with a pot the size of a cauldron and placed it above the fire.

"Her stews are the best in the village," her husband said.

"That's really sweet," she said, with affection in her eyes.

"It's the only reason I put up with her," he said, and he and his friend laughed while she playfully hit them both and took a seat by the fire.

"Tell us a story, then, Exiluk," the muscular giant said. "Us giants love a good story."

"What kind of story?" Exiluk said.

"How did you get here? You said you'd travelled the world. Tell us about that. Or tell us about something amazing you've heard. I dunno. We love a good story."

"Okay, let me think," Exiluk said. The stew began to bubble and the scents of meat and vegetables overwhelmed his hunger.

"What about the others?" the wife giant said. "They'll wanna hear a story too. We should get everyone around the fire for this."

"You're right, especially the kids, what a lovely experience to hear a story from a goat man," her husband said. "Oi," he raised his voice. "Everyone, come around our fire. We've got a visitor here to tell us a story."

Giants emerged from their homes, chattering, staring in wonder at Exiluk as they gathered around the fire. Exiluk sensed a sliver of disappointment deep inside of him. These giants were simple and kind, and there were no palaces or treasures to be seen.

CHAPTER 3

ASH

Ash stood straight and attentive at King Ingamar's side. He coughed and spluttered, wiping mucous onto a red serviette. Its stench was repulsive. She took it reluctantly, trying her best not to appear disgusted. She disposed of it and rushed back to his side.

"Father, you should rest. Why do you insist on dining with us when you can barely breathe?" Princess Serene said.

"Too stubborn and proud," the Wild Queen said. She gulped dark red wine from a crystal glass. "More," she demanded. Tilly hastened to give her more wine. Deep reddish purple wine rose in the crystal glass with the satisfying sound of liquid being poured. The Wild Queen was named as such because it was thought to be more suitable to call a queen wild than crazy. Ash's mother was the Queen's personal maid, and it seemed to Ash she was the only person to have compassion for the Queen.

The King grunted and waved his hand. He didn't approve of the conversation. His beard was grey and long and his hair was thin. His body was skinny and deteriorated. *Such a feared man, yet so fragile,* Ash thought with hatred for him. The King was cruel and had no respect for servants, or anyone.

Prince Gideori, his son, youthful and strong, was a powerful witch like his father was said to have been when he was younger. Gideori said, "Fear not father, I will respectfully represent the family and the kingdom at the Goaner wedding."

The royal family of Ul Nirin had recently received an invitation to the Goaner wedding. The wedding would unite the daughter of the minister of Avenia with the son of a mining mogul, and it seemed to be the focal point of palace gossip. Ash had noticed tensions in the witches' words in recent days.

The King grunted, "What do I care about giants!" Uncontrolled black and red mucous seeped from his mouth onto his grey beard.

Though they didn't state it publicly, it was clear that the witches of Ul Nirin didn't like the idea of powerful giant families uniting in Midvale.

Ash pulled a serviette from her pocket and held her breath, wiping... Flash. Stone floor. Confusion. The King had struck her. Aching cheek. Aching elbow and hip.

"Did I give permission to approach me?" the King said.

Ash dragged herself to her feet, seething. Through clenched teeth, she managed, "Your Majesty, I apologise. You did not give me permission to approach you. I acted impolitely." The last time the King had drooled on himself, he had hit her when she had asked for permission to approach, saying she should have cleaned it up right away to maintain his dignity. *I wish he would just give up and die,* she thought. The thought was wrought with guilt because she knew that a small part of her really meant it, though most of her wouldn't wish death on anyone, not even witches and giants.

"Well," the Prince said, "attend your king!"

"May I approach, Your Majesty?"

"Get on with it," the King grunted.

Ash did as she was told. The mucous smelt like death itself. It was no wonder the family wanted their father to stay in bed. Nobody would want to eat with that smell invading their senses. It was so harsh she could barely think clearly when she got a strong whiff of it.

"Father, you see, once Toarer Goaner marries Naara Darthik you could say the ministry and military are married to all the mining in Avenia. That level of influence is somewhat unprecedented in the Nine Lands, and I need to nurture our relationship with the giants to make sure we can make the most of it," the Prince said.

Prince Gideori was charming on the outside, and most cruel and narcissistic on the inside.

"Did you not hear me, boy!" The King backhanded his silver goblet, and it flew across the table, red wine covering everything. "I do not care about giants," he grunted.

Ash and Tilly rushed to clean the table. Supper time had been much like this for months. Ash would have been more satisfied with the family's suffering if it hadn't meant that they would take most of it out on the servants, which of course, they did at every opportunity.

Princess Serene was the only one who didn't treat them awfully. This whole time she had sat quietly and rigidly, seemingly deep in thought, away in her mind. She was often like that around her family, which was interesting because she was vibrant when she was alone with Ash.

The kitchen servants placed silver tray upon silver tray of delicious and delightfully presented food on the table. A whole roasted bird, surrounded by all sorts of brightly coloured vegetables. Grapes, olives and cheeses, and more wine. The family picked at it ungratefully while Ash's mouth watered.

The King's disgusting scent found her and reminded her that not everything in life is as it seems, no matter how privileged one might be. The King tore into a leg of chicken and the fat splattered and dripped onto him. He stuffed a tomato into his mouth and it squelched as his teeth broke its skin, red juice spitting a distance onto the table, and the rest dripping through his beard. He coughed and choked, clearing his throat and spitting into another serviette.

The King's family looked at him with shame and sadness, and the air was filled with sorrow. Ash wondered what the city would think if they knew how glum nights at the palace had become for the rulers of Ul Nirin.

Something seemed off to Ash, and it wasn't just the King's deterioration, but she couldn't put her finger on it. She examined the room: the creamy sand-coloured stone, the intricately carved patterns repeated throughout the stone with precision, the red, orange, yellow and white mosaic tiled floor, the lanterns with their detailed filigree metalwork and magic honey-yellow glow, the rare charms and herbs and runes and artefacts. Now that she came to think of it, it all appeared somewhat busy and chaotic. She had never seen it that way before. Until then, she had always considered the palace to embody the ultimate sign of power: wealth and magic.

The Prince looked beyond his father to Ash and smiled creepily at her. She cringed and an indescribably sickly feeling filled her. He had begun taking a fancy to her and she feared where it would lead. The Prince was known to like young servant girls and boys. Humans and witches were forbidden to reproduce together, so she would be forced to drink wombrott potion and become infertile. The experience was said to be worse than being plunged into the underworld. She didn't want to think about it. *I wish he would die too,* she thought. *I wish they would all die.* Guilt. *Perhaps not Serene, she doesn't quite deserve to die.*

Princess Serene chewed her food slowly, her eyes still glazed and not paying attention to the supper. The Wild Queen downed more wine. The King's energy was spent and he could barely keep his head up. The main course was removed from the table and desserts were placed upon it.

Prince Gideori took a slice of apple drizzled in cream and honey with lilac petals and he winked at Ash as he slowly wrapped his lips around the apple. He was a handsome man, yet repulsive.

I wish that apple was poisoned. I wish he would die.

The Prince licked and sucked the cream off the apple slice.

Ash found herself still watching, slightly mesmerised, as if in a light trance, and thinking, *I wish the apple was poisoned. I wish the apple was poisoned.*

The Prince bit into the apple, chewed it, and swallowed. Nothing. And even though Ash knew it was impossible for her to do magic, she was still disappointed.

One day, I'll get some poison, she thought. *One day soon.*

A horrific groan, a scream of intense pain. Shock, and silence, except for the snoring King whose head had drooped as far as his neck would let it.

Then another scream as the Prince grabbed at his throat and his stomach desperately. He became grey and yellow, and black veins showed through his skin.

Impossible, Ash thought, amongst all the commotion of servants and family members now frantically attending to the Prince who writhed and convulsed and screamed in pain, as if his body was battling a demon.

"He has been poisoned. My son has been poisoned," the Queen screeched, madly. "Lock the palace down, nobody leaves." A guard rushed off to obey the order. The Queen screamed, "Put these servants in the dungeons. They have poisoned my son. They are all going to pay for this." She sobbed. "Call the healer, quickly."

The Princess said calmly to a guard, "They are innocent until proven guilty, remember that." Tears dripping down her cheek, she crouched over her brother, who was stiff as a rock, and she began an incantation.

A strong guard grabbed Ash so forcefully her neck whipped backwards, and before she could find her feet, he dragged her through the great hall and gallery and down to the kitchens, past the armoury and servants' quarters, out through the courtyard, and down a rusty ladder and into the dungeons.

She wanted to protest, to say she had done nothing wrong. *Did I? It's not possible,* she thought. The guard threw her into a dark, dingy cell. It was damp and stuffy, and it stank. A shadow moved. She flinched. Her eyes adjusted. It was a bony old man sleeping in the corner. Tilly and the kitchen servants were thrown in soon after. The cell felt crowded. The gate clanked shut and the guards left.

They stood in silence, in shock and disbelief.

Tilly began to sob, "They're going to execute us, aren't they?"

"Whoever did it must own up to it," Stefin said.

"You're the cook," Molly said. "You prepped all the food. It must've been you."

"Hang on a minute, I didn't do it, there's no way I'd have done it," Stefin said.

It couldn't have been me, could it? It must be a coincidence. It must be. You can't wish poison into an apple. Ash decided she wouldn't say anything. It was too absurd to think she could have done it.

Molly said, "You went with the Prince to Garaduk, we all know they hate the north, they put you up to it."

"Don't be so ridiculous. They monitor everything coming into the palace, how could I have got poison in? It must've been one of the guards," Stefin said. "I wouldn't ever poison the Prince." He was desperate and angry.

"The guards never touch the food," Molly said. "You did it." She trembled as she spoke.

"Shut up," Ash screamed. Her voice cut through the dungeon and an eerie silence followed. Fear and uncertainty filled the air, an uncomfortable horridness she wished she could run from.

It wasn't long before a guard came and unlocked the gate and grabbed Stefin. "You first," he said. "All we want to know is who put you up to it. That's it. You can make it easy for yourself."

"But I didn't, I didn't, please." Stefin's feet flapped and scraped and jarred against the stone floor as he vainly tried to resist being dragged out.

"What'll they do to him?" Tilly said, between sniffles and sobs.

Ash shook her head as if to say, *I don't know and I don't want to know. Neither do you.*

The old man in the corner scraped himself awkwardly and weakly into a seated position, his back against the rough rock lining the cell. His eyes were whitish grey and glazed throughout, no pupil, no iris. He grinned, showing only a few teeth, and said, "The rule of witches will unravel to the essence of truth. The prophecy." His eyes glowed white, and he pointed at Ash. "You," he said. "When the darkness and chaos come for you, dance, don't run." His eyes dimmed and he rested his head back against the wall, muttering to himself. "Dance, don't run," he whispered. "Dance, don't run."

"Nutter," Tilly said, nervously.

And then the screaming started. Stefin's screams and groans and cries stretched across eternity, and every change of tone and pitch and length in each scream spoke of a new torture.

The screaming stopped. The silence was unbearable. Each moment of silence, a moment closer to their turn.

The screaming started again. Weaker, yet more desperate.

More unbearable silence. Ash felt vomit surge through her and she instinctively swallowed the first clump because being sick on palace grounds was forbidden under all circumstances, and then she remembered she was in a cell in the dungeons and she was sick everywhere. Her stomach stung and her throat throbbed, and her mouth was left with a sour taste. She salivated heavily. The smell was sickly and sharp.

They came for Molly next, and her screams were twice as horrid. It was impossible to tell how much time had passed and how long Stefin and Molly had endured their tortures. Time was irrelevant, more suffering had been dealt than a person should have suffered in a lifetime, and Ash's blood boiled with fury and despair.

❦

Ash and Tilly were dragged to the torture rooms together. The guards had clearly become impatient, and they must have wanted to get it over with quickly. There was blood everywhere. So much blood, all over two tables and the floor. There were potions and powders and herbs in vials and surgical implements of all types. The low light from only two little lanterns made it feel all the more sinister.

Tilly fought and screamed as they strapped her to a table. Ash lay on the other table without a fight. The guard guided her hands into the straps and fastened them. Her legs were bound next. They cut off her clothes. A guard turned her head and pinned it to look at Tilly. "You will watch each other squirm until one of you talks," he said.

"Girls," a crooked voice said. "I am the interrogator." He was an old man and he appeared fragile and feeble, yet there was a wrongness about him that spoke of evil. The way his bones were shaped. His posture. His skin. He looked as if he dined on suffering. "This can be a lot easier for you if one of you simply tells us who it is that wants the Prince dead. It is impossible for a servant to gain access to a poison as powerful as that with which the Prince was struck. No, this is a more serious matter than a rebellious servant, and we think one of you knows exactly what we need to find out."

"We don't know," Ash said, firmly.

"Somebody knows. These things do not happen by chance, do they?"

"It could have been one of the guards." She couldn't stop trembling, no matter how hard she tried to calm herself. The guard holding her head banged it against the table. White flash. Pain.

"Oh, of course," the interrogator said, "if we have to interrogate the guards, we will." He took a vial of black powder from the wall and pulled out the stopper. "I think I will start with her, she seems more *susceptible*."

He poured the black powder into Tilly's mouth, and she wriggled and struggled as the guard held her down. "No hope in struggling, dear girl," he said, soothingly, in a way that chilled the damp air. "Even the slightest darkroot powder in your blood will conjure all sorts of suffering in the mind and body. See?"

Tilly's body went limp for a moment. She was lifeless, and then she cried a cry that spoke of the most unbearable suffering on earth, and her eyes turned hollow and black. Something beyond pain, beyond sorrow, something so much deeper and darker. The interrogator touched her on the forehead and caressingly whispered an incantation, and Tilly calmed to a gentle, hopeless sob.

"Trust me, girl, that was just a taste of what you will feel until you tell me everything," the interrogator said.

"Please," she begged. "I don't know."

"Perhaps a little nonmagical interrogation will persuade you further. It is only a matter of time until you tell me something, after all," he said. He was measured, calm, and methodical. He took a tool, took her shaking hand, and gripped her fingernail with the tool. Yanked it off. She shrieked.

Ash couldn't bear to watch. She closed her eyes, but Tilly's pain invaded her mind. The shrieks haunted her. *What can I do? Even if*

I confess, they'll kill us both to make an example. She was confused, her thoughts raced around in a woozy swirl, and her blood rushed loudly in her head. She felt panicked and traumatised.

The interrogator tore each fingernail and each toenail from Tilly, and he seemed to enjoy every moment. "This might be painful, but it is somewhat harmless," he mused. "Consider it a warmup for the devastation to come." He put the nail extractor down and picked up a knife. "Now the fun stuff." He made an incision into her stomach, and she groaned. He poured a powder into the incision, and she wailed.

"Wait. Wait!" Ash said. "I did it. I poisoned the Prince."

"There we go then," the guard holding Ash said. "I knew it was her."

"Intriguing," the interrogator said, peering closely into Ash's eyes. "Why exactly did you poison the Prince?"

"Because I'm sick of the way we get treated. I'm sick of being a slave!"

"My dear," the interrogator said. "You are no slave. You serve the magic, you serve the royal family, you live in the palace. Without us, you would be in some whore house, or dead. Without the witches' advancements, you humans would be living in the dirt like animals."

Ash was sick of hearing it. She closed her eyes and said nothing, wishing for it all to end.

The interrogator stuck his bony finger into Ash's mouth and his taste of evil made her instinctively wretch. With practised ease he poured a liquid into her mouth before she could react and close it. It tasted harshly bitter. "Truth potion. Incredibly hard to make. Extremely rare," he crooned. "Now we will see if you really are telling the truth."

A rush of relaxation rippled through Ash's body, and she felt light and good. Her muscles felt loose and deeply relaxed. She felt warmth and well-being, and detached from all the pain and trauma. Everything that had just happened seemed like a distant nightmare that couldn't affect her anymore.

"Now tell me, *dearest*, how did you poison the Prince?"

"Uh... I... wished for it," Ash said.

She had a vague sense that she should be minding her thoughts, but she felt so pleasant and relaxed that she couldn't care about or control anything.

"You wished for it?"

"I wished he would die. I wished the apple was poisoned."

"You are smart for a human. Games of semantics can evade the truth for some time, yet it will not help you here," the interrogator said. He took a hammer and approached Ash. "Now tell me, why you did it, how you did it, and who put you up to it. Be very specific, and very truthful, or I will crush your kneecap."

"I wished he would die. I did it because he deserved it. Nobody put me up to it. You deserve to die too," Ash said. She couldn't help herself. She didn't mean to say it. The truth potion gave her no choice.

"Hmm," the interrogator said. He peered into Ash's eyes. She peered back, vague, distant, and uncaring. She only hazily noticed the revulsion churning in her stomach. He put the hammer down and pondered. "So, you are telling me you *wished* the poison into existence?" He picked up a rod of metal with a wooden handle. "You see, if I crush your kneecap, you could become unconscious from shock. I do not want that. Not yet." He rubbed his fingers together and a flame appeared from them. He heated the poker with it until it was red and white. "They say fire magic is chaotic and uncontrollable. They say it makes you mad. I do not *feel* mad." He pressed the poker onto Ash's bare stomach and the relaxing and numbing effects of the truth serum instantly vanished, and her stomach seared painfully while her skin crisped and melted.

She clenched her jaw trying not to scream, trying to contain herself. It was impossible, and she screamed louder than she ever imagined she could. Her piercing howl shook the room. Glass smashed and pieces exploded. Rock crumbled and crushed. Metal screeched and clanged. The interrogator collapsed. The table shattered. She thudded onto the ground as rubble fell on top of her.

CHAPTER 4

THEO

The slaves worked hard at the site, and it was starting to look more like a wedding. The large, elevated platform on which Toarer and Naara were to be married had been embellished in drapes of exquisite lace and cascading blooms. Its edges were lined with live vines in varying shades of grey and green, and interwoven with delicate flowers in a variety of soft pastel colours. The whole wedding site was decorated with delicate glass spheres on fine silver chain that were to be filled with fireflies on the day of the wedding. It was elegant and charming.

Theo was helping paint subtle motifs said to bring good fortune to newlyweds on the platform. He had a knack for painting, so Mistress Mildred had always said. He was grateful for the job because painting relaxed him. He couldn't stop wondering what Toarer had been about to say. *What could change everything?*

A giant appeared, armed and armoured with the colours and emblem of House Darthik: green, black, and red; a snake with its mouth and fangs wrapped around a dragon's tail, and the dragon chasing the snake's tail, creating a circular form. The giant nodded at Kirakai.

Kirakai cracked his whip. "Stand respectful, you sorry excuses."

Theo put his brush down and stood sharp. The party arriving included Toarer; his bride-to-be, Naara; and her mother and father.

Kirakai welcomed them.

Naara's father was the lord minister of Avenia, a well-known and powerful figure across the Nine Lands. Avenia was the most wealthy and influential of the Nine Lands, due to its abundance of resources. It was rich in rare minerals, good woods, and useful plants for potions. The wedding, exploiting these resources, promised to be the most spectacular in all history.

"Back to work," Kirakai said.

Theo feigned work while watching them stroll and nod and talk together.

"Cutting it rather fine, aren't we, taskmaster?" Naara said. "I thought you said you had military efficiency. Have you lost it in your old age?" Naara was a highly-ranked military official and she loved taking digs at Kirakai, who was old and who claimed to have been in the military. Some said he professed to be a forgotten hero, and his bitterness was because his life had descended to that of a mere taskmaster.

Kirakai lashed his whip on a dwarf's back and the poor dwarf whelped and whined in pain and shock. He had done nothing wrong whatsoever.

"There will be discipline for all of you if we're not done by sunset," Kirakai grunted. "Almost fifty of you and you can't even prepare a wedding. Master Goaner should sell you to the mines and get new stock. You will be working in the pits where you belong if you don't look alive sharpish." He lashed three more servants at random.

"We *did* offer to help with the wedding," Larani Darthik said to Lord Minister Fimni Darthik. They were particularly bony, tall, and thin for giants, which made Naara's distinctively bold stature quite intriguing and even more intimidating.

Lord Minister Darthik scowled at Larani. The wedding politics were clearly wearing thin on him.

Theo could see Toarer putting on a brave face. Toarer hated watching the servants being punished. Showing any signs of disagreement or dissent would make things a lot worse for everyone, so Toarer always hid it. Sympathy for servants was worse than blaspheming the First Giants. "The site looks excellent," Toarer said, in his gentle and kind voice. He faced Naara and Kirakai, but his eyes addressed the servants. Toarer had a way of calming things, almost by magic. Yet, according to the lore of the Land, giants couldn't do magic, just like humans and dwarves couldn't.

The sky was pale blue with wisps of clouds. The sun was unusually forgiving. It had given way to a gentle breeze that carried rich scents of freshly worked wood, fresh lake water, flowers, and paint.

Theo found himself trying to will magic into existence. His thoughts about the lore had made him desperate to prove them wrong. *We're not inferior!* He willed and willed, angrily. He wanted it so badly he felt desperation all over his body. *Something, please, anything*, he thought.

Nothing. Yet he couldn't help feel there *was* a hint of something. He just couldn't explain it, and he barely believed it.

"Theo," Avira whispered. "Are you alright?"

Theo shook his head to ground himself back to reality and started painting again. "I'm fine," he said. "Just tired."

"Your eyes went into the back of your head," Avira said.

He shrugged.

"You *do* realise that this wedding will be one for the history books, don't you?" Naara's tone was deliberately facetious. "If we have to postpone it because it is not ready... You can't even imagine the consequences."

"There's no question. It will be ready," Kirakai said. "I will work them to death if I have to."

He would, Theo knew it, and a terrible feeling loomed over him. They would never be ready by sunset, and it would be another night without food or proper sleep. He was sick of feeling worthless. Worthless because he never did anything to escape or better their lives. Worthless because the giants would kill him without any bother at all.

Little Squeak ran up to Kirakai and squeaked a message to him.

"Kitchen master wants you four to get the wines and beers from the cellar. Get to it," Kirakai said.

Pika, Tico, Avira, and Theo rushed off behind Little Squeak, along the primed path through the woods and into the gardens, which were immaculate with well-curated colour and shape, and which smelt divine. Bees buzzed and butterflies fluttered. Large, velvety soft petals created a visual splendour. Several servants tended the gardens, perfecting them for the coming guests.

Four old and worn-out dwarves decorated the garden entrance to the manor with flowers and pot plants. Two exhausted human slaves on ladders, slumped and with shaking hands, carved new patterns into the stone archway. "What do you mean the snellsilks haven't arrived yet?" Mistress Mildred shrieked from somewhere close.

In the entrance hall past the garden, exquisite tapestries depicting major historic events draped the towering walls. The largest and most prized tapestry was of the Battle of the Conjunction, the last battle the giants and witches fought before creating an alliance of peace and prosperity across the Nine Lands. Between the tapestries hung imposing paintings of the Goaner family in golden frames.

Scents of wedding foods wafted from the kitchen and were sublime. On entering the kitchen, Theo's senses were captivated by luxurious, rare, and exotic ingredients that had been sourced from far and wide to prepare pickles, chutneys, berry compotes, cured meats, and herb-infused oils, vinegars and liqueurs. The juiciest of berries, the crunchiest of apples, the best cuts of meats, and herbs—such fragrant herbs! Lemony, peppery, sweet, and rich—all intermingled with the sweat of the servants who toiled and slaved to prepare everything on time. Giant-sized bowls, trays, and other containers were filled to the brim with deliciousness.

Theo's mouth watered and his stomach ached with a hollowness he despised. He thought about not having dinner and he resented it. It almost made him want to work harder, but that would mean Kirakai had won and that he would have taken everything he possibly could from them.

"Finer, chop them finer," kitchen master Tibbel said, rushing around, observing several servants. He winked at Theo as they passed through the kitchen to the cellars.

Little Squeak handed Pika the cellar key and said, "Kitchen master Tibbel said you'd know which ones to get," and ran off.

"I don't..." Pika said, but Little Squeak had gone.

Tico took the lantern that burned next to the cellar door and Pika unlocked the door. It was marvellously odd that the kitchen master had asked them specifically to help, and Theo was nervous and intrigued.

Orange from the lantern seeped into the dark grey stone as they descended the stairs. Shadows crept over them with the movement of the lantern. Theo welcomed the damp coolness after the sweat and toil of working the gardens.

The cellar was full of barrels piled on the rough stone floor and shelves and racks stacked with bottles and preserved foods in jars. A note had been pinned to a barrel. Pika took it and said, "It's from Toarer."

Tico grunted a half chuckle. Pika couldn't read. Servants couldn't read. Parchment wasn't used for casual notes. And he clearly had no idea about Toarer and Pika. Theo felt a pang of guilt. They had left Tico out. He would feel hurt and betrayed that they had kept something so big from him. *What have we even kept from him? Pika's the one to blame here, so secretive, so conspiring.* The thought agitated Theo. He didn't want Tico to blame them for the mess Pika was creating.

"I'm being serious," Pika said. "Toarer has been teaching me to read and write."

"What?" yelped Tico.

With a sickening lurch, the reality of what Toarer had revealed hit Theo hard. He hadn't really processed it all. He had just been running away from the reality, as if it hadn't existed. *That's all I ever do*, he thought. *Ignore it, run away from it. Coward! I should have thought this through.*

Now he had seen it, it was all different. Heavier. Undeniable. A servant reading. Toarer had taught Pika to read. Reading and writing were severely forbidden for slaves. If anyone found out, they would all be tortured. Upon confession, executed. Others would be executed for good measure, to set an example.

The lore said that reading and writing would be wasted on

humans and dwarves because their brains were too small. Unlike witches and giants. And so, it was banned, with the severest of punishments. They were committing treason. Treason! It felt too strange, too unbelievable to be true.

"What're you talking about?" Tico said, his face and voice full of desperation and confusion, exacerbated by the shadows of the cellar.

"Listen, this is important," Pika said, gently but firmly, commanding control of the situation. A calming silence. "The note says, 'I think it is time you told them everything, and gave them the choice,' and I agree. It's time." And looking somewhat contrite, he added, "I'm sorry for keeping you in the dark."

"What choice?" Tico said, impatiently waving the lantern. "What are you talking about?" Tico's features were harsh for a dwarf, his face was thinner and bonier than most. As the lantern moved the harshness intensified, hardened by shadow.

Light and shadow followed the rhythm of his hand around the cellar, over the rustic wooden casks, glass jars and bottles, and wooden tubs, the dusty stone floor, and spider webs. The darkness of the cellar pressed in on them. The lantern stopped moving.

"Since Toarer got engaged to Naara, he's been spending time winning the lord minister's favour, and he's managed to get access to the ministry's restricted literature.

"Much of it is touted as outdated and disproved narrative, and their newer versions are supposed to have been corrected with more accurate accounts, but we think there could be truth to the debunked stories. We've found sources from the lore of different civilisations that corroborate certain things." Pika took the lantern and burned the note. Calm orange flames glowed, wrapping around its edge and spreading. He dropped it on the floor and let it burn. "We believe that everyone is capable of magic and that the witches suppress us to make sure we never try it. We're capable of as much as them, and perhaps a lot more."

"Ludicrous," Tico said. "Absolutely ludicrous. What's got into you Pika?"

Anger met with confusion in Theo, which caused the fire inside of him to intensify. He wanted to throttle Pika for taking such a big risk. For spouting such nonsense. *Humans and dwarves can't do magic!* Yet he wanted it to be true so badly he felt a different kind of fire battling the fear. Some inexplicable energy that excited and irritated him, and then it calmed him, wrapping around the rage and dissolving it. The calm confused him. It was an unusual feeling for him. It's mystery threatened to agitate him, though there was already so much to deal with, it didn't get a chance.

He watched Avira's intense expression, locked on Pika. He wanted to know what she was thinking, and his vision blurred, and he had to take an intense, deep breath.

Pika took something from his pocket. "Look. I've got this," he said. He opened his palm to show a glass orb with smoke and faint light swirling in it. "It's a teleorb. It can take whoever touches its mist to any place they know well enough to picture in their minds."

"I've heard of them," Avira said. She was taken aback, trembling. "The witches use them to travel distances. If you get it wrong, it'll rip your guts from your stomach. Even the strongest witches have to train for a time to use them." She shook her head. "You know if you get caught with that, you'll get a thief's execution."

"Right. I don't intend on getting caught with it," Pika said. "We could use it to get beyond the barrier."

"No. The barrier disarms unauthorised magic," Theo said. Whatever calm his body had managed earlier was waning. *Beyond the barrier. He's nuts. Mad. He'll get us all killed.* Pika's optimism was ghastly. Threatening.

"This one's authorised," Pika grinned.

The smoke and light swirling in the orb was mesmerising, gripping, as if it were coaxing Theo towards it. He wondered if the others felt it. Avira's eyes and expression said to him, *What do you think?* He shook his head. He didn't know what he thought.

"Where did you get it then?" Tico said. Tico was tense, agitated, fists clenched, jerking his knees on the spot. The lantern flickered and the shadows clawed at them.

"Never mind that. I need to give you a choice."

"No, Toarer's note said to tell us everything," Tico hissed.

"You're right. I won it in a card game."

"Ugh, I wish I'd never asked," Tico grunted.

"It's a story for another day, and we'd better hurry now, someone'll wonder where we are soon."

As if on cue, there was knocking on the cellar door. Not heavy or aggressive knocking. Energetic knocking. Strange. *Had someone been listening to them?* The timing was incredulous. Theo felt sick. They had been caught. It was all over before it had even begun. *Why would the person knock, though?*

Pika put his foot over the burned note.

Door opening. Footsteps, fast and light, coming down the stairs. Theo's heart dropped like a boulder. Everyone froze awkwardly. Little Squeak emerged from the dark stairway into the cellar.

"What you talking about?" he squeaked, innocently. "Is this where you hide when you don't want to do work? I hide up a tree, it's much nicer. You've been here ages. I'll show you the tree if you want?" He was a chirpy boy at the best of times, and he was awfully bouncy now.

"Are you alright, Squeak?" Pika said, clearing his throat and attempting to sound normal.

An adult would have noticed their tension. It was awkward and horrible, like a slow cut. But Squeak somehow fluttered through it all, oblivious.

"I had a big, big, big, big big big spoon of honey. Now I feel like a bee." He ran in small circles with his hands out, like a bee.

Everyone laughed and Little Squeak giggled, still circling like a bee. His cheer was infectious, and Theo breathed a welcome sigh of relief, enjoying the small, unexpected moment, and dreading the conversation they would have to return to.

"Don't tell anyone, will you? We don't want people to think we were avoiding work, we only wanted a little rest," Avira said, calmingly putting a hand on Squeak's shoulder. "It can be our secret. And we won't tell anyone you sneaked some honey."

"Yep yep, our secret," Squeak said, and he ran back up the stairs, making the sound of a bee. The cellar door closed with a bang.

"I don't like this," Theo said. "We'll get caught." Now that Little Squeak had gone and all the cheer with him, Theo felt awfully heavy and horrid again. The darkness didn't help, and neither did the dusty, musty smell. It was as if the walls were closing in on him, slowly, but surely. He found it hard to catch his breath. *Don't be weak, not now, Theo.* The swirling smoke in the orb whispered a strange, incomprehensible sound, as if ghosts were talking from the beyond, calling. He shook his head to ground himself.

Tico grunted and said, "We'd better get upstairs."

"No," Avira said. "We need to hear this. Pika?" She was shaking, and there was an immense determination in her face.

"Here's your choice," Pika said. "If I can figure out a way to use this orb to get beyond the barrier, beyond the forest of Darpirith, somewhere far and safe, will you come with me?"

"There's nowhere safe," Theo said. "The watchers will find us."

"I've got a plan. We'll be safer beyond the barrier than we are here. You'll have to trust me and Toarer, he's with me on the plan, remember. When I can tell you more about it, I will. I can't now, we shouldn't be down here any longer.

"There'll come a point where the decision must be made. It could be in a few moments, or a few months, I can't tell you when." Pika slipped the orb back into his pocket. "You'll need to decide very soon, because when I crack this orb, we're either in the smoke together, or we're not."

They all looked at each other cautiously. Avira smiled, yet it looked as if she was fighting back tears. Theo understood. Hope. Despair. Their dismal lives, the torture, it may all finally be over. And it may all be about to get a whole lot worse. They might be executed. He was so overwhelmed he felt faint again, and his vision blurred. *Pull yourself together, Theo. Don't be weak. You can't even handle information, never mind a quest.*

"I wish I could give you more time, I wish I could tell you everything I've learnt. I know it's the biggest decision you might ever make, and that there's so much to take in, and you have to put so much trust in me. I'll respect any decision you make. Yet, know this. I'd feel much better about the fate of my quest with the three of you beside me in the wide world beyond the barrier than without.

"The choice is yours."

CHAPTER 5

EXILUK

A stew of vegetables and meat wafted up a delightful aroma from the huge bowl in Exiluk's hands. He hadn't realised how hungry or drained he truly was until that moment. He took a spoonful, and it was warm and thick and delicious.

"Tell us a battle story," one young giant said. He was the size of Exiluk.

"Pirates," another said.

"Romance," someone said.

"What do blue goat men like to eat?" an adult asked, looking down at Exiluk from his seated position on the floor.

"Our people eat simple foods of mainly fish and frogglehorn from the swamps and a type of mild, nutty, chewy grass from the plains," Exiluk said. He thought of all the lavish and gourmet foods he had tried on his travels and found he had no wish to go back to plain eating.

They chattered amongst themselves about what kind of story they would like to hear until Exiluk said loudly, "I know a story you will all like."

The giants quietened, their faces kind and endearing.

"I will tell you of the time I met Skup, the pirate king who fell in love with Elenor of the Aerie. Elenor was snatched by Badr, ruthless leader of the Duna Saqaa."

"Ooh," the giants gasped. One said, "This'll be good. Pirates are mad to be on the sea. We don't like the sea."

"I was on the hot and sweaty island of Cynthia, drinking and relaxing in a bar by the ocean when I met Skup, the rugged, scar-faced pirate king," Exiluk began. He felt a murmur of guilt at the memory of drinking alcohol. The keradin did not intoxicate themselves for pleasure. He pushed the guilt aside.

The giants were silent, absorbed, and the huge stew pot above the fire continued to simmer and bubble while the fire crackled, and flames danced with the air. A gentle breeze swept across the land.

"The pirate bar was rough, and there was something pleasing about that roughness. Aged wood from wrecked ships, trinkets from seafaring adventures, dimly lit lanterns casting eerie shadows on the weathered wooden beams. The floor was uneven and covered in sand. The smells of sea salt, tobacco, and aged rum, were intoxicating. Skup carries a scimitar around his waist because pirates are always getting into trouble, it is in their nature. Pirates call trouble, and trouble calls pirates. He stood next to me at the bar with some of his crew behind him, and he said, 'We'll take a few barrels for the journey,' to the barman. He turned to me, and he said, 'I've never seen a creature like you, and I've travelled every land there is in my time.'

"I said, 'We keep ourselves to ourselves in our villages, because we have everything we need there.'

"He said, 'What're you doing here then?' in his hardened pirate voice.

"'I felt a calling, and I followed,' I said.

"'Like us pirates, that's how we do it too,' he said, and he slapped my back affectionately. 'Get the horned man a drink,' he said. So, we drank, and laughed, and we became friends."

Exiluk took another spoonful of stew. It was still warm and he relished the soft, long-cooked meat and rich flavours. "Skup couldn't stop talking about a woman of the Aerie. It was strange to see a pirate man, so ruthless and hardened made so vulnerable by his heart. 'She's so beautiful that light follows her and she's as delightful as all the happiness in the world. Her soul is so pure and kind. Her hair is long and it glows. Gems glisten from around her green eyes. Have you ever seen an aerie, Exiluk?' As he said it, I could feel the pain and emptiness he felt without her.

"I shook my head. I hadn't heard of the aerie before then.

"Skup downed a swig of rum and said, 'Gems grow on their bodies, real gems in all colours! And they're the most prized gems in the world because when they're at their brightest, they burn themselves out and turn to dust and fall to the ground. When you take it off the skin before it has turned to dust, though, it lasts forever, the most incredible and rare gem you can find. But to take an aerie's gem is to take a part of their soul.'"

"Woah," a giant said.

"The pirate dragged the last few drops from his bottle and slammed it down on the bar and said, a bit woozy and drunk, 'Elenor has been promised to marry Llasas, a prince of the Aerie. But she doesn't want the marriage, it's an arrangement by her parents,' he said.

"'I'm sorry,' I said, waving at the barman to get Skup another drink. Skup grinned at me, 'Luck has it that she's been snatched by desert bandits, and they want five chests of aerie jewels to get her back.'"

The gentle giants gasped and cried in horror, and Exiluk realised their kindly nature had been quick to understand the implications of the terrible ransom. "I felt that too," he said to the giants, experiencing a rare moment of sympathetic compassion, something he hadn't experienced much at all since leaving the swamps.

"'The aerie don't believe in fighting,' Skup continued, 'so they'll either cough up the price, and that'll be devastating to them, or someone else'll have to save her,' he tapped his chest, grinning.

"The barman put a bottle in front of Skup and the pirate took a big glug, golden beads of rum dripping off his beard, and he said, 'I'm going to free her and we'll sail the seas and capture her bounties until our very honourable end.' Skup's smile is a little crooked and charming at the same time.

"He put his hand on my arm and squeezed. 'Are you a fighting man? You're big and strong. We could do with some more muscle.

Ah, not man, I mean keradin. Are you a fighting lot?' He looked at his scimitar around his waist. Its leather sheath was worn and tattered. The small part of exposed metal by the hilt shone a brilliant silver.

"I said to him, 'Keradin don't fight. We don't believe in harming another under any circumstances.'

"He looked at me like I was strange, and he said, 'Even when someone has harmed someone you love, or they've stabbed you in the back?'

"'Even then,' I said." Exiluk remembered sensing Skup's mind. Skup had been disappointed that Exiluk wasn't a fighter. Pirates were rough and fighting was in their blood. He remembered Skup trying to think of a way for him to join them. Skup had liked Exiluk.

And before Exiluk could collect himself, he remembered her helplessness as the life seeped from her and he was horrified. He pushed the image away and it was as if it was a story about someone like him, not him. And he felt alive. Powerful. A figure of tales. *Tales of the insignificant are seldom told,* he thought. Pride battled with guilt for a short moment, then he focused his mind and returned his attention to the giants. This time the dissociation was a bit easier for him, and with that ease came a pleasant relief.

"'Yet, Skup, I have a sharp mind, I am a tactician, I can help you pave your quest so it is easier and less dangerous,' I said to him, and his eyes lit up because he wanted me to join him on the adventure."

The giants muttered amongst themselves, "He's mad. Questing with a pirate, so brave." The fire blazed and radiated heat. The sky was a clear and darker blue. The sun had set. The first stars shone white. The air was cold, and if it wasn't for the fire and his now dry, thick robe, Exiluk would have been shivering. The giants seemed hardened to the cold, sitting comfortably, eyes curiously on Exiluk.

A giant said, "Why did you volunteer? You barely knew the pirate, and the sea and pirates and bandits are so dangerous."

"For the same reason I am here. Some things simply call you."

"Not us, we like it here in the south, it's quiet and lovely and we have everything we need," the giant said.

"Should I finish the story?" Exiluk said in a kind, yet slightly forced tone. The words, *quiet* and *everything we need*, agitated him. That was something they had always said in Si'hantikup.

"Yes," all the giants cheered, so loud the air rumbled.

"The sea was rough, and the ship was getting battered by big waves and the pirates loved it. I wasn't so excited by it, but Skup said, 'This is nothing, keradin, we've sailed through storms that felt like we were in the pits of the underworld.'"

The giants gasped.

"We got through the storm unscathed and anchored near cliffs with layers of yellow and red rock. The sea was flat and light blue, it was truly beautiful.

"Skup and his crew sharpened their weapons while I looked at a map of the area. He said, 'She's calmed for us, it's a good omen.' He was talking about the sea. His blade sang as he slid it across the sharpening stone, and he said, 'This'll cut through bone like butter. It's goblin steel infused with dragon blood.'"

The giants cringed and said, "Urgh," and "Err."

"He put his blade down and pointed at the map. 'We're here, in this sheltered bay. We'll leave the ship here as it's nicely hidden. We can get ashore easily and the bandit's camp is somewhere around here,' he moved his finger north-west, 'about half a day's walk. Leave soon and we can get there by sunset and slaughter those damned snatching bandits and save...' he took a deep breath with wide eyes, truly in love, 'her.'

"'How many of them are there? What defences will their camp have?' I asked Skup. I feared his judgement was clouded by his heart.

"He said, 'What does it matter, keradin, we're more than fifty of the best fighters on the sea.'

"'What if there are five hundred of them?' I asked. Skup was unruffled. He said, 'I reckon we could take 'em.' I said, 'What about ten thousand of them?' and his eyes lit up and he said, 'Now that would be a fight! Then she'd really know how much I care about her.' I knew then his judgement was clouded by his heart."

Some giants muttered, "Clever, so clever." The wife giant stood quietly and ladled stew to several giants with empty bowls.

"I said, 'Send two of your fastest to scout the camp. We need to know their defences and numbers.'

"He said, 'For a creature who doesn't fight, you sure know how to fight.' And I said, 'I have a well-trained mind, that is all.' He said, 'Well I don't want to wait all that time. We'll take the challenges and fights as they come. I'm not bothered by a bit of blood, and nor are my crew.' He raised his voice, 'We're not afraid of a bit of blood, are we, crew of the Elenor?' The whole crew cheered and bashed their weapons together and drummed on the wood of the ship."

Exiluk remembered the excitement he had felt at that moment, there was nothing like it he had ever experienced before. A wild rush. "It was so exhilarating I had to calm myself. 'Patience is the greatest virtue of all, and the wait will be worth the lives saved. Just imagine if this goes wrong, what will happen to Elenor?' The pirate considered this and said, 'Fine. I'll do it for her. I'd do anything for her.' That much was obvious."

"Wow, that's so romantic," a woman giant said. "Why can't you be patient with me?" she playfully whacked the giant next to her.

"We've lived hundreds of years and I've been with you for most of them, I'm not sure you know how much patience that's taken."

The reply was a grunt and a giggle, and they looked to Exiluk to continue his tale.

"The scouts weren't back by the time we thought they would be, and Skup insisted the crew go look for them. I reasoned with him the desert may be harder to travel than the sea, and we should give them more time. If they weren't back by midnight, we should go. He agreed, so we waited, and worried as darkness crept over the ocean." Exiluk waited to build the tension, and he could feel the giants' anticipation.

"Two pirates returned later that evening, one was bleeding from the leg and the other was shaken up. 'A giant scorpion half the size of a man,' the shaken one said. 'Never seen anything like it,' he panted, as others tended to his injured comrade's leg."

The giants' eyes widened and they looked at each other with a mix of awe and disbelief. "A giant scorpion," a young giant cried, holding onto her mother's sleeve and moving in closer to her.

"Scaredy-boo," her brother teased. The other giants turned and shushed them, eager to hear the rest of the story. The fire crackled and flickered, casting shadows and light. Its flames swaying and leaping like lively spirits.

"Once the leg was tended to, we made our plans using the scouts' information and set out."

"You went?" the wife giant said. "I thought you would watch the ship or something safer than going with pirates to fight bandits."

"I was looking forward to being on dry land again, and I wanted to watch the events I had helped plan, it seemed only right. So, we walked through the cold desert night to some dunes overlooking the camp. It was a stark camp, and untidy, with pointed yellow-brown tents scattered unevenly and some of their spoils littered about. Banners fluttered in the soft night breeze. The starlight and moon beamed over the camp, and fires scattered around it made it easy enough to see it in sufficient detail in the dark. There were no defences, but there were hundreds of bandits and I knew that if the pirates rushed in there it would be a bloody battle, no matter how good they were at fighting.

"Skup said, 'We can take em.' I said, 'Send your stealthiest pirate in there to start a fire. As a tent burns, they will be distracted. Burn a few more for good measure. Then get in there and save her. That tent has the most guards around it,' I pointed, and I said, 'She will be in there. Your focus should be on getting in and out with her safe. The faster you are, the more chance she has of staying safe.' Skup nodded in agreement and relayed the plans to his crew.

"A pirate slipped down a dune and into the night, and we waited. There was shouting and uneasiness from the camp as an orange glow erupted. Skup and his crew moved quickly and quietly, their weapons drawn, and I didn't even realise that I had followed them. It must have been all the excitement and fear."

Exiluk had been supposed to stay hidden safely on the dunes. He had not been a fighter. He remembered a feeling he'd had the whole day leading up to that moment. A little murmur inside of him that said, *You wanted to experience a battle. You yearned for the thrill of it.* He fought with that memory. It made him extremely uncomfortable. Battle was not the keradin way.

"In some kind of daze or trance, I followed behind the swift sea of pirates sweeping into the bandit camp. The bandits were a rough and weather-beaten lot, dark skinned, dark-haired, and the men had long, thick beards. They were putting out fires and panicking. Fighting broke out. Metal clashed with metal and sparks shot about.

"I hid and watched as they moved through the camp, blasting through the bandits who got in their way. Skup led the pack, and he sliced through bandits like they were nothing. The pirates were relentless and powerful and crude, and they made easy work of the first bandits, but as more bandits started flooding in, things got tougher. They were surrounded but Skup led them forward, fighting through the crowd of bandits and getting closer and closer to the tent Elenor was in.

"And then she shrieked, so loud as if she was about to die, and everyone looked to the tent to see a hulking beast of a bandit holding her with a knife to her throat and a gem in his hand. She bled from her cheek where the gem had been torn from her. They say it is a pain and sorrow worse than a thousand griefs."

The giants looked terribly upset and empathetic.

"The fighting had stopped, and the leader of the Duna Saqaa said, 'I won't lose half my clan to a bunch of pirates. One move and she dies. I'll make you watch as I rip each gem one by one.' And Skup howled, 'Elenor! No, let her go. Let her go now.'

"His crew looked confused, as if it was the first vulnerability Skup had ever shown them, and Skup noticed the sentiment so he pulled himself together and said, 'That wouldn't be wise, bandit, look around, you've lost three times as many as we have, and we've barely broken a sweat.' The pirates laughed and jeered, and one barked at a bandit and the bandit flinched, and the pirates laughed some more.

"Skup said, 'Why don't you put that knife down and fight

me, one on one, man to man. Or do you need your whole crew to protect you?' The bandit laughed and spat on the floor. 'Why would I bother? You're half my size and I could slaughter your crew and take Elenor. You know what these gems are worth, you pirate scumbag?'

"Anger flamed in Skup's eyes as if from the underworld. He said, 'There will be stories told of this day. Do you want to be known as the bandit who cowered from a fight and lost hundreds of his clan, or the bandit who fought the best pirate in the world? I wouldn't even have to think about it. That's the difference between you and a true leader. A true legend. My legends will last forever, bandit. You couldn't even dream of it.'

"The bandit pushed Elenor to two guards who held her. He went into his tent and returned with two golden scimitars that would have looked beastly if they hadn't been so beautifully polished and rich. They glowed in the night. 'Your *tale* ends here, pirate,' he said. The bandit was muscular, powerful, and menacing, his scimitars were truly daunting.

"He charged at the pirate with incredible agility and leapt. Golden scimitars came hurtling down like a meteor from the skies. 'Legends will be told…' Skup sidestepped, angled back, swung his scimitar, and embedded it deeply into the bandit's back, 'about me.' One swift move and the duel was over."

"Wowww," the giants gasped.

Exiluk remembered the bandit squirming desperately in anguish as the blade wreaked havoc in his spine and Skup twisted and turned it to make it worse. He couldn't word that part to the giants.

"The guards let Elenor go and Skup ran to her and wrapped his arms around her tightly and lifted her off her feet and she wept, her tears glowing silvery and ethereal in the night."

"Is she a pirate now?" a child giant asked.

"Yes, and they live happily ever after," Exiluk said.

The giants clapped and cheered. They poured drinks and served food, and the mood was very jolly. Many came to Exiluk and thanked him and patted his shoulder affectionately. He smiled and nodded, yet he felt as if a darkness had crept over him.

The rest of the story wasn't one that Exiluk liked to recall, but there were times he struggled to banish the events from his mind. Now, he wished he hadn't told the story. He had mostly dissociated his dark deed from the story until now.

Skup had been so emotional and mad and confused. Once he had held Elenor enough, he sent her back to the ship with three of his crew, unsheathed his scimitar, and began a killing spree. With their leader dead, and full of fear, the bandits were no match for the pirates, who felt like legends. Exiluk saw a bandit run off and hide but thought nothing of it. As the slaughter came to a close, Skup had said to leave a few of them to scarper so they could tell the legend of Skup and his crew. A handful of bandits fled, shaking and falling in terror.

The one who had hidden earlier reappeared stealthily with a bow and arrow and aimed at Skup in the darkness. Exiluk, in an uncontrollable urge, had picked up an axe and rushed the archer. She saw him and changed her aim. A vicious pain shot through Exiluk's left horn, as if half his head had been torn off. In a desperate act, he plunged the axe into her heart. In that moment, which felt like an absurd eternity, he knew he could never be the same again. Her eyes. He could never forget the desperation in her eyes as she met death. It plagued his thoughts and his dreams, and he could never truly forget because his deformed horn would always remind him of the time he had swerved death and dealt it in the same instant. He remembered the rush, the pure thrill of it, exhilaration and shame and power. It was indescribable. So vivid. So lucid. So... he hated to admit it... incredible. He felt so guilty and confused. He closed his eyes and focused on the darkness, just for a moment, and then to the sounds of the giants chattering and enjoying themselves, and those feelings of guilt eased away.

They drank and ate and talked, and all the giants were keen to hear about Exiluk and his travels. It was tiring. He had gathered that the land from the mountains to the sea was called Craddock, and that there were a few small settlements scattered around. Most of the cities and more developed parts were on the other side of the mountains, especially in the middle and the north of the Nine Lands. Even these giants called those parts the lands where witches and giants rule.

"To get to those parts you have to go to Garaduk Eastport and cross the river there. It's about two days northeast from here. Find the river and walk east until you get there," the muscular giant said, with a roasted leg of meat in his hand, held by the bone. "That's with big legs, it'll probably be longer for you."

Exiluk nodded. "And what about the mountains?" Their magnificent form was just about visible in the darkness.

"There's nothing in those mountains except snow and the ghosts of our ancestors, the First Giants. You don't want to go there, they don't even like us, never mind a strange creature like you."

"What do you mean?"

"The First Giants were noble, good, and wise, and much bigger than us. They were put on this world by the stars a long time ago, and their job was to fill the world with earth, water, fire, air, and souls. There were earth giants who nourished the lands, fire giants who gave warmth, water giants who made the rivers and oceans, and air giants who gave breath to everything. Soul giants put spirit into everything that lives. And that's how the world came about, and it was good." The muscular giant tore at the meat and chewed it in his big mouth. "The world's a bit of a horrible place now though, and most giants are a horrible lot."

Exiluk remembered the woman he had killed. He scrunched his head to expel the memory. "You seem like an exceptionally nice lot to me," he said.

"You wait until you get to the cities, you'll see what they're like. They're greedy and mean."

Exiluk imagined palaces of gold. Bold, brave giants and luxuriously dressed witches who ruled valiantly.

CHAPTER 6

ASH

Ash woke in a daze. The room was full of dust and debris. She wasn't sure how much time had passed. Tilly lay limp under rubble and shards of wood. A piece of wood had pierced right through her womb. Blood pooled all around her. "Tilly," Ash cried. She could feel no pulse, and no breath. Tilly was dead. *I killed her. What's wrong with me?*

Shocked, and as if in a dream, she found her clothes, and only then remembering they had been cut, she covered herself as best she could. The burn on her stomach caused by the interrogator's heated poker stung ferociously. She passed the cell and noticed the old man was gone. She climbed the slippery, wet and rusted dungeon ladder into the courtyard, her wound splitting open with each reach for a rung.

Shouting and chaos bombarded her senses. Horses neighing wildly. Servants with weapons swarming the guards, crushing them, mauling them. Stones and rocks being slung, cracking heads and bones. Flashes and blasts of magic. A mob flooding through the gates. So much destruction. *Mother!* she thought, and she rushed towards the Queen's quarters.

She raced through the kitchens with their shelves upended and their contents on the floor, sacks of flour and grain torn open, tables overturned, and servants stuffing preserves, meats, and fruits into sacks and baskets. She raced onwards into the great chambers where there was havoc and looting, but on a smaller scale. The guards were just about in control there. *Not when that mob gets here,* she thought. She raced up the stairs, her burn stinging and leaking blood and pus. *It looks a lot worse than it is, the pain is easing,* she told herself.

She turned a corner and ran into three servants holding Princess Serene who was screaming. Ash stood shocked. As much as she despised the royal witches, it was momentarily disconcerting to see the tables turned. Her overwrought mind watched in a stupor as a fourth servant, Edgrin, pressed a hot branding iron into Serene's forehead, above her eye. The crescent moon mark of the Palace of Ul Nirin. The mark of ownership.

"Now you'll die a servant, just like us," Edgrin laughed. He sounded far away to Ash.

She isn't like them, though, Ash thought. "No, not her," she heard herself say.

"Wot?" Edgrin turned, shaking the hot iron. "You can't tell us what to do, you're either with the rebellion or you're one of them."

"I said," Ash said. She could feel anger and hate and raw energy pulsing through her, and she welcomed it. Everything that had happened, was all too much. "*Not her.*"

"Not her," Edgrin said, looking around confusedly, as if he had forgotten where he was or what he was doing. The three servants let go of the Princess and they all walked off.

"Why did you do that?" Serene said. She was ashen and shaking, her lips trembling, her eyes teary. "Why did they listen to you?"

Ash felt extremely tired and disconnected, the raw energy subsiding as quickly as it had arisen. She shrugged and shook her head. Serene took her hand and pressed it in gratitude and led her towards the royal bedchambers.

"I have to find my mother. I need to know she's safe," Ash said.

"I will tell the guards to bring her to us. It is better that way." Serene led her down the looted hallway with its broken mirrors on the floor, and its embroidered wall hangings, heirloom ceramics, and precious metal ornaments missing.

A barrage of guards blocked the way to the bed chambers, wands at the ready.

"Let us through," Serene said.

"No servants beyond this point, Princess," Varamin of the King's Guard said.

"She saved my life. They branded my face, and they were going to kill me," Serene said. "Now move."

The guards stepped aside.

A guard opened the door to her chamber. She said to Varamin, "Send for a teleorb, and bring her mother here, make sure she is safe."

"You can't orb anywhere outside the city, Princess. The barriers are up by command of the King," Varamin said. "Forgive me, Princess, I am not sure I heard you right. You want me to bring the *servant's* mother here?"

"Dare you to disobey me, Varamin?"

"I am tasked with your safety above all, and these are unprecedented times. Never in history has the palace been breached." Ash felt his strength, position and power to be commanding, but he didn't seem to influence the Princess.

"Bring me the orb, and her mother," the Princess commanded, slamming the door.

Ash stood awkwardly, uncomfortably, but the rebels and looters hadn't reached the Princess's room yet and so it stood clean, tidy, peaceful and inviting, and her traumatised mind and aching body yearned to surrender to it.

Serene walked Ash to the bed and gently laid her down on it. "I know you could not have poisoned my brother. You were behind my father the whole time."

It was like sinking into a firm and welcoming cloud. She expected herself to have to fight sleep, but the guilt of having wished the Prince dead and being unsure deep down whether she had killed him or not, tormented her mind into an intense restlessness. *I couldn't have, be realistic,* she thought. *I can't do magic.* Her mind raced back and forth in an overtired, overwhelmed and unclear manner between guilt and disbelief, giving her no peace. "Why didn't you defend yourself with magic when they branded you?" Ash said, still somewhat disoriented. She could hear clattering, shouting, and booming coming from a distance.

"Uh…" Serene said. She appeared taken aback. "I had no wand, no potions or powders, and magic without them takes a concentration I could not muster, not with all of them dragging me around." She slumped onto the bed next to Ash and let out a huge sigh, pulling a turquoise silk cover over them both. "Everything is going to be different now, isn't it? No matter how this all ends."

"Yes, I think so," Ash said. The bed's canopy draped sumptuously around the arched headboard, its regal silver latticework encrusted with warm-toned jewels. Silky sheer curtains billowed softly against the wooden lattice doors that enclosed the Princess's balcony.

A knocking at the door shook them. Varamin said, "I have your orb, Princess."

"Enter," the Princess said. "What about her mother?"

"We are still trying to locate her," Varamin said.

"She's not with the Queen?" Ash asked, panicked.

"Hurry *up!*" was all Serene said.

Varamin appeared surprised, most likely to see the Princess and a servant lying so casually on a royal bed, and most likely perplexed that a princess would want to save a servant and her servant mother. He handed the Princess the orb. "You will not need it, your highness. Even a thousand servants could not get past the King's Guard. Everything will be under control soon."

As he spoke, Ash could hear the cracks and whizzes of magic and she could faintly smell its scent, a bit like tangy, acrid burning. The cries and yells of the rebels and the guards increased in intensity.

"Bolt the door, as a precaution," Varamin said, leaving swiftly. The fighting sounded fierce, yet Varamin's commands were calm and calculated, which was reassuring.

"They say Varamin is one of the strongest mages in the Nine Lands, perhaps only second to my brother, and before he was ill, my father. We will be okay, won't we?" the Princess said.

"You will. When this is over, they'll go back to torturing me. My life was never okay," Ash said, sensing a harsh bitterness in herself. She pulled her torn clothing from her stomach and showed Serene the burn from the hot metal. The wound was pus-filled, inflamed, and horrible.

The Princess looked appalled. "I am truly sorry," she said, softly.

They lay together silently. Awkward tension pressed down on Ash. The air felt thick and her heart felt heavy. She knew the Princess wasn't responsible, but she felt angry and resentful towards the royal family.

"I really hope my mother is safe," Ash said.

"I am sure she is with the Queen, safe in her bedchambers," Serene said. Her relaxed tone was reassuring.

Resting on the Princess's bed felt like the calm before the storm. Ash experienced a profound realisation that things weren't going to be okay. Her whole world had been turned upside down, and she couldn't shake the fear that she had caused it all by killing Prince Gideori. *I couldn't have. Don't be so stupid. You can't do magic. Tilly, too.* She couldn't control her thoughts.

The fighting was louder, closer. Ash could hear struggles, grunts and gasps right outside the door, and it was impossible to relax, despite the soft and comfortable bed. And then they bashed on the door, shouting, "Kill the Princess."

The Princess clutched Ash's arm in fright, her breathing quickened. "Do you want to come with me?" she said, almost in a whine. "We will find a way to escape the city. If the servants overthrow the whole city, I am as good as dead. If the guards regain control of the city, it will not be good for you. You saved my life. I owe you a chance." She spoke as rapidly as her breathing. Ash's frayed nerves caught on to the Princess's fear and she had to swallow and take a deep breath before she could gather herself.

"Humans have no hope in the Nine Lands, so don't impose false hope on me," Ash said, coldly. The door was being bashed and smashed heavily. "I don't want to leave without my mother." Ash realised the Princess needed her, that she was too scared to act on her own, and it gave Ash a small sense of satisfaction.

"We have no choice. Your mother would want you to live. We can come back for her."

"No," Ash said, shaking her head, but trembling as she realised there was no other choice. Wood shattered from the door, and the bolt rattled and clanked more loudly and loosely after every thud. "I can't leave her. I don't want to leave her."

The Princess's hand felt so soft and gentle and sincere as she took Ash's hand. "We will come back for her, I promise," Serene said.

Wood splintered from the metal that held the bolt in the door. The door rattled and banged and more wood splintered. The Princess broke the orb and the smoke wisped around them and entered Ash's mouth and nose. A cooling sensation seeped into her face, her throat, and her lungs. Colours, whirling, rushing sensation. Nausea. Intense pain. Thrown all about the darkness. Spots and stars rushing past her. Blackness.

～⁂～

She came to consciousness near the city wall in the servants' slums, Serene kneeling over her. A pile of vomit by her head. The air smelt, and it wasn't just her vomit. Rickety, shoddy buildings of stone and wood surrounded them. She had forgotten how servants lived beyond the palace. She rose and felt extremely weak. The Princess looked garishly rich in the surroundings of the slums. "The first dead body you see, take their clothes and ditch yours," Ash said.

"A dead body, I could not," she said.

Ash laughed, looking at the branding on the Princess's forehead. It was red and raw, fresh. An explosion, out of sight, but within earshot, filled the air with smoke.

"I thought you had to know the place you port to," Ash said. "What do you know of servants' slums?"

"I know more about Ul Nirin than you could ever imagine," Serene said, stiffly. "We need to get out of the city."

Ash gritted her teeth and ran, pushing through the nausea and weakness. It didn't take long to find an abandoned dead man and woman. Ash clumsily ripped their clothes off, while Serene watched in horror, but she took the robe from Ash and reluctantly changed her clothes, complaining of discomfort and itchiness. Ash swapped her torn clothes for the dead man's tatty and smelly robe.

She led them towards the main gate. It was half open. There was fighting. A body was impaled on a wooden spike. *Flashback of Tilly dead in the dungeons.* She felt even more sick.

Guards were grappling with the mob, and it was messy. She grabbed the Princess's hand, and they sprinted like the wind, and nobody stopped them. They dodged colliding bodies and fiery magic. Clanging weapons, angry shouts and fervent cries filled her head. The conflict and turmoil stank of sweat and fear. So close to the gate. She couldn't believe it. Bang, she stumbled, something had made her legs feel as heavy as stone. A guard down the street had cast a spell on her. The Princess drew her wand and stood in front of Ash to protect her. Ash crawled backwards trying to get under the gate.

The guard laughed, "Servants can't do magic. Where did you get that wand, it looks precious." He seemed so amused by a servant holding a wand that he lowered his guard.

Serene made a sign in the air, the pattern lingered for a moment and a bolt raced from it and sent the guard flying. "I am not a servant." She dragged Ash under the gate and helped her limp into the cover of bushes. Plumes of smoke rose from within the city walls.

They watched the gate and listened, wondering what was happening inside. The smoke, the commotion, the blasts, and the screams all slowly reduced over time. There was no way to know who was winning. Some servants fled from the city and guards chased them down on horses. One had got close to the bushes before a guard cast a spell wrapping her in vines and dragging her back.

"I'm not waiting here to be found by the guards," Ash said, getting up and scrambling awkwardly through the thickets.

"Don't go, please," Serene said. "The guards will have things under control soon, and I will make sure they do not harm you."

Ash continued, pushing through the shrubs and bushes, sharp

spikes grazing and cutting her skin.

"I command you to stop!" the Princess wailed.

It wasn't the authority that stopped her, it was the desperation. Ash had never heard a witch sound so helpless and desperate. She knew that feeling all too well, and it didn't sit well with her. The Princess was nothing like a princess now, her servants clothes and her branded face made her almost indistinguishable, aside from much healthier skin and eyes. Mucky, and in the bushes, she was clearly dismayed.

She never hurt any of us, Ash thought. *Yet she never stopped them from hurting us.* "You'll be okay, Princess. Varamin knows you were branded, he knows who you are. Just go to the King's Guard when this is all over, they'll have you back in your perfect palace in no time." Ash took a deep breath and turned her head, feeling a fiery anger mixed with heavy sorrow. "You'd better look after my mother until I come back for her."

"Do not leave me," the Princess sobbed.

She's a princess, she'll be okay, Ash thought, as she wandered into the unknown.

It was a strange feeling to be free and overwhelmed with fear at the same time. Never had Ash had the chance to wander the lands, and she was elated by the sense of opportunity. She walked through meadows with a variety of flowers. Daisies stretched their delicate white petals towards the sun, their yellow centres attracting bees and dragonflies. Clusters of lavender released a mild soothing fragrance and violet irises mingled amongst the tall grasses.

Tall and broad trees dotted the meadows. She found an orange tree and took one from it. Tore off the skin and devoured it, her face covered in the juices. She was incredibly thirsty, hungry, and tired. She devoured another orange and drowsiness overcame her. *Don't sleep here,* she told herself. *Must. Keep. Going.* As she said it, she sat against the tree and she was reminded of how much her body ached, so heavy with exhaustion. *I have to go back for mother. How, though?* She was drifting off. *They'll execute most of us. Not mother. Mother would have been sensible. The Queen would have summoned*

her to the royal bedchambers or she would have stayed in the servants'
quarters. She's wise like that. Ugh, what a mess I've got myself into.

When she woke, the sun was setting and the air was much cooler. She was achy, heavy, and tired, but grateful that she didn't feel sick anymore. Insects and animals buzzed and chirped and ticked and sang, and the plants shimmered peacefully in the gentle breeze. She walked. Quietly and carefully, hidden by nature, unsure of where she was going. She just knew she couldn't stay there. She felt compelled to move, to get away, and to find a way to rescue her mother.

She heard a woman's voice in the distance and she dropped to the ground, hiding. The woman began singing. It was so beautiful that Ash felt warm and soothed and comfortable, despite doing her best to stay alert. A man's voice joined the chorus and Ash was so enchanted by the harmony she couldn't stop herself creeping towards the sounds. It was as if she was entranced. The music felt too good to be bad. Too blissful.

Three tall, pale figures with long whitish blonde hair and whitish blue eyes sat around a fire. Two sang, and one began to pluck what looked like a harp but was more intricate and complex. The sound was delightful and energising, so magical. Ash knew from the tales of the land that these were elven beings and that this was the famous elven band. Three horses grazed behind them.

She had heard them play in the palace once. The sound of their music had spread throughout the castle so that even the servants in the kitchens and servants' quarters had been able to enjoy their singing. She recalled stories she had heard of the elven band. Some said they were sent from a place called the aether to save the earth. Some said they were banished and disgraced and sent to earth to suffer the ways of the mortals. Others said elves were only half immortal, only certain things could kill them. The music stopped.

The male singer said, "You may join us." He looked directly towards Ash.

She felt exposed. Caught off guard, she edged backwards as carefully as she could, trembling.

"I see you with the sound. I see your soul and your heart, and you need rest," he said. "Join us, you are in no danger here." He swigged from a skin and breathed out heavily before going back to his beautiful chorus. The words were from a language Ash had never heard before. A rhythmic, ancient-sounding language. Powerful and wise.

The fire was warm, and the elves gave her a blanket to help her rest. She nestled into it as deeply as she could. It made her feel safer, as if it provided a magical barrier that no evil could get through. The elven music was otherworldly, and now more than ever, she understood why they were the most prized entertainers in the land.

The music they played now was so much better, so much more entrancing than that which they had played in the palace. Even though her eyes were closed, she saw shapes, colours, and swirls with each sound, and each shape seemed to mean something to her, speaking to something deep inside of her that she couldn't quite put into words or thoughts. The music stopped, giving way to the sounds of a fire crackling, and nature, and the stillness of the night.

She opened her eyes to see the flames of the fire flowing in orange and yellow, and the wood glowing red at its edges, pulsing with the breeze, and the grey smoke swaying with it.

"I am Nilinriall," the elf man said. He swigged from the skin and the harsh scent of alcohol followed his harsh exhale. The female elf glared at him, her eyes following the skin. "This is Gwynnestri, and Dillinir," Nilinriall said, pointing first to the female elf and then to the other elf.

"Ash," she said, not wanting to talk, simply wanting to listen to more of their music. The healing effect had been remarkable.

"We are on our way to Avenia, the High King has summoned us to play for him," Gwynnestri said. Ash could tell she was trying to be friendly. "Where are you going?"

Ash smiled, not because she was happy, but because she didn't know how else to respond. "I need to get out of the Nine Lands," she said. "I killed Prince Gideori and some guards, and... my friend. The slaves rebelled in the city. There was so much fighting. I ran. But I have to go back for my mother. I have no idea what to do." She wasn't sure why she spurted everything out so openly, so bluntly, and she instantly regretted it. She didn't know what the elves would think or do, or even if they were truly friendly.

The stench of alcohol on Nilinriall made her doubt it. He was so much more worn out and lacklustre than the other two, though she noted he hadn't lacked vibrancy when he sang.

"Don't worry about him," Gwynnestri said. "He has a good heart, even if he has lost his way."

Ash realised she had been staring at Nilinriall for some time while her thoughts had run away with her.

Nilinriall drank more. "You are the ones making me go back there. I wanted to forget about her, about us." He drank some more.

"The wedding in Avenia is not for some time, brother, there is plenty of time for you to prepare yourself," Dillinir said. "Now you can finally free yourself of the shadows you cast upon yourself. This is the Way."

"Now is not the time," Gwynnestri said. "We must focus on our friend."

The elves contemplated something together and spoke to each other in what Ash assumed was Elven. Gwynnestri said, "There is an essence of great power in you girl, and we do not sense deathsong. Are you sure you *killed* someone?"

Ash stared at the fire, concentrating on its constant flow of light and movement, trying to shake the image of Tilly impaled on the shard of broken wood. And blood. She felt sick, and the anger inside her horrified her. One of the horses stomped its foot and neighed. "I'm sure," she said.

"Sleep now, and we will play," Gwynnestri said. "Elvensong heals."

Ash lay next to the fire and the sounds of the elven band made her comfortable and sleepy. She stared at the stars in the blue-black sky and the silver moon that bathed them in soft light. She remembered the rare summer evening she had sat with her mother on the wooden bench in the kitchen gardens, and her mother had braided her hair while they chatted quietly, eager not to draw anyone to them.

The setting sun had cast a golden hue over the gardens and she remembered the scents of rosemary, chamomile, and lavender. Ash had listened intently to her mother telling her the tale of the elders who put the stars in the night sky and gave each one unimaginable magic of fire, water, earth, air, and aether, which is the realm of magic, and how sometimes a tiny star would fall and bring its magic to earth for all to use, not just witches. When her mother had leaned in and whispered words of encouragement and love, reminding her of her strength and potential, Ash had felt a profound sense of warmth and security, much like she felt now with the elves. *Mother is great with her stories,* Ash thought. *I wish they were real. Why do fairytales and dreams have to be the only things of excitement in life?* And with those thoughts, her dreams were plentiful and pleasant.

Raised voices and tension woke her. Instantly alert. Heart beating hard. A well of anxiety.

"We can't help her!" Gwynnestri hissed. "I wish we could." And then she realised it was the elves arguing amongst themselves.

Nilinriall slurred his words and spilled his drink as he gulped. She heard it but didn't look. She was afraid of being noticed. He said, "Ugh," and she heard him shake the skin and groan. It had run out. "We can take her to a smuggler, we can save her," he said.

"We cannot," Gwynnestri said. "It is too dangerous. We are too conspicuous and we would get noticed with a stolen servant, and our purpose is in Avenia now." Her words were stern and filled with intent. "Did you not dream of a burning cocoon at the wedding, and of the butterfly that came from it?"

"You know I did. We all did. But we are lost and we cannot rely on dreamsong." He tried swigging from his empty skin again, and groaned when it returned nothing. "We have time until the wedding, so why can't we help this poor girl?"

"The dreamsong called us to Avenia *now*, Nilinriall, not in several moons. We have no time, the strands of fate have bound us. We must continue on that path, not this one. This is it, Nilinriall. Finally, our calling. We all felt it."

Nilinriall grunted. "How many times have we tried to understand why we were sent here? How many times have the High Elven told us we cannot return, with no explanation? I am done, and I want to help this girl."

"You are blind drunk! How can you expect to be sensible? You want to run, that is all you have ever wanted to do," Gwynnestri said. "I am not going to let what you did so long ago compromise our destiny. We *will* go back to Avenia and you *will* face whatever waits there, whether it be a flaming cocoon or butterfly, or both, or *anything* else. You will face it." Gwynnestri was so resolute that Ash knew, simply *knew,* there was no way to convince her otherwise. No way to convince them Nilinriall was right, that they should help her, or at the very least, that they could help her.

The elves were silent, giving the stage to the waning crackles of the fire and the chatter of insects. Ash was curious about what she had heard, for a while, and then she drifted off.

※

She woke to the scent of freshly burnt wood and the sounds of birds singing. The elves were gone. She felt alone and helpless. Hopeless. She sat on the fallen tree trunk the elves had sat on and stared into the wilderness, daydreaming and thinking about what to do next. She realised her wound wasn't stinging anymore and she raised her clothes to look. There was only smooth bare skin, nothing to show there had been a horrible burn. *Elvensong is healing,* she thought.

A harsh, hurried voice. "This way," the woman screeched. "They're close. We've got one." The sounds of running footsteps. Bushes rustling and twigs snapping. Commotion and clamour.

Ash threw her blanket down and ran. Bushes leapt out at her, biting. Branches and leaves forced her to duck and swerve. Her breathing was so fast and deep she rasped on each inhale. A heavy force bashed her in the back and took all the wind out of her. *No, no, no!* She lost her balance and landed with a thud. Stunned. She lay gasping, desperate for air.

A woman peered over her, panting, smiling a crooked smile. "Look at what we have here," she said, waving her wand in Ash's face. A man appeared by the witch's side. Both were rough and tatty looking, and stinking. Unusual for witches. "Another runaway. Seems we're in luck lately, Arduk."

"I'm not a runaway, I belong to the palace and I'm making my way back there. If they find you've stolen palace property, you'll be hanged."

The pair appeared concerned.

"They'll torture you before they hang you, I've seen it so many times. It won't be long before the watchers catch on to my trace." She hadn't even thought about the watchers until now. The thought gave her chills. There was no escaping. They *would* eventually find her.

"She's got the palace brand," Arduk said. "Maybe we should return her."

"They won't give us anything for her, you twit."

"But Bettie, I don't wanna be tortured."

"We'll rebrand her, it's fine. Tie her up and take her to the rest of 'em."

"No, please. You're making a big mistake. I'm the King's servant. They'll make an example of you," Ash said, as Arduk tied her hands together.

"The city's rioting, kid," Bettie said. "You're the last thing the watchers'll be looking at. A pretty, exotic little thing you are too. We'll get a good sum for you somewhere far from here, I'm sure of it."

I wish they would die. I wish they would burn. I wish the world would end. I wish I would die.

She was so confused and distraught, and she felt such a fire inside of her she was sure something would happen like it had when she had killed the Prince, and the interrogator, and Tilly. *Tilly.* But nothing.

Nothing, because it had all just been a coincidence. Nothing, because she really couldn't kill people with her mind. How absurd to even think it. Yet how could so many coincidences happen in such a short amount of time? And why could she feel something so *firesome* inside of her?

I wish they would die, she continued.

Nothing.

There was a sense of relief and a sense of disappointment. She wanted the power. She wanted the abilities. She didn't actually want to kill people, though.

Arduk fastened a rope around her neck, and he held the end of it. "You can either walk with us or I'll drag you. Your choice."

They walked through the bush to the road where there was a single file of slaves lined up and chained together, and a couple of slave snatchers giving them grief. She recognised Serene.

"I am telling you now, I am the princess of Ul Nirin. Take me to Varamin, now!" Serene said.

The slavers laughed belligerently. "You're nuts," one man said. "We've heard some stories in our time, never a branded servant pretending to be a princess."

"I am telling the truth," the Princess whined and sobbed and shook her hands, rattling the chains around her wrists.

"She's got the entitled attitude of a princess," the man laughed. "Palace servants getting too comfy by the looks of it. We'll soon have that out of you, sweetheart."

Serene sobbed. "I will prove it to you, I *am* a witch, I can do magic. Give my wand back, I will show you."

"No!" Ash said.

Serene looked up and the moment she recognised Ash, her face filled with hope. "She will tell you. She is my servant."

"That's funny," Bettie hissed, pushing Ash to the back of the line. "We got no servants here from the palace. You've got to be lying." She tied Ash's neck rope to the servant in front of her and fastened chains to her wrists.

"This is outrageous, you will pay for this," Serene said. "Tell them, Ash!" she pleaded.

Ash turned her back on her.

Bettie stormed at Serene and slapped her so hard in the face she fell, rocking the servants she was attached to. Princess Serene gasped as the rope around her neck tightened with the sudden movement. She clambered to her feet, choked and distraught.

Bettie said, "If I turn in a branded human who was witnessed trying to practise magic, I get a hundred silvers and they hang you. That's a lot more than I'll get for a whiny little bitch servant who won't keep her mouth shut," she spat. "Now look here, look around you, everyone knows their place. Can you hear that?" She put her hand to her ear. "They're all quiet. They all know how to stay alive." She grabbed Serene's chin and shook it roughly. "You wanna live, darling?"

Serene nodded, and then she was so full of sorrow she couldn't keep her head up.

"Good," Bettie said.

CHAPTER 7

THEO

Theo lay on his grubby mat plagued by his thoughts. Kirakai had ordered Avira to serve him in private and Theo hated every possible thought about it, and he hated himself for not doing anything about it or even having the courage to talk to her about it.

Pika's choice played on his mind too. It was absurd to think they could escape the Nine Lands and live safely. He resented Pika for bringing it up, a false hope of something that would never happen. He had heard Pika tiptoeing off earlier, no doubt to Toarer. He wondered what they were doing. Wondered when they would get caught. He dreaded the thought.

Tico grunted loudly in his sleep and it sent Theo's heart racing. The dwarf rolled over and grunted a little more before settling. Theo tried to quieten his thoughts by listening to the faint rustle of blankets, the occasional shift in position and the soft, rhythmic breathing of the servants. He usually appreciated the hushed atmosphere and the sense of space it gave him. But not tonight. His thoughts were troubled.

If Pika and Toarer were gone, it would be catastrophic. Yet that was the inevitability. Toarer was getting married and leaving Blackhill Manor and Pika was going to use the orb to escape. Theo suddenly had the feeling he had no choice but to go with Pika, and yet it left such an ugly clump in his throat he just couldn't get himself to agree with it. He wondered if Avira would go without him. He really didn't like that thought.

He drifted into middling consciousness between sleep and restlessness, and his worries about Avira and Pika and everything else took on distorted images and sequences that jumbled his mind. For a while, he was aware of being half asleep and half awake.

Something surrounded him, trapping him. Yet it was protective and comforting. He felt secure and nurtured, as if he were a butterfly in a cocoon. It was warm, dark and tranquil. A pleasant sort of darkness, not the ominous kind.

In an instant, flames tore away the feeling of safety. Red and white fire blazed all around the cocoon, all around him, and he felt the heat and the evil as he desperately wriggled and pushed, trying to escape. He pushed through the cocoon with his legs, and flames burned him.

He opened his wings and flapped them in a panic. The movement extinguished the flames on them and he flew through the fire. Endless, untameable flames. Each flap of his wings enraging and enlarging the fire around him. It was hopeless. The flames were tearing at the edges of his wings and burning his legs and he was in agony. He flapped and flapped with all his might until it was all too much. His flight waned. He gave up. Plummeted towards the ground, into the flames.

Something pushed him upwards. A butterfly. One, then another, and another. Three saviours in the form of delicate creatures. He felt an instant bond with them. No words were exchanged, yet their sentiments of curiosity and love were clear. This novel sensation struck Theo deeply, for he had never truly known the feeling of being loved. They flew him high, away from the raging fire and into the refreshing embrace of clear, open air. They fluttered playfully around him and it was exhilarating. Onwards and upwards they fluttered into the stars, and the magnitude of the cosmos and the world below him left him in awe.

"Theo?" Avira said, concerned, holding him.

He was on the ground outside, at the edge of the lake away from the wedding site. The air was cool and fresh. The still and tranquil lake reflected silver moonlight. *What?* he thought. He was covered in sweat and confused. He couldn't remember going to the lake at all. He only remembered struggling to sleep, and the dream of being a burning butterfly. He felt strange, and wondered if he was still dreaming.

"You were sleepwalking, and your eyes were in the back of your head again. I didn't know what to do. I was on my way back from..." She stopped herself. She hugged him tightly and he felt bliss for a moment, before the weight of everything closed in.

He wanted to ask about Kirakai, but he didn't have the courage. He diverted. "There must be something wrong with me. The fits, and now sleepwalking," Theo said.

A thick, murky shadow drifted from a tree above them, and he flinched, pointed, and trembled. "The shadow," he gasped. It disappeared into a tree, as another shadow came from behind a trunk, closing in on them. Theo scurried backwards as it advanced, inching closer until it eventually dissipated into the lake.

Avira was too calm. "There's nothing there, Theo. I'm here. It's only me. It's okay."

It was only her. There were no shadows. He shook his head, trying to gain a sense of reality. He calmed a little, and it felt good to relax. "I'm going mad. I'm useless," he groaned. He still couldn't work out whether he was in a dream or not. It felt real, too lucid to be a dream, and yet it was so surreal to be out by the lake at night with Avira. The lurking shadows made it even harder to know what was real and what wasn't.

"There's nothing wrong with you, Theo. You're exhausted, that's all. It's not surprising your mind is playing up." She was close to him, and her eyes were compassionate and sincere. "Have you thought about Pika's choice? We can't stay here. We have to go." A tear ran from her eye, catching the silver moonlight and glistening as it trickled. A heavy silence followed.

The thought of trying to escape paralysed Theo. He was convinced it would go terribly wrong or they would get killed. They would be caught and tortured. He tried to think of their freedom, but the risks weighed heavily on him and tied his stomach in a knot. He struggled to muster words. "I wish it was that simple," he finally said. "But I don't think it's a good idea."

"You want to stay here? Let these things happen to us over and over again until we die? Ugh, maybe you *are* mad, Theo," she said. She slumped to the ground, her face wrought with sadness. "I can't do it anymore. Promise me you'll come with us, Theo."

"I..." he said. It was a promise he desperately wanted to make and keep, yet he had no confidence he could keep it. His heart wanted to say, *Yes, of course, I'll go with you, Avira. I never want to be apart from you.* But his fear and doubt said, *No, no, no, you can't, you'll get killed. We can't escape. Only fools would try.*

Her expression demanded everything of him. She needed him. He needed her. He needed her support, her strength, and her kindness. He couldn't lose her, it would be the end of him, but he couldn't make a promise he couldn't keep. He said nothing. She tried to hide her disappointment, though he could see it clearly. She shifted to lie next to him and she stared into the stars. He was tense beside her, hating himself for his lack of courage.

There were countless stars in the sky that night. Some steady and small, others bright and twinkling, and some clustered so close together it created an ethereal, glowing cloud. The few clouds in the sky were soft and light and edged in silver moonlight. The night air was brisk and tranquil. A mellow popping sound came from the lake as fish rippled the surface.

"How can something so beautiful be so cruel?" she said. "The world, I mean." She took his hand, gently.

"I know," he said. They lay and watched the stars and the moment felt deep and magical. It felt like there was nothing else in the world except the two of them and the beauty of the night sky. Theo relished the warmth that radiated from Avira's body. A shadow swept over him, and it shook him back to reality. He didn't want to say anything about it. His mind raced around all the bad things it could catch onto and he couldn't stop it. Avira squeezed his hand.

"Do you ever think about your parents?" she said.

His thoughts changed direction and he was grateful. "No, not anymore. It seemed pointless after a while. I'll never know my mother, though I used to wonder what she might have been like. We'll never know who my father is, nobody does," he said, still captivated by the vast starry sky above them. "Do you?"

"I miss mine very much. When they sold my father, I was so sad. I was so young I barely remember anything except for the pain. That's still vivid. And when my mother was sold, it was too much for me. I turned into a ghost. Something in me numbed and died. It hasn't been the same since. I dream of finding them again, maybe by chance or maybe by purpose."

You'll never see them again, he thought, thinking himself realistic and pragmatic. "Maybe," he said, trying to hide the doubt in his voice.

"Do you ever dream of what life would be like without giants and witches?" she said.

"Not a lot," he said.

"I do, every day," she said. "I dream of having my own little home near meadows and a stream, and making delightful meals every night with real food, and having kids and playing hide and seek in the woods with them and telling them stories and singing them to sleep before spending all night with their father talking about the deep wonders of the world."

Theo imagined himself with her and their children, free in beautiful lands in their own beautiful home. He found himself experiencing a desperate hunger more intense than he had ever felt before. He yearned for the life she described. But he knew it would never happen and he suspected she wasn't dreaming of a life with him at all. She deserved someone better than him in every way. He felt so bereft he wanted to cry.

They lay holding hands, picturing lives so impossibly removed from theirs that it was hopeless.

"I'm sorry," he said, eventually.

"What for?" she said.

"I'm weak. I always let you down."

"Ugh, Theo! You are *not* weak. We all have our weaknesses. That doesn't mean we're weak." She put her head on his chest. "You're kind, you're thoughtful, you're careful, those are all great strengths, and I admire you for them. You need to start recognising your strengths or you'll never find the courage you need to..."

Theo waited for her to finish.

"The courage I need... to what?" he said.

"Nothing," she said. "Everyone needs courage, don't they."

He could tell she was avoiding something. No matter what she had been about to say, it was clear to him that he needed to find the courage to promise her a new life beyond the barrier. A good life. One that she deserved.

He imagined the wild and dangerous rush of porting from one place to another by magic, and the sense of freedom in the wide world beyond the barrier. No giants to torment and torture them. No witches. No Kirakai. No slop. No exhaustion. No starvation. Infinite opportunity.

But the vastness of the world out there intimidated him. He worried about not finding food, about dark shadows chasing them, about being captured again, about being battered in relentless ice storms or getting lost in a hot desert without water or shelter, about Avira finding someone she deserved and abandoning him, about being alone beyond the barrier with nothing and no one. He pictured the porting going wrong and their insides being ripped out. It was all too much. The sliver of excitement and optimism was crushed by anxiety.

The sublime moment of peace and connection with Avira had been ruined by his thoughts and it devastated him. He felt as if everything good would be tarnished by the bad, many times over, as always. *When will it end?* he thought.

"I wish we could lay here every night," Avira said. "It's so stunning." She tightened her grip on his hand and nestled closer into his chest.

"Me too," he said. A gentle breeze rustled the leaves. The odd insect chirped in the distance. A pleasant scent came from the lake and its surroundings, of water and plants and earth. He closed his eyes and the eerie silhouettes of the woodland disappeared into a comfortable, timeless contentment he wished he could revel in forever. *I would sell my soul for this,* he thought, carelessly.

"Maybe we could do this every night, beyond the barrier," she said. "We have to go back to our quarters now. I don't want to."

Theo didn't want to go back either. He couldn't bear to go back. He decided that the dream of being a butterfly was a blessing. It had led him to this blissful moment with Avira. Half of him was screaming at himself to ask her to stay the night there with him, and she would say, *What about the whip?* He would say, *To the underworld with the giants, I would sell my soul for you. Let this moment never end.*

The other half of him forced himself to stand up. As he did, he felt so heavy and wrong and upset with himself. He gave her his hand and helped her to her feet. They hugged tightly one last time. The fat and dark shadow of the giant manor loomed over them.

CHAPTER 8

EXILUK

Exiluk headed to the mountains. The stories about the ghosts of the First Giants were much more intriguing than Garaduk Eastport, which was more of a military base that controlled goods going in and out of the Nine Lands, and a place for merchants to stop over before returning to the mercy of the ocean.

The wind bit fiercely when it gusted, and a light snow fell. The mountains towered ahead, dressed in white, black, grey, and brown, and seemingly barren except for scattered trees and bushes without leaves.

The trail meandered through uninhabited steppes dotted with yellow, brown, and violet flora. The grassland stretched for miles ahead leading towards the mountains. He walked for an age, but quite contentedly, enjoying the new terrain and the brisk air. His stride was occasionally hampered by broken ground, which had been undermined by the burrowing of hare-like creatures. They sat at the entrance of their burrows and watched his progress with interest, whistling to each other. The distant calls of unseen birds created a harmonious backdrop to his solitary walk, immersing him in a meditative rhythm. Snowflakes spun in the wind, rising and falling with each gust.

A circle of stone arches stood on the weather-beaten rocky mountainside, silent, heavy and ominous. Exiluk examined it closely, noting the size, shape and alignment. He imagined that even a horde of giants would have struggled to carry those rocks.

Perhaps the First Giants could have, he thought. He traced the circumference with his eyes and noticed faint engravings running down the centre of the stones. He ran his hands along the surface, slipping his fingers into grooves and along smooth and rough stone. He compared it to the one he had seen in the forest of Darpirith, which had been a source of wonder, mystery and magic for the keradin. That stone circle had been a wonderful mesh of colour covered in green moss, lichen, red and blue mushrooms, green vines, grey and brown branches, and red leaves.

This stone circle before him appeared desolate compared. It felt like a doorway, a portal. Each arch was formed by two tall stone pillars with a horizontal slab across the top. The pillars stood next to each other at slight angles to form a circle. There was a hint of magenta in the grey-black rock. The rock glistened with a light layer of frost and snow. It emanated a strange energy that felt so profoundly mysterious and so ancient Exiluk couldn't connect with it. It scared him to know there was a power that he couldn't understand. A power he may never understand.

Old teachings of the keradin said there were artefacts on many worlds that dated back to the elders themselves, and that some of those artefacts were used in the making of the worlds and contained unimaginable powers. The stone circle before Exiluk felt as if it was one of those artefacts. The forest of Darpirith was deeply magical and of immense power. *Perhaps those powers are due to the stone circle there,* he thought.

Disconcerted, he walked on. He found a worn path of stones and rocks laid into the ground and followed it. The path was wide, as if made for giants or some other big creature. He walked and walked, ascending the mountain.

The air was crisp and invigorating. He made good progress. What looked like birds of prey circled high above and seemed to follow Exiluk for a while, no doubt making sure he didn't venture too close to their eyries.

He was high upon the mountain. The view of the landscape below, in muted colours of brown and yellow and blanketed in a thin layer of snow, and the silvery sparkle of wintered trees with their bare branches covered in frost, and the glistening sea under the pale winter sun, was almost dreamlike in its beauty and tranquillity. The mountain felt sleepy and majestic, like a mythical giant.

He heard talking, a deep voice, and he slipped behind a rock. There was a dirt path curving around a bend, intersecting with his stone path.

A dwarf on a giant's shoulder was reading a map. He said, "We've found it, look, the stones. The pattern matches the key on the map. We've found the path!"

"Shh, I don't want to draw attention to us," the giant said.

"I don't think there's anything on these mountains, Toarer, we haven't passed a single living thing for days," the dwarf said.

"Doesn't that worry you, Pika?"

"I'm more worried about the mindwatchers than some evil creature following us."

"I am sure it's fine, the nearest tower is nowhere near here," the giant said. "Still, it feels quite ominous," he muttered, with a slight shudder.

As the giant stepped onto the stone path, he stopped, and both giant and dwarf absorbed the scenery as they looked down from the heights of the mountain over the vast plains and endless sea.

"I've never seen anything so magnificent," Pika said, awed. "The world is full of wonder! Thank you, oh thank you for taking me with you, Toarer."

"Your life is at risk." Toarer shook his head. "If anyone found out what I have dragged you into... Don't thank me for that." They both went silent, their brows furrowed in concern. "No being should be restricted from seeing the world," he gestured towards the glorious expanse before them, "even if we have to take down a couple of empires to make it happen." The giant and dwarf laughed. "I don't like the idea of being executed, though," Toarer added, and he tried to laugh it off but it seemed to Exiluk their mood had changed.

The giant walked on. "It's so hard seeing how you get treated and knowing if I say anything you will just get it worse," he said. "And you four mean more to me than my family," his voice cracked.

"Oh Toarer!" The dwarf wrapped his short arms around the giant's head and sighed.

Exiluk, deeply intrigued, followed from a safe distance, hiding amongst the rocks and crevices of the mountain face. He thought about the wonderful simplicity of the keradin way, and how it engendered kindness and happiness. *There is certainly more suffering outside the swamps,* he reflected. He thought about all the excitement he had experienced on his travels and it made his pulse beat quicker and his senses heighten and his stomach flutter, and as he craved for more he thought no more about the peace and happiness of life in the swamps. *Onwards,* he thought, relishing and revelling in the adventure. The giant's stride on the more established paths meant Exiluk struggled to keep up. He was tired, breathless, and sweating, doing his absolute best not to be noticed.

After a while, they left the stone path and took a rough trail up the steep mountain, the dwarf leading the way now, checking the map every now and then. It was much easier to keep up now the giant couldn't take advantage of his full stride. They reached another stone path. This one was older and narrower and clung to the edge of the mountain, and at times the giant nearly lost his footing.

Eventually, they stopped by a cave opening, and Exiluk crept closer. The arch had engravings above it, but they were worn and distorted, and it was too difficult to discern clear shapes. The dwarf said, "Look, some of these patterns match." He pointed at the map and at the carved, faded runes.

The giant had to crouch to get into the cave entrance, and after some moments he exclaimed, "Pika, look at this one, it's too small for me, it must be dwarven!"

"We don't know that, don't get your hopes up yet," the dwarf said. "It could be anything, could be mines made by slaves."

"There would have been official records. No, these lost tales have been accurate so far. I think we have finally found it," the giant said.

"You will have to go in yourself, I am afraid. If you want to, that is. I can guard the entrance for you."

"Of course, I want to."

"If you see anything dangerous, just run. Promise me that, please?" the giant said.

"I will."

With the giant in the way, Exiluk had to wait it out. His curiosity was piqued. He wondered what the map was for, if they were on the hunt for some of the treasure Captain Greavis had spoken about. *But why would a dwarven slave risk his life for treasure,* he wondered. *What use could he have for it?* Exiluk waited for what seemed like an eternity until the sun had set and the stars emerged, and the air got significantly colder. The giant lit a fire in the cave entrance and soon drifted off, snoring.

The glowing, burning wood cast a warm, soft light about the cave and shadows danced on the rock walls and ceiling. There wasn't much space to get past the giant. Exiluk pressed himself against the cave wall and crept slowly. There was a small entrance to a tunnel, he had to crouch to get through it, and on the other side he could just about stand normally. He followed it into the darkness. The tunnel went on and on until he could see the ending and faint firelight. Exiluk crept slowly.

He slipped into the room at the end of the tunnel. It was massive and magnificent, except its contents were sinister. Two giants' skeletons lay sprawled amongst dozens of scattered, deteriorating dwarven skeletons. They were strewn about in a chaotic and contorted fashion, as if they had been fighting or fleeing. Exiluk wondered how giants could have got in there recognising they certainly couldn't have fit through the way he had come. There were only a few broken bits of weaponry and shattered armour dotted amongst the skeletons. *Someone came and looted,* Exiluk thought, also noticing places in the walls and pillars that appeared as if stones or gems had been plundered. He crept on, eager to learn what the dwarf was after.

He entered a long hall with tall pillars lined along its edges.

Each pillar had elaborate patterns and a series of runes carved into it that he couldn't understand. The aesthetic reminded him of a sophisticated and ancient civilisation. The walls were covered in equally elaborate carvings and decorations. There were holes where it appeared stones and gems had been taken out of the décor. A few fire lanterns glowed. At the end of the hall was a gargantuan carving of a dwarf on a throne stretching from floor to ceiling. An entrance to another cavern ran through the statue.

As Exiluk entered the next cavern, he found himself on a platform that ran the edge of the cavern along all four sides. It was equally as grand with its carvings, but smaller. Stairs in front of him led down to another platform, which in turn led to a further platform below, and so on for countless levels. Skeletons scattered the stairs. Exiluk could see the faintest glimmer of light coming from below. He followed downwards, into the depths, feeling vulnerable as he was exposed on the stairs. There were entrances to many tunnels and hallways on the way down. He ignored them, aiming for the light below.

He reached an entrance with a torch burning on the wall. The tunnel was long and rough with rock and dirt, and many other tunnels stemmed from it. He continued until he found some stones polished flat with runes carved into them. The runes glowed with a vibrant, magical outline. Some were light blue, some whitish, and some golden. They had been activated. At the end of the tunnel, a bulky wooden door was open, and he saw an abundance of gold gleaming. He couldn't believe his eyes.

Stealthily, he hid behind the doorway and peered into the room. No sight or sound of the dwarf, so he snuck in and hid behind a treasure chest overflowing with jewels, gold coins and ornate goblets. The entire cavern was treasure. The walls, the floors, everything but the ceiling was covered in it.

There were all sorts of objects from statues to amulets to rings to coins to weapons to goblets and everything in between, and many objects he didn't recognise. They were made from gold and silver and other precious metals and stones, and many were of stone and metals he didn't recognise. Their colours and textures and depths and power were tantalising. He could barely take it all in. He had never seen anything so magnificent. Gems on the walls glowed bright, giving the whole cavern light.

Where's the dwarf? he wondered, also worrying how he might take enough treasure with him to be satisfied and how difficult it would be to come back for it all. *I will figure that out later,* he thought. *As long as I get back here before the giant and the dwarf. Hmmm. I will need to find people I can trust. Worry about it later.*

He waited a while for signs of the dwarf, eyeing the vast treasures before him, his heart beating eagerly. These weren't mere objects of vanity made of gold and silver. He sensed energies, harmonies, powers and resonances amongst the treasures. Metals and gems of otherworldly radiance. Crystals beaming with magic. Amulets embedded with black stones with smoky swirls. Swords and shields of white with a pearly rainbow wash. Rune engravings with powerful, ancient meanings. It was too much to appreciate in one go.

The more time he spent there, the more he had the sensation that the room and its treasures were whispering to him with a power too ancient and sacred for him to understand.

Aside from the gleaming, nothing in the cavern moved. He crept carefully so as not to make a noise. He smiled, realising he had found enough wealth to last him a thousand lifetimes and more. *How could I possibly go back to the swamps after finding something like this?* He caught himself. *No. This is not the keradin way. I will go back to the swamps and cleanse my mind.* The thought of a cleanse, the thought of feeling pure again, he knew he needed it. He knew it was right, and it was the keradin way. *No matter the context, no matter the action, you can regain your integrity, you can find a balance,* he remembered master Zotikup saying. And yet as he remembered those words, he felt a murmur of defiance. It was small, almost imperceptible, and it said, *No, you will not. It is not the life you want. What do I want?* he thought. *Look at that amulet!*

The amulet was on a gold neck chain. It was round and had a

stone that appeared as if it was a window into the skies at night. Only once had Exiluk seen the stars like that: the night he saved Skup's life. The night he... He expelled the thought, expelled the feeling. Focused on the now. Quashed the deep guilt inside of him. Pictured the stars, the vivid, immense, incredible stars of the desert sky. The vastness. His own insignificance. It helped him feel okay about it all. *Nothing really matters*, he said to himself, and yet he knew he was distorting the teachings. He didn't care, it helped. He picked up the amulet and ran the stone between his fingers. He felt energy running through him, and as he placed it around his neck, that energy intensified. He felt alive, magical, powerful. *If only I knew how to use it,* he thought.

It makes sense to take everything I can carry without bringing attention to myself, he thought, filling his pockets with rings and gems and placing many fine jewels around his neck and wrists. Each one made him grin more widely. *What fortune!*

He found a black chain mail vest made from a metal that looked as if it was constantly swirling like an oily puddle rippled in a breeze. Despite it being light, he felt weighed down by it as if the power it oozed was too strong for him. *I will get used to it,* he thought, as he slipped his robe back over the mail vest.

What if the dwarf catches me? What if I can't leave with all these delicious jewels? I have been stupid. I should be more vigilant. Just a couple more, he thought, as he eyed a ring with a gleaming orange gem and slipped it into his heavy pockets. *What if he closes the door and locks me in? I need to know how to activate the runes. I need his map.*

He found a mirror about the size of his hand, not made of silver but something blacker, yet equally as reflective, and he peered into it and saw his glowing blue eyes and his horns. *Wait, my horn! It has grown back!* He saw his hand in the reflection and he ran it over the horn and his hand could feel the broken end. In the black mirror, he could see his hand running over a complete horn. *How strange,* he thought, as the disappointment seeped through him. His horn was still broken. *I had better get out of here and hide somewhere so I can follow the dwarf.*

Some irresistible trinkets called to him on his way out and he stuffed them into his bursting pockets. He heard rock grinding on rock, slowly, heavily, and dropped prone with an awkward metallic clank. A secret opening was widening in the rock at the far end of the cavern. He slipped into deeper cover and watched the dwarf reading what looked like his map. No, this was longer and thinner. It was a scroll. The dwarf was so immersed in the reading he almost tripped.

Exiluk made haste and slipped past the thick wooden door on the way out. He found a tunnel to hide in from which he could watch the dwarf exit. He sat and waited. Body heavy with loot. *How could I have been so stupid?* he thought. *I almost got caught. Don't turn greedy, Exiluk.* He waited and waited, wondering where the dwarf had gone and how long it would take him to return. He couldn't go back to the treasure for fear of the dwarf spotting him. He didn't want to push his luck any further.

A voice and the sound of something scraping on rock. Exiluk peered around the edge of the tunnel to see the dwarf running a small, thin wand along the shape of the runes. He was reading and muttering to himself as he manipulated the runes. The blue glow dimmed and disappeared on the rune he was scraping the pattern upon. The dwarf moved to the next one. This one was glowing pure white, until it dimmed and disappeared into the rock. The dwarf pushed the bulky door closed and it took all his might, then he went back to the runes.

Once all the runes were deactivated, the door disappeared, and it appeared as if it was just a dead end of a tunnel, rough rock and dirt. Nothing more. Without the glowing runes, it was much darker, except for the dwarf's small torch casting orange and brown around him. The dwarf put the map in his bag, fastened it tightly to his back, and left briskly. Exiluk followed, keeping a long distance, struggling to be swift and silent, weighed down with his new treasures.

"Toarer, Toarer, I found it, I found it!" the dwarf said, as he reunited with the giant.

"I can't believe it," the giant shrieked, rumbling the cave. "This changes history. It changes everything. I can't believe it."

Exiluk snuck closer so he could see. The dwarf appeared elated and exhausted, as if he hadn't the energy to process the situation. The giant was so excited he was shaking and restless, his fingers crossed together as if he was praying, hands moving up and down restlessly.

"There were hundreds of tablets in the library beyond the treasure. I couldn't take them, but I copied what I could onto scrolls." He patted his bag and smiled. "Us dwarves, we're not stupid and we're not weak, Toarer. Everything we've been told is a lie. We were once..." he paused. "Incredible... You should have seen it in there. The size of the halls and the carvings. The treasures. It was... unbelievable."

The giant appeared somewhat reserved. "We have so much work to do now. The ministries and rulers won't like this at all. They will kill us before we..."

"Let's not think about that now," Pika said, as he sat down, leaning against the cave wall. "We've got this far, we'll find our way further. I need just five minutes of..." he yawned, and his eyes closed. "Rest," he just about managed to say before his head drooped and he drifted off.

This is my chance. I will wait for the giant to fall asleep and I will take the map.

The giant took the dwarf's bag and put it on his lap and sat up straight, attentively.

He can't sit like that forever, can he? Exliluk thought.

Time passed and the giant's attentiveness didn't waver. The discovery had obviously meant an awful lot to him. This made Exiluk agitated. He wanted that map. He needed that map. *It is fine, I will find an opportunity,* he thought. *This may not be the time. The time will come.* He thought about how excited the dwarf and giant had been and he couldn't help feeling excited himself. If what they had discovered could change history, then Exiluk could be a part of history. *I can make history,* he thought.

History is made by heroes. He thrilled at the thought, and becoming aware of that thrill, he thought about how he was changing, that he no longer wanted peace and tranquillity. He sought thrills and excitement. He had a vague sense that this should bother him, but he ignored it.

A sliver of daylight entered the cave and Exiluk found himself stirring out of a sleep he hadn't intended falling into. The dwarf and the giant were talking and gathering their things. Exiluk waited until they had left and then buried some of his treasures, and then he followed their footsteps in the freshly fallen snow, thankful that it would have hidden his tracks from before.

CHAPTER 9

ASH

The elvensong had given Ash more strength and rejuvenation than she had expected. She was grateful. She had needed it. They had all been rebranded and they had been walking south by day and sleeping on the cold ground by night with only enough food and water to survive. The rope around her neck had worn her skin raw. She was hungry and tired, and she could see the others were much worse off.

South of Ul Nirin led to Eliniar, passing from the predominantly witch-dominated empire of Lor Kithin to the mixed kingdom of Midvale. Although the High King of Midvale was a giant, leading some to consider it a land of giants, plenty of witches lived there too. Being a servant of the palace had its perks. She had learnt more about the Nine Lands, their trade, and their rulers than most servants ever would. More than some of the masters too, she assumed.

Serene had whimpered and cried for most of the trip, and no matter how much the slavers hit her she hadn't been able to stop. That had angered them more. Ash had spent most of her time wishing the slavers would die, especially Bettie and Arduk. But the slavers had not died. Nothing extraordinary had happened at all.

A soft orange sun rose over a pale blue sky and the morning breeze sent chills through Ash's skin. They had been walking since first light. Eliniar was greener, colder, and wetter than Ul Nirin, especially the further south they went. *I wish Bettie would die.*

Bettie deserves to die. All the slavers deserve to die. Nothing. She was convinced that whatever had happened in the city must have been a coincidence. She had no powers at all. Yet she couldn't shake the feeling that she had killed Tilly, and she felt so horrible about it. *Why won't it work on these slavers? I wish Bettie would die. Bettie deserves to die.* She had got past the guilt of wanting someone to die. She was so infuriated.

"There we are," Bettie said. "Lord Sully's plantations. He'll have some of you for a good bag of coin."

Servants worked the land in the distance, just tiny figures on green and brown. A large, symmetrical house stood in the centre of the vast expanse of land.

It was well known that plantations were hard work, second only to the mining pits, and Ash began wishing she was back at the palace. She missed her mother. She had thought about her a lot, every long day they had walked. She had dreamt about her many times, some pleasant, and some plunging her into a frantic and ceaseless searching, but never finding her.

The manor stood three storeys high, its bricks a pale sand colour and impressively uniform compared to most other houses Ash had seen. Bricks of precious stones formed long vertical and horizontal lines, spread far apart from each other and seemingly at random. The precious bricks were semi-translucent with a glossy shine, and textures of white and grey were splashed through their inner form. Many mullioned windows spanned the width of every floor. The crystal panes that had been cut and polished to perfection had a rich blue-grey tint. At the front and centre of the house, wide terrace steps led to a long, rectangular and shallow pool of crystal-clear water surrounded by finely kept gardens. At a distance from that house stood several smaller and simpler buildings.

Ash and the other servants were lined up outside a barn. Betty gave each of them a quick slap to bring colour to their faces and told them to look alive, sharp. The taskmaster exited the barn. He was dour and mean looking.

He examined them. *Not me, please,* Ash thought. *Don't choose me.*

Not a plantation. He pinched the arm of the man in front of him. The man had a bit of muscle on his arms, but he was old and thin.

"Hmm," the taskmaster said. "You worked a plantation before?"

The man shook his head. Bettie cracked a whip over the man's back and he whelped and tensed. "Don't lie, your brand was of a plantation master in the north."

"He will do, I will take him for five coins."

"Five!" Bettie shrieked. "He's worth twenty-five."

"He is old, and these are stolen goods. Lord Sully won't pay market price for stolen goods, you know that." The taskmaster moved down the line. He wasn't interested in the next one, an old lady who looked frail and near her end. He stopped at Serene. "This one is particularly healthy, if not a little sorry," he said. "Where did you get her?"

"I'm the p..." Bettie had flicked her wand and sealed Serene's lips shut. Serene protested and struggled but the sounds were muffled and her words inaudible.

Bettie said, "She told me her last lord was *particularly* fond of her and he kept her well." She flicked her wand again and Serene's lips returned to normal. "She's got hell of a tongue on her though, and a wild imagination, so I'll give her to you for just ten."

"That's a fair price, Bettie, and you never give a fair price. What are you hiding?"

"I told you, she's a talker and she's got an imagination. Look at her, she's young and healthy and I'm sure Lord Sully'll like the look of her. He'll be pleased with you."

The taskmaster nodded and moved on, bargaining for some, and denying others. Ash wondered where those who hadn't been bought would be taken next. Since Serene had been bought, Ash decided she wanted to stay there too. She wanted at least a sliver of familiarity in her new life. The taskmaster reached her. He was tall with a strong build and a harsh face. He looked down on her. There was no brand on his face. An employed taskmaster, a witch. Someone who did it because he liked it. A cruel type.

There were also human and dwarven taskmasters in the Nine

Lands who had willingly sold their integrity to serve their masters. *Traitors. Cowards,* she thought. She couldn't decide which sort she despised the most.

"Do you know housekeeping?"

She nodded.

"Field work?"

She nodded again. It was a lie to make sure she was bought.

"Do you know your age?"

"Around fifteen."

"I'll give you ten for her," the taskmaster said.

"*Come on*, Rorxis, you gotta give me a little more than that. She'd go for thirty-five at the market, look at her. She's got something about her. She's got grit, I can tell you. She's stronger than all of them here. And she does what she's told. No complaining."

"Fifteen, take it or leave it."

There was a cruel irony in that somehow, so quickly things had changed, and Ash had become more valuable than the princess of Ul Nirin.

Ash's hands hurt. The herbs they were picking were particularly prickly and rough in places and they had to fill twenty baskets per day or go without supper. Serene was inspecting her own hands, which were brown and red from blood and dirt. Her eyes were watery. She had gained the strength not to cry out anymore. She caught Ash's gaze and Ash tried to smile. There was nothing to smile about. The work was gruelling and mind-numbing, the weather unpredictable, the hours long, and they were deprived of proper rest and adequate nourishment.

Ash had just dropped off her twentieth basket and she sighed with relief looking over the field, admiring the pink disc of the setting sun. Serene arrived at the drop-off point and Ash nodded at her.

The taskmaster said, "Twelve, looks like you will go without supper."

"I have not eaten in days. It is making me weak. Please, let me have supper and I will work much better."

The taskmaster drew his wand and flicked it at the Princess. She shrieked and keeled over onto the ground and writhed. "I am not sure how your last master ran things, but *nobody* talks back to me here, you got it?"

Serene lay on the floor whimpering.

Ash wanted to shout at the taskmaster, but she knew it would only make things worse. The anger in her was almost unbearable, and she just managed to contain it. She helped Serene up and brushed the dirt off her clothes, though the dirt merely smeared rather than coming off.

"Twenty baskets a day and you will eat. Otherwise, you are not a profitable worker. I don't expect you to understand business. I expect you to understand orders. Now get on with it, and if you don't do twenty baskets by lights out, I will put you in the pits, and you are not having food tonight even once you have met your quota. That will teach you. Where your entitlement has come from, I can't fathom." The taskmaster shook his head.

Ash felt deeply sorry for Serene, and she was confused and conflicted about those feelings. Serene was a witch. Witches took slaves. Serene was finally getting a taste of her own cruelty. Ash didn't want to feel sorry for her. She felt sorry for every human and dwarf that had spent their whole life suffering like this. Serene had barely suffered a day compared to them.

Some servants were lucky enough to have been chosen for housekeeping, which was much easier work, and Ash wished Serene had been chosen for that. Although, it was said that Lady Sully was a jealous and unpredictable witch who dished out punishment gleefully and randomly. Their young child was said to be a sadistic and strange boy who was best avoided, for he would try to turn you into a newt or toad, and often get it wrong or forget about you and never turn you back.

Ash sat in the servants' house with her back to the wall and ate her food. The food that the plantation workers had to eat was much worse than the servants' food at the palace. She longed for a real piece of meat, or a vegetable that wasn't slimy and about to rot. The sloppy vegetable stew they ate every night tasted tangy, as if it was about to ferment.

The mood in the servants' house was always deeply glum, almost morbid. It was as if all the spirit had been sucked out of them. They were all just lifeless beings repeating the same work every day. They barely talked to each other, barely even looked at each other. There was one boy who was chirpy, but everyone ignored him. Sometimes they scowled at him.

The sense of community amongst the palace servants had been much better. As Ash thought about the palace, she missed her mother, and it hurt so much that she tried not to think about it.

She kept an eye out for Serene, a part of her hoping the Princess would find a second wind and finish her twenty baskets before lights out. The other part of her told her not to care. To forget about the Princess and focus on herself. She needed to figure out a way to escape. She had been so close to some kind of freedom for just one night and she refused to believe that was the only freedom she would ever have. The thought of it all made her rage.

The chirpy boy came and sat on the floor next to her. He looked younger than her, but she couldn't tell by how much. The floor was cold, and made of rough-wood planks. The boy was scrawny and pale. *Likely from the cold south,* she thought. He said, "I'm Nifty. What's your name?"

"I'm Ash," she said.

Nifty tucked into his bowl of food. "Where'd you come from?" he said.

"Ul Nirin," she said.

"Oh yeah, what's it like up there?" he said, slurping. "You wanna bit more supper? I always feel sorry for the new girls like you, must be hard fresh on a plantation." He looked at her cut up, dirty hands.

"Don't feel sorry for me, I don't need your pity," she said. She held her empty bowl out.

Nifty poured a little food into it and smiled. "I've been 'ere all my life, as long as I can remember, anyway," he said. "Everyone's glum but I don't allow it in me. It's not so bad when you look at the right things."

Ash looked at him blankly. He was clearly a bit mad to think that. She had concluded that plantation work was as close to the underworld as you could get without being in it.

"I got food, shelter, and I get to spend the days outdoors in the sun and with nature. Could be a lot worse, could be in a whore house or mining the pits."

She wanted to say something friendly. Despite finding him strange, she recognised he clearly had good intentions and was trying to be nice. She couldn't find any words.

"What'd you do before they brang you 'ere?" Nifty said. "You not eating that?"

"I was a servant in the palace and I'm here with the princess," she said wryly, looking at the cold food in the bowl, still desperately hungry and wanting to devour it, even knowing it was tangy and slimy.

Nifty laughed endearingly. "Well, when they come and rescue the princess, take me with you, would you?"

Ash tried to smile. She wondered who had won the fighting in the city. She wondered if they were looking for the Princess. Perhaps that was their only hope. Perhaps the Palace of Ul Nirin would search for the Princess and eventually find her. The Princess would save Ash too. She owed her one. Ash's heart sank, she wasn't hopeful at all.

After a while of sitting together, Nifty nodded to Ash courteously and left her, presumably to go about his evening. Ash sat alone until Serene walked into the servants' house looking weary and she slumped into the corner with Ash. Serene stared blankly as if there was nothing around her.

Ash gave Serene the food Nifty had given her. She was extremely grateful, and she finished it desperately within seconds, and licked the bowl as if she was trying to draw energy from the wood. They were silent for a long time, their backs to the wall, watching the other servants in the house. It was more of a barn than a house.

Blankets were scattered all over the floor where they slept. There was a large, dirty bowl of water on one side for washing. The water smelt so bad that Ash preferred to stay dirty. *At least we were required to be clean and well presented at the palace,* she thought, eyeing her dirty, cut up hands. She felt a sudden rush of emotion thinking about it all and she hugged Serene.

Serene burst out crying, and they held each other tightly. "We have got to get out of here," she whispered, almost inaudibly, trembling. "I cannot survive this."

"I know," Ash whispered, her lips close to Serene's ear. "You're not a servant, you're the princess of Ul Nirin. Don't let them take that from you, no matter what happens. What do you need to become strong again?"

"I need rest, and food, and somewhere to practise, and ingredients for potions. We will never manage it, it is hopeless. They will hang us before we stand a chance," Serene said, crying again.

"How does it work? How do you do it?" Ash whispered.

"There is a magic inside witches, we learn to cultivate and command it. Focus it and channel it. It is inside objects too, things like bones, wood, gems, and herbs. Magic lore is complicated," she whispered.

"Don't worry, we'll get you strong and we'll get out of here, and we'll make them all pay," Ash said.

Serene shrugged, disbelieving.

"But for pity's sake, don't show anyone that you're educated, and be careful about what you say. If Lord Sully learns he's got an enslaved princess on his plantations, he'll be smarter to kill you than to send you home. Try talk a bit more like us, would you?"

The workers' bell rang just before sunrise. Ash remembered that she had been dreaming she could fly, and as soon as she had discovered it in her dream, she flew away and was finally free. It had been exhilarating, and she had felt powerful beyond measure. As she remembered that sense of power, she also remembered she had learnt to conjure spells, and that while she was flying, she blazed fire, dark shadows, and fury and chaos down on the guards, ministry, and soldiers of each of the lands she flew over. Waking to learn it was all a dream was desperately disappointing, yet it left her with a chill she couldn't shake.

Everyone got up and got ready to trudge to the fields. All were quiet and dreary except Nifty, who said, "Morning," to anyone and everyone he could make eye contact with. Ash felt too tired to give him the credit he deserved. She merely nodded when he greeted her. Those who had completed twenty baskets the day before were given breakfast. Ash and Nifty shared theirs with Serene.

Darkness was subsiding to sunrise. The air was cold and refreshing, the sort that cools the throat as it goes in. She walked beside Serene and Serene took her hands. "Look," she said. "Thank you for the food."

An intense warmth filled Ash's hands and travelled through her whole body, even her frozen toes felt good. She looked at her hands closely. There were fewer cuts and scrapes on them. Serene's magic had healed them. She put her arm around Serene as they walked.

Nifty caught up to them and said, "'Ello, I'm Nifty." He shook Serene's hand. "Woah, you got soft hands. I'm guessing you've never worked the plantations before. What they got you in the fields for?"

"Serene," she said, avoiding his other questions.

"I noticed you struggling yesterday," Nifty lowered his voice, "and 'coz we'd never met I didn't know if it'd be rude to offer help or not, 'coz if we got found helping each other we'd get in trouble. Now we're acquainted, if you need help later just give me a nod. We'll swap baskets when nobody's looking." His grin was endearing.

"That's sweet of you. Thank you, Nifty," Serene said, seemingly very touched by his kindness. Ash noted that Serene was trying to talk more commonly, and although it sounded a bit awkward, it was a lot less princessy.

Nifty skipped ahead down the path with an abundance of energy.

"He's peculiarly jolly, isn't he?"

"A little mad, probably," Ash said. They giggled. Ash admired his spirit and kindness, and that admiration conflicted with her. She whispered, "Don't get close to anyone here. We don't know who we can trust."

The work was monotonous, picking herbs, day in, day out. The same routine in a constant loop. Sun up, hands in the soil, fingers gripping stems. Over and over. The time dragging on, slowly, indifferently. No ending in sight, just the herbs, the soil, and the unchanging routine of the day.

Ash used the time to think about how they could escape. Serene needed somewhere she could make a wand and potions, and somewhere she could practise her magic. It seemed hopeless, the servants' house was always packed after work, and they would soon notice her gone if she was away for anything longer than a toilet break.

"You know what potion they use prickleroot mostly for?" Nifty popped up from nowhere and gave her a fright. "Oops, didn't mean to scare you, thought you'd 'ear me from a mile off." He picked the plant as he walked, ensuring to pull all the roots from the ground and take the whole thing as they had been instructed to do. "Gas," he said, a cheeky look on his face. He looked around, presumably making sure the taskmaster wasn't watching them talk. "All these fat witch lords and giants with nothing better to do than eat all day. Apparently, this stuff fetches a fortune 'coz of how much tummy trouble there is."

"Disgusting," Ash said, and they laughed together.

Nifty's basket was almost full, and he subtly swapped his with hers and nodded at her with his cheeky grin.

She swapped it back. "No. I don't need help."

He looked a little upset for a moment and then smiled and went on his way. Ash felt bad for rejecting his kindness, but she didn't want to take any risks. She didn't want to get close to Nifty. *Any extras will be a burden in our escape,* she reminded herself.

She watched Nifty swap his full basket with Serene's half-empty basket and Serene appeared eternally grateful. She would get a full slop supper for once. *Good, she needs her strength. We need her magic,* Ash thought.

∼≈∼

The work had been grinding and mundane, as always. Ash had lost track of how long they had been on the plantation. It could have been a couple of moons or more, it made no difference.

The three sat together at supper. Nifty's company was pleasant, if not a little irritating now and then, though overall his infectious energy made Ash smile. She resented herself for liking him, but it was impossible not to. Nifty stopped talking for a short moment as they ate.

"Nifty, you've been here a long time, haven't you?" Ash said.

"Sure 'ave. Longer than I can remember. And it might be that I'm 'ere 'til I die. Sad the way of the world it is but you 'ave two choices no matter what. You either make the most of it or you get the least of it. I'm not gonna let 'em give me the least of it so I make the most of it."

"Right," Ash said. "So, when you want some peace and quiet, just somewhere to be alone without being bothered, where do you go?"

"Oh yeah, I've got a place. And since you've been so kind to me past few days, I'll show it to you. Nice little place it is, peaceful and secure."

Ash was excited, and she tapped Serene's leg with her foot, but Serene ignored her. Serene looked dazed. She hadn't touched her food. The bowl of slimy slop was still full.

"What's the matter?" Ash said.

Serene's lip trembled and tears streamed down her face. It was the first time she had cried in a while. "I can't do it anymore," she said. "I've been trying, really, I have. I'm not made for this. I thought it would get easier, but I'm just not capable. I hurt every day, my stomach can't deal with the food, and I'm just so... broken. I am not one of you, remember."

Some of the servants had overheard her. Serene's last sentence had been spoken as if by a princess. So proud, so entitled. Fortunately, the tears and the breakdown had somewhat masked her power, entitlement, and privilege.

"Fine, you've never worked a plantation, but you'll get there," Ash said loudly, trying to hide the Princess's indication of there being something more to her.

"I won't," Serene said. She banged her head on the wall, hard, and the thud made everyone silent. She did it again, and again, and she wept as she banged her head again. Ash and Nifty grabbed her and stopped her from hurting herself any further. Ash's hand felt blood through Serene's hair.

"Let me go!" Serene said. She slipped quickly and nimbly through their grips, and edged towards the door appearing defensive and embarrassed.

"Don't run away, Serene. They'll make you pay," Nifty said. Never had he sounded so serious.

Serene's eyes spoke of desperation. She was going to run, there was no question. And Ash could see that Serene welcomed the ultimate consequence. They exchanged a final harrowing stare and Ash mumbled, "Please come back before lights out?"

The Princess stormed off into the night.

"Give her some time, she'll be back," Nifty said, reassuringly.

Things were awkward and tense in the servants' house and the wait was excruciating. *She wouldn't have run away,* Ash thought. *She just needs some time alone.* Although she truly hoped for it, she felt as if she was lying to herself.

"I'm going to find her," Ash said. Nifty followed.

They searched the farm buildings, the bushes, and the woods, and they tried calling for her without drawing any attention to themselves. She was nowhere to be found. They searched the fields and the further fields, and still nothing.

"She wouldn't 'ave actually run away, would she?" Nifty said, hesitant, worried. "That's a death wish."

"Where else can we look," Ash said, desperate.

He shook his head. They had looked everywhere. All the cheer had drained from Nifty's face, and Ash didn't like it. The fields shimmered softly under a silver moon. A bird chirped in the distance. A larger bird swooped over high in the sky. They walked back towards the servants' house slowly, worried.

Each moment that passed was more excruciating. If Serene wasn't back by lights out, the taskmaster would notice, and it wouldn't be good. *Not good at all,* Ash thought. The time for lights out would be so soon. She took a pile of blankets from near her, and some servants scowled at her. She scowled back so vehemently they looked away and carried on their gloomy evening.

She scrunched the blankets into the shape of a lying body and spread another blanket over it, her heart racing. She sat next to the pile with her arm on it.

"Smart," Nifty said.

Footsteps. *Serene?* Hope ignited with a frantic heartbeat.

"Come on now, runts, lights out," the taskmaster said.

Ash's heart sank. The taskmaster entered and began his count. His eyes flicked to each member and his lips moved for each count. He passed Ash and his lips moved and she hoped that he had counted two. Ash and sleeping Serene. The taskmaster stopped counting and thought about something for a moment. He ran the numbers again.

Ash was so nervous she felt sick.

The taskmaster stopped his gaze and counting at Ash, looked at the blanket and said, "Ah," and counted in his head.

Everyone in the room was tense and Ash worried the taskmaster would notice. Everything felt wrong and heavy and horrible.

"Wait," he said, scowling at Ash. "You think I am stupid, don't you?" He walked slowly, each footstep loud and daunting, and he looked down on the sleeping Serene and frowned. He ran up and booted the blankets and they flew at the wall. He laughed and said, "I knew it. You can't fool me. Where is she?"

"Toilet," Ash said.

"I don't believe you," he said. "I want all of you here, right now, whether you are in the middle of your business or not," he shouted, so loud that everyone shuddered. "I will give you the count of five.

One... Two... Three... Four..." he paused.

"I don't hear running," he said, his hand to his ear. This was all a game to him, and he loved an opportunity to play up. "Five!" He smiled. "We have a runner, haven't we?" His laugh was slow and nasty, and the sound cut the air. "You two," he pointed at two male servants, "get the snarler ready. We've got a search on our hands. Ohhh this is going to be something."

Everyone was struck with horror. Speechless. Paralysed.

He pointed at Ash, "And no supper for her for two weeks." He flicked his wand and Ash was struck with pain and terror all over her body.

The pain was a horrible, itchy burning. She frantically tried rubbing it away but it wouldn't budge.

The taskmaster lowered his wand. "If you *ever* lie to me again, I will put that curse on you for a whole night, do you understand?"

Irritation lingered on her skin, but her flesh and bones no longer felt it. She was shocked and weakened, and she couldn't look him in the eye, despite wanting to show strength. She tried to scowl at him, but she couldn't muster much more than a frown.

The taskmaster and the two servants left the house. Ash whispered to Nifty, "What's a snarler?"

"A horrible beast that can find anything it's got a scent of."

Moments passed and a growling, snarling, grunting beast could be heard. When it barked and howled it was like a wolf and what she imagined a dragon to sound like, but more choked and guttural. The taskmaster was laughing loudly, and Ash could picture the grin on his face. Chains clanked and dragged.

Soon it was outside the servants' house and the clammer of chains and the servants screeching and grunting trying to tame the beast was terrifying. Ash could hear it all, and picture it all in her mind, and it wasn't pretty.

The taskmaster entered the servants' house, slowly, proudly, and grinning. "Which one is her blanket?"

Nobody said a word.

"Which is her blanket!" he screamed. "I will let the snarler tear you apart one by one until you show me."

One servant woman said, "I'm sorry master, we'd tell you if we could, but they're all mixed up. Look." She pointed at the pile that the taskmaster had kicked.

"Give me something of hers then," he grunted.

The servants looked at each other with confusion and dismay, and then frantically looked about, and Ash hated them for it.

"This is what she wore when she came here, I remember it," one said, throwing it to the taskmaster.

"There we go then, we will have her back here in no time." He took the tattered robe and left. The door slammed behind him. The sounds of the snarler intensified, excited by her scent. Chains could be heard being grappled and unlatched, and off it went— grunting, snarling, groaning, and howling—until it couldn't be heard any longer.

Time stood still and Ash felt heavy and horrid. There was no hope now. Without Serene, there would be no magic. With no magic, no escape. No escape, no chance to find her mother.

Every servant in there was full of disgust, hatred, and sadness. Yet not a single one spoke of how unacceptable things were. There wasn't a smidgeon of hope in them. She wondered if humans and dwarves had always been like that. *Are we truly as weak and stupid as our masters say we are?*

Ash was so dismayed, so distraught, and so horrified. She was at a loss. She wanted to wish for magic, wanted to change what was happening. Wanted to wish the taskmaster dead. Wanted to burn everything down. *It's no use*, she thought. *What's the point? I can't do magic.*

The servants got into their sorry makeshift beds. Ash and Nifty waited in darkness, and it was unbearable. Nifty put his hand on her arm and she recoiled, rejecting his attempts to comfort her. They waited and waited. Too much time passed.

"We'll find a way to help her," Nifty said. "This ain't the end for her. We'll find a way."

"How can you be happy every day living like this! You're mad.

You're twisted and messed up to be happy. *Here.* What's wrong with you?" She didn't know where the words had come from, and she was mortified to have lashed out at Nifty like that. His reaction made it worse, like a scorned child struck out of nowhere. Moonlight came through the cracks in the shutters and the poorly constructed walls. It was just enough light for her to see his pale shadow shrinking, scorned.

Her whole body was on fire with rage and anguish and shame, and everything in the servants' house shook.

"Earthquake," she heard someone say, as they stirred from their sleep and she stormed out into the night. She found refuge in a bush. She curled into a ball with her head between her knees and her arms wrapped around her shins, and she squeezed herself angrily. The tension, contortion, and pain were cathartic as she screamed—loud, long, and hard. Wind rustled in the bushes, and the dark and cloudy sky obscured all but a few stars and the bright, almost-white moon.

Her thoughts kept her company. She hoped Serene would be able to conjure magic and kill the snarler, but deep down she knew that wasn't going to happen. There would be too much pressure for her to be able to conjure magic like that. Once she realised that, she tried to avoid thoughts about Serene.

She wondered what was happening in the city. The city guard had probably gained control over the rioting. Humans and dwarves couldn't overpower magic. Not with stones and trade tools. Not with hunting arrows. It was useless. Hopeless. Every time she had tried to be optimistic, it had backfired. Things had just been getting worse and worse. That thought made her cry.

Mother must be okay, though, she thought. *She would have been sensible and avoided the fighting and done as she was told, and she's probably serving the palace now in a favoured position. Everyone likes mother, she's too kind not to be liked, even by witches.* She missed her mother dearly.

"Ash?"

She was surprised to hear Nifty's voice.

"I hope you can 'ear me. If you don't wanna talk to me that's fine. I just wanna'd to make sure you're back before taskmaster notices. If taskmaster sees you're not about when he does his rounds again, he won't be happy. And if you do wanna talk to me, I'm 'ere."

Ash stayed put. She could see Nifty through the bushes. Half of her hoped he would just leave her. The other half of her needed some comfort, some reassurance. She crawled out of the bush. "Can you show me your hiding place?" She wasn't entirely sure why she had asked that. Serene would likely be executed for running away, and without Serene there was no need for a hiding place to practise magic.

Nifty smiled. "I thought you were mad at me."

"I thought you'd be a lot madder at me..." Ash said. "What I said..." She paused.

"Don't be silly. Only person who can make 'emselves unhappy is 'emselves and I don't plan on spending my life mad at people, what'd that solve? Not a lot as far as I can see it."

Ash threw her arms around him and held him tightly. "You really are nuts, you know that? You're the craziest person I've ever met, and in a good way. You're amazing." Her chest tightened, realising she was becoming too fond of Nifty.

Nifty looked completely taken aback, almost frozen. Ash guessed nobody had shown him any affection before. She looked at his wide eyes and worried she had embarrassed him or upset him. Then his face broke out into the biggest smile, and they both laughed.

They walked the path towards the fields and at a point around halfway, Nifty slowed. He searched for something at the edge of the path walking up and down, examining the floor carefully. "'Ere we go," he muttered to himself, and they went off the path into the woods. He counted nine trees as they walked, and behind the ninth, he dug his heel into the ground a few times until the sound changed from a muffled thud to something a little more wooden and hollow. He dug up some leaves and dirt to reveal wood and a rope. He pulled the rope and the wood lifted. He grinned. "Dug this place out when I was younger." He gestured for her to go. "You first, I'll close the hatch behind us."

Ash was apprehensive, but her curiosity was much more powerful, so she found her way down the ladder in the dark. The wood of the ladder was impressively smooth. As she reached the ground, she found herself on a flat, hard surface of good, sturdy wood.

Nifty followed her in and closed the hatch, and everything was pitch black. "I'll light a lantern, just a mo."

She moved out of his way, carefully feeling around with her hands, worried she would touch a rat or a spider's web or something slimy. Her hand found the wall, also smooth wood.

There was a twisting, creaking noise, and then a lantern glowed colours of orange and golden honey. The lantern was a contraption of a crystal that let tiny amounts of potion through a dripper. When the potion hit the crystal, magic formed and it glowed. It was like the lanterns in the palace, except much less fancy. When enough potion had dropped onto the crystal, the whole room was bright.

Ash gasped. She was in a miniature home, a really nice home. There was a mirror on the wall. There were shelves with ornaments, vases, and vials. There was a pot. He had taken broken glass and stones and embedded them into the wooden planks on the walls to make the most beautiful patterns. And a pile of blankets to rest in! It was incredible. Unbelievable. "How's this possible?" she said.

Nifty's grin was humungous. "Little by little, they don't notice something missing. Something breaks and they throw it away. Well, I find a way to mend it and use it. I always wanted my own little home and life's what you make it, ain't it? I can't go buy something like a lord can but that don't mean I can't 'ave a little something. You just gotta do a little bit every time you can. When they killed my..." he stopped abruptly and the joy washed from his face. "When they killed my dad something in me changed and I was so miserable and ill for so long, and it was so horrible one day I woke up and I said, *Never again. I'm not letting 'em win.* So I worked out all the ways I could win and I made it happen." He smiled again.

"I just don't understand how it's possible to achieve something like this. Don't you worry about the mindwatchers?"

"Not 'ere on the plantations I don't. Lord Sully don't play by the rules. I reckon he's tinkered with some protection spells, you gotta if you're buyin' servants on the cheap. I've always thought what I want and never got into trouble for it. Plus, I reckon they've got a lot more to worry about than a boy in a hideout," he laughed.

Ash wanted to cry but she held it in. Nifty was a whirlwind of emotions and she had enough of her own to deal with, although she couldn't help admiring him. She felt a heavy knot in her stomach at the thought that they would have to leave him here when they escaped, and an even heavier tighter knot formed when she realised their chances of escape were gone. "Why would you take me here? It's so precious. You barely know me."

He looked at his feet and blushed. "Oh, I dunno. You asked me for somewhere you can be alone. No one's ever really asked me and if you don't ask you don't get, do you? And I thought it'd be nice to share it with someone one day. It's a nice little place and it'd be a waste to 'ave it just for myself. You're welcome to come down 'ere whenever you like. Not that you'll ever 'ave much time. I sneak off at night after everyone's asleep mostly, and 'ave a little sit in 'ere when I need time alone, and then get back before the morning bell rings." He pointed to a pile of blankets on the floor, presumably where he liked to sit and relax.

Ash examined all the implements on the shelves. She was sure there was enough to make potions and much more. It was the perfect place for Serene to practise her magic. *Serene!* Her heart was crushed. *If only she hadn't run away. We were so close. She would have loved this place.* Ash swallowed a lump of sorrow and said, "I can't thank you enough, Nifty."

"If you're happy I'm happy. I figure that if you can be happy for others and not just yourself you've got a load more chances a day to be happy."

She found herself throwing her arms around him again, and she hated herself for it. She pulled herself away. "We'd better go before taskmaster realises we're gone."

CHAPTER 10

EXILUK

The giant carried the dwarf on his shoulders and Exiluk tailed them ensuring he stayed out of sight. All he wanted was a chance to get the map. *But why do I want that treasure so badly?* he asked himself. *It is not the keradin way. There are some things a keradin has never tested himself against. What cavern of treasure has a keradin ever found? It is not fair to hold myself to keradin standards beyond the swamp.* He felt sense in his words and yet a part of him knew he was deceiving himself.

They reached the other side of the mountain, and Exiluk crept to an edge making sure he wouldn't be seen. He looked out onto hills covered in tall, thin trees with dark trunks and few leaves, and pristine, ivory-white snow. Scattered amongst these trees were some remarkable ones with grey-hued bark and rich copper foliage.

Between the wooded slopes, clearings revealed colossal stone buildings, larger and more imposing than any castle, pyramid or monument he had ever seen. Their minimal exteriors—simple, almost sleek—made them seem even more gargantuan. Each structure stood solitary, evoking wonder in Exiluk. *How many giants inhabited these immense buildings? How many dwarves and humans had toiled to build one? Did witches too live within these magnificent walls?* These marvels appeared as if they had taken centuries to craft, and they appeared as if they would sit there, lifeless, for millennia to come.

The giant and dwarf took shelter in a shoddy wooden hut that appeared not to have been used for a long time. It was large enough for a couple of giants. Hardy-looking, rough, reddish-brown vines and pale moss grew over most of its exterior. Exiluk curled up snuggly between some bushes against the wall outside and waited, listening. He was cold, but he could bear it. The air was clear and crisp, the sky overcast. Smoke came from the chimney inside the hut.

"How long will we need to stay in Okuden?" Exiluk heard the dwarf say.

"You know I hate these formalities. I will tell them we are late because we got lost and that we can't stay too long due to the wedding. I get the impression the Okudenians hate these formalities more than I do. They will be happy to see us depart for Avenia soon, I am sure."

"It's going to be torture going back to civilisation after feeling so free with you. Thank you for these days, Toarer. I'll never forget them."

"Pika, you are talking as if there won't be more. This is just the beginning."

"Now that we know, now that we really, really know, what will we do, Toarer?"

"We have to be so careful, Pika, and even with what we know and what we now have, it won't be easy. Most giants and witches like the way things are, and even if we told them the lore of the Nine Lands has been adulterated, would it be enough to change their ways?"

"It has to be!" the dwarf hissed.

"Naara fantasises about uniting the Nine Lands under one ruler, a giant ruler, of course. Telling someone like her that dwarves were once a mighty civilisation wouldn't change her at all. She is so besotted with the idea of giant superiority, I doubt she would even stop at the Nine Lands, you know."

"That's a chilling thought," Pika said. "In a way, it's a good thing you're being forced to marry her. You might have a chance to calm her down a bit. And her father's much more reasonable, isn't he?"

"He is, yet he is just a palace puppet. I doubt he could persuade many to see things as they are," Toarer said. "Don't worry, though. We will find a way." The giant had a kind, coaxing voice. "We will find a way."

"On the tablets in the Cavern of Knowledge, there were writings of a broken alliance between the Old Dwarven of Ormynydryth and the dwarves that were here. We can find them and reclaim the alliance. Then they'll have to help us!" The dwarf's voice was trembling with excitement and fear.

The giant yawned loudly. "We will find a way when we get back to Blackhill."

Exiluk listened intently to everything they were saying. As he understood more and realised they hoped for their freedom, his old keradin trainings and teachings stirred his heart. He had only known freedom and kindness, and here was a dwarf who had only known cruelty and subjugation. The fire crackled and popped, and the smoke that came out of the chimney was thick and smelt of wet wood. Exiluk wrapped his robe tighter around himself, thankful for the thick keradin hairs all over his body. The night got later and colder.

He hadn't heard talking or significant movement for a while, and the giant's breath was rhythmic and slumberous. As carefully as he could, he got up and crept to find a gap in the wood so he could peer into the cabin. His eye pressed to the wood, and with the help of the glow from the fire, he could see the shape of the dwarf lying with his hand over his sack, no doubt guarding the map. It was almost as if the dwarf had one eye open. The giant slept on his back, his stomach rising and falling slowly.

Could I sneak in and get it now? Maybe. Is it worth the risk of being caught and thwarted by the giant? Unlikely. Patience, Exiluk. Patience is the keradin way. That thought made him feel proud to be keradin. He was still patient. Even if he had been losing his way, that was something he hadn't lost yet. *I will remain patient, and my time will come.* His thoughts ran with him. *Maybe I don't even need the map, or any more treasure. I have much buried, more than someone could ever expect to gain in a lifetime and more. Generations worth! Maybe I will just follow the giant and dwarf and be grateful for the experience. Whatever happens, their story will be a great one.* As he entertained his barrage of thoughts, he found an enclosure to sleep in, pulled his robe into a comfortable position, and drifted off.

Exiluk followed the giant and dwarf to the foot of the mountain and beyond into the sparse, snowy woodlands with tall, thin trees and little vegetation. The giant no longer carried the dwarf on his shoulders, and the dwarf had to struggle to keep up with the giant's strong strides. They travelled directly towards one of the stone monuments that towered into a sky of thick, purple clouds.

Three armed giants met them on the path. "Who goes there?" one said, she wore furs and armour.

"I am Toarer of the Goaner family, and I have come to visit Prince Damek and Princess Leorli of Okuden. They are expecting me."

"Lord Toarer, we expected you many days ago," the giant said.

"Indeed, we found ourselves a little lost. Perhaps my mother and father were right, I should have travelled with a caravan," Toarer laughed, awkwardly.

The giants stared at him blankly. "We will escort you to the palace."

The giants strode fast, and the dwarf now really struggled to keep up. They had no regard for him. The good giant looked back with empathy in his eyes for the dwarf. Exiluk assumed that the good giant couldn't do anything about it due to the necessity of keeping up appearances.

Ancient carved stone in hues of grey, beige and almost black formed a gargantuan palace, one of the monoliths Exiluk had seen from the top of the mountain. Up close it was colossal and brilliant and seemed to be a building of an age gone by. Even the grandest palaces and castles he had seen across the world didn't have the same sense of history as this one.

He hung back behind a mound, peering over its edge and marvelling at the structure as the giants entered. The pillars exhibited an array of geometric shapes—cubes, triangles, pentagons, and circles—interwoven with long tusked animals, bears, eagles, and other forms that left Exiluk intrigued and mystified. Two giant statues marked the tall, granite arch entrance. The dwarf appeared as a mere tiny creature trying to catch up to the giants.

He studied the palace's exterior for some time, and then he noticed himself feeling bored. Boredom was something he was getting more familiar with. Keradins were never bored. From the earliest age he could remember learning to focus his mind so sharply that boredom wasn't possible. *My mind is weakening, sure. Yet it is still stronger than these giants, sure again. It wouldn't hurt to strengthen it a little though, especially as I return to the swamps.* The thought of returning to the swamps aggravated him.

A thump and a flash of light. He found himself lying upwards with an armoured giant towering over him. The giant grabbed his leg and dragged him along the rough and bumpy ground, up some stairs and into a big, empty hallway of dark stone. An ache formed in his head as the dazed feeling wore off. Control of his body returned to him and he tried to wriggle free of the giant's grip but the giant was too strong. The hallway was so vacant it felt ominous and the stone so ancient he felt an obscure force coming from it. He was dragged through huge rooms that weighed down on him a sense of history and mysterious, powerful grandeur.

He was searched and everything except his robe taken off him. *My treasures!* he thought, as he was thrown into a bare stone room and the door was locked behind him.

Exiluk was angry at himself for he had lost his awareness. He had got so caught up in thoughts and mental ramblings that he hadn't even noticed a giant sneaking up behind him. *I have lost all my skill*, he thought, *and that is not the keradin way. Even if I am straying from the keradin path, I should use the skills to my advantage. Why not? One's own advantage may not be the keradin way, yet if the skills are there, why shouldn't they be used? Anyone with a mind can use them after all.* He sat against the wall and began mind-strengthening practices.

The room was austere, its dark stone walls rising to a stark seamless expanse of a ceiling. Light filtered sparingly through narrow, slit-like windows, casting faint beams that barely illuminated the room. The granite floor had been worn smooth with time and use, and the surface bore marks of age with subtle cracks and uneven patches. The room was cold.

A giant entered and said, "What were you doing spying on the palace? Where are you from?"

Exiluk cleared his mind and searched for a thread of the giant's mind. He couldn't sense anything. "I wasn't spying. I am from the other side of Darpirith, and I am on my way home. I travelled the world for many years and I wanted to explore this land before finally going back."

"Hmm," the giant said. "Darpirith is deep and full of crooked creatures and mysteries, nobody passes through Darpirith. You are lying."

"My kind live and breathe the forest, we know it well."

"Where did you get those treasures, if not as a payment to spy on us?" All the while Exiluk was searching for the thread of essence in the giant's mind and he found something he could sense ever so slightly. He connected a thread of his essence to the giant's and he sent influence into the giant's mind.

"Those are treasures from many adventures during many years of travel, ask anyone who has travelled for long how many treasures they acquired."

The giant thought about it for a moment and Exiluk could feel his influence on the giant's mind.

"And wouldn't I be paid for spying after the assignment, rather than before?" He could feel the giant's sentiment changing.

The giant thought about it some more, and left the room.

That was the first time Exiluk had coaxed another being's mind purely for his own benefit and he felt guilty about it. Guilty and excited. *What else can I achieve with mind control?* he thought. *Is it worth corrupting my soul like the keradin teaching's say? I don't feel corrupted. I feel good. Practise more, Exiluk. Strengthen your mind!* A flash of flesh and metal, blood and spirit ripped through his mind. His heart beating wildly, he pushed the memory away as hard as he could.

Taking deep breaths, he calmed himself. Breathing more calmly, he sat against the wall and strengthened his mind. A series of exercises focusing on different things as intently as he could, and catching onto threads of his essence and growing them. To the untrained, these threads would be invisible and intangible. To the keradin, they were as clear as day. He saw his physical form and he saw his essence, and the more he focused on their relationship the stronger his essence became. It looked like an egg of flowing light and energy with thin threads reaching from it.

The room darkened as night crept through the slit windows, windows too small for anyone to escape through. Two giants entered. One held a torch so close to Exiluk's face he could feel the searing heat. He said, "We are going to keep you here until we have decided whether you are a spy or not."

Exiluk quickly caught the giant's thread. He said, "You don't want to do that." He tried to catch the other giant's thread too, but he couldn't coax them both.

The giant with the torch turned to the other and said, "We don't want to do that."

The other giant looked at him strangely, and said, "What are you talking about?"

Exiluk sighed. There was a time his control of mind-threads was so sharp he could make a creature do anything. Yet he would never have used his skill in that way back then. *How ironic,* he thought. "How will you determine that I am not a spy?"

"That is none of your business," the giant said. "I bet the woods are crawling with spies like you."

"I assure you there isn't a single keradin in those woods. If you can't find any, will you set me free?"

"That is none of your business," the other giant said, looking at the other. They both nodded and left the room.

Later, the door opened, a tray of food slipped in and the door closed again. Exiluk ate his meal of stale bread and watery vegetable soup, and went back to his mind-strengthening practices. After some time, despite not having practised in a long time during his travels, he felt quite comfortable and impressed with his progress.

Days slipped by, and he began to get frustrated. The giant and dwarf were likely getting away with the map and he didn't want to lose them. The isolation had proved a fortuitous ally though, for he was able to strengthen his mind more easily without distractions. It was strange to feel frustrated and yet sharp of mind. That had always been antithetical to a keradin, yet he was experiencing it. He dispassionately observed the frustration, and the frustration was compelling him to do something drastic to get out of there. *When my mind is strong enough, I will do whatever it takes to get out of here,* he thought.

Several more days of isolation and practice saw his relationship with his essence increase significantly. He called, "Hello!"

No response.

"Hello, is anyone there? I need to talk to someone right now. I want to confess to being a spy!"

No response.

"Did you hear me?" he shouted. "I want to confess to being a spy. I will tell you about your enemies." He sat back and waited and harnessed his essence.

Three armed giants entered the room. He caught their mind threads with ease and searched to see if there was a recollection of telling others about his capture. He couldn't find that sentiment. They had kept it a close military matter so as not to risk alerting their enemies and hadn't even reported it to the king yet. Exiluk said, "You want to set me free, you want to give my things back."

They looked at each other confusedly, and one said, "Get his things for him."

A giant left the room.

Exiluk wanted to smile but he had to keep his focus. "You have realised I am not a spy at all, haven't you?"

"He is not a spy, that is obvious," one giant said.

The other nodded. "Obvious."

"When I have my things back, you will escort me out of here and leave me to go on my way."

"It is the least we could do," a giant said.

This time Exiluk did smile.

The giant who had left the room returned with Exiluk's things and apologised for taking them. They led Exiluk to the exit and he was smug about how well things were going. Now that he wasn't upside down, he could admire the palace in much more detail.

He was led through cavernous hallways with towering, stone columns that had been carved with meanings he couldn't decipher—shapes and patterns arranged in ways that clearly meant something. The ceilings were high and vaulted, and how they had been engineered he couldn't fathom. The floors were of patterned stone, and the walls were plain, heavy blocks of dark grey.

So close now. Focus. The threads. Only the threads. He continued wrapping the threads of his mind around theirs, and they walked with him towards the massive arched entrance of the monumental palace. He wanted to look back, wanted to see if anyone was watching them, but he couldn't. He had to keep moving forward. *Stay focused.*

They passed through the arch, through the palace grounds, entered the woodland, and Exiluk said, "You can leave me now, knowing I am not a spy and knowing you have done the right thing."

"Stop!" a giant said, running after them. "What are you doing with the spy?"

"He is not a spy, we are setting him free," one of Exiluk's escorts shouted back.

"Whose orders?" the giant said.

The three escorts looked at each other confusedly.

"The boss told you to," Exiluk said.

"Irast's orders," one of the escorts said.

"Stop, now!" the giant said.

"Keep walking with me. You will protect me, because I am innocent and it is honourable to protect the innocent," Exiluk said, briskly walking deeper into the woods. His mind felt strained and drained. He wouldn't be able to keep them under his control much longer.

The giant chasing them caught up, his heavy trod loud and close.

The giant drew his sword. The metal sang and groaned as it ground out of its sheath.

"We will protect him, he is innocent," one of the three giants said. They raised their weapons and blocked the other giant from getting near Exiluk.

"What has got into you? You have gone mad. Take the spy back to the palace at once."

The three escorts looked at each other confusedly again and lowered their weapons. The confusion turned into frowns of disbelief, and they appeared as if they had no idea where they were. A light snow fell around them. The forest was cold and quiet.

Exiluk felt sick, he had pushed his mind's essence too far. He wanted to collapse into a long sleep. No, not want, *need*. His mind was shutting down. He grappled with it and pushed it as hard as he could and in a wild frenzy of mind that he had never encountered before, he said, "Kill him."

The three escorts swung their weapons. The giant defended one with his heavy sword and the ground shook with the force, but the other two landed, one in the side of his leg and the other in his neck. His flesh spat blood as he collapsed to the ground, his eyes filled with shock and horror, his crimson blood staining the pristine snow.

Exiluk's vision was blurring he was so exhausted. He fought his exhaustion with the last of all he had and said, "You did the right thing. The giant was in the wrong. It is best that you hide the body and nobody hears of this." He imprinted that thought into the giants' minds with all his might and then he ran as fast as he could, thinking, *Why did you do that? Why did you push it so far? What have you done?* And he regretted the weight of the treasures upon him and the inevitable consequences of what he had just done. He knew deep down that the consequences of his killings would be severe, he didn't need to be keradin to know that. And he ran as fast as he could, for as long as he could, and he felt exhausted and exhilarated and the shadow growing in him was on fire. Something in him felt more alive and more powerful than ever and he revelled in it as he ran and ran, until he collapsed into nothingness.

CHAPTER 11

THEO

Theo and Avira lay on Toarer's bed. Avira rested her head on Theo's chest. He felt so comfortable and tingly he dreaded the moment the work bell would ring. They had just eaten Toarer's leftover breakfast. It had been delicious.

Toarer was looking out of his open window longingly. Theo felt sorry for him. He knew that Toarer was often sad and conflicted, and Theo knew those feelings all too well. Toarer said, "Pika told you then?" He turned from the window and his expression was sincere and caring. "Please go with him. I have never been able to forgive myself for what we have done to you. It would make me so happy to know I helped you become free."

"We're scared," Avira said. "We *have to* go though, don't we?"

"Come here a moment," Toarer said. He helped them onto the window frame. A vast land of green and golden hues sprawled out in front of them under a pale blue sky. They looked out onto the lake, the woods, the plantations, the wildlands, and the mountains in the distance. "I had a dream last night. Everything you see now was shared by all of us, there was no servitude, no violence, and there were cute little houses for all of you, nice ones. I was so happy. Then I woke up. But the thing is, it felt so real it must be meaningful. I can't shake it now. We have to make it happen."

Avira took Theo's hand as they looked out over the land. He thought about his dream of being a butterfly and the sense of freedom he felt once he had broken away from the flames. The morning breeze tickled his skin. He felt a strange sense of hope brewing in him, a small, almost invisible, *Maybe.* He didn't like it at all. Hope meant disappointment. He had learnt that many years ago. "It's impossible. A dream, nothing more," Theo said.

"Don't say that, Theo," Avira said. "Everything starts as a dream, a hope, an idea, doesn't it?"

The giant put his big, heavy, comforting hand on Theo's shoulder. It radiated warmth. "I understand Pika hasn't had an opportunity to tell you our plan, but I assure you, it's a good one." Toarer's endearing optimism and calm transitioned to hesitation. "I can't tell you every detail though, the mindwatchers could find your thoughts." Toarer's eyes sparkled as he continued.

"Before the giants and witches ruled, dwarves lived in the mountains of the Nine Lands. They were a mighty civilisation with a close connection to the magic of the earth, and they could coax ores from rock, and craft like no other. But although they were strong, they were no match for the giants and witches, who together were relentless and powerful in battle. All the dwarves' riches were taken and the dwarves that didn't escape were enslaved."

"It sounds like a fairytale," Avira said.

Toarer smiled. "I have seen enough to know it's true. There are records of old alliances with other dwarven beyond the Nine Lands, and we think Pika can convince them to help us," he said, a little triumphantly.

Theo and Avira stared at Toarer, taking it in. *Help? They might get help?* Theo felt a glimmer of hope threatening him again, and he could feel the excitement in Avira. Her hand had become warmer, sweatier, and she held his hand tighter. She was so optimistic. *So naïve,* he thought. "If the dwarven of the Nine Lands lost to the giants and witches, what makes you think any other dwarven can succeed? How do we even know they're still there? No matter all of that, they can't care. They would have tried to save us already."

The giant laughed gently, squeezing Theo's shoulder in a reassuring way. "I have always admired your sensibility, Theo. Sometimes we just have to take a leap of faith, though, don't you think? Pika needs your help. Please, go with him."

"What help can we be?" Theo said.

"Theo, I won't have you thinking like that anymore. You are strong. You have put up with Kirakai all your life. You have worked hard every day, harder than any witch or giant ever has. You have endured so much, and you have never given up, despite it seeming so hopeless. Nothing can stop you. You have grit, I am certain of it. I couldn't think of a better trait for a quest like this."

I suppose there's something in what he's saying. We have done those things. Maybe I do have grit. He felt the hope strengthening and he shook the thought away.

"I've always liked that about you, too," Avira said. "You always get on and do it, whether you like it or not. The others give up, they do a poor job of it all, the bare minimum. You don't."

The words touched him. He fought hard to hold off tears. One threatened to slip from his eye. He looked away from her. He had always thought he was pathetic, that Avira pitied him and saw him as weak. "You're stronger than I'll ever be," he said, a little choked up.

"Let's be strong together," she said. "I have to get out of here, please come with me. Pika needs you and I need you. We all need you."

Theo wiped his tears as surreptitiously as he could. He struggled to find words and he resented that. He wanted to say, *Yes, let's go.* He wanted it more than anything and yet those words were simply too difficult for him to say.

"I have something for you," Toarer said, taking his big hand out of his pocket and opening his palm. Two intriguing trinkets lay in his hand, roughly the size of a human thumb. Each trinket was a cloudy blue crystal, wrapped in three threads of cream stone. The crystals' edges gleamed a rich, translucent blue. "Go on, they are yours."

"What is it?" Avira said, hesitant.

Magic in human hands is dangerous and chaotic, Theo thought, reciting the lore.

"Pika found them in a hidden dwarven cavern, and inscribed on a tablet it said, 'To protect.' We don't actually know what they do, but I want you to have them, to protect you on your quest."

"What if we don't go?" Theo said.

"Have them anyway," Toarer said.

"What if the watchers find them on us?" Theo said.

"There are magic trinkets all over the Nine Lands, they won't know humans are holding them."

"They could catch our thoughts about the trinkets, or what we're looking at, can't they?"

Toarer looked closely at the trinkets in his palm, curiously, smiling, intrigued. Toarer's adoration for them made Theo feel less concerned. Toarer said, "Theoretically, they could. Though only dozens of witches strong enough to be watchers, and with thousands of slaves, I am sure you have little to worry about. They can't listen to all your thoughts at once. Lately, I have realised they are more of a deterrent than anything else. They are there to scare you." Toarer pushed the trinkets towards them and Avira took one, and Theo took the other.

It glowed brightly in Theo's hand, a white light at the centre and blue on the edges. Theo panicked and threw it on the bed.

"Wonderful!" Toarer exclaimed.

Avira's trinket didn't change. She shook it and eyed it all around. Nothing. Rolled it in her fingers. Nothing. "Take mine," she said.

She handed it to Theo and it glowed. She smiled. "What does it feel like?"

"Energising, I guess. I feel strong. The stone is cold." He gave it back to Avira and the light disappeared.

"Looks like you're magic," Avira said, laughing. "You *are* special aren't you," she murmured.

He doubted it, but something astonishing had happened, and he couldn't deny it. Yet he worried that it only meant he needed a protection stone because he was weak. He worried about what he might need protecting from. Yet the thought of a magical stone that could protect them made him feel a little more comfortable about the unknowns of the quest they might embark upon. He climbed down from the window and took the trinket from the bed.

It glowed again, and he felt calmer this time. It made him feel strong and determined. His worries didn't overwhelm him so much. He began feeling more optimistic about everything. It almost felt as if he knew, really *knew* everything was going to be okay.

The work bell rang. Theo put the stone in his pocket and the thought of another day under Kirakai's whip filled him with defiance.

"I will try and see you again before the wedding," Toarer said.

∽✦∾

Kirakai cracked his monstrous whip in the air, and this time Theo didn't shudder. The servants were prepping the wedding site. Theo felt better than usual. Stronger, and clearer. He hauled a tree out of the way with Pika.

"You're as strong as a dwarf today, Theo," Pika said, winking at him.

Theo grinned.

Kirakai cracked his whip over Theo's back, and it seared with pain. He dropped the tree trunk expecting to writhe on the floor as the giant's whip often made him do. The pain disappeared quickly. He shrugged, picked up the trunk, and carried on. Pika appeared confused. Avira grinned at him.

The whip tore at Theo's back again and he ignored it. Sure, the pain was excruciating for a moment, but he didn't care. Pika tried to hide his grin.

"Oi, Blondie, what's the matter with you?" Kirakai whipped him once more. He could feel the skin opening and blood trickling down his back, soaking into his torn clothes in a sticky mess.

"We've got to get this wedding ready, don't we. The more you whip us, the harder that's going to be," Theo said. It was the first time he had ever stood up to Kirakai and he expected wrath. They carried the log, paying no real attention to the giant.

The giant whipped the air and it sounded like a bolt of lightning and thunder. He whipped again and again, perturbed by Theo. Theo, his back turned to Kirakai, winked at Pika. Pika laughed, but abruptly stopped himself, making sure the giant didn't catch him.

Crack, crack, crack, the whip roared in the air, and Theo felt like he had got to Kirakai. He felt as if he had gained a small victory and it felt good. They put the tree trunk with the other fresh wood and Pika pat him on the arm.

He turned to find Kirakai towering over him, close and intimidating. The giant picked him up and turned him upside down and carried him towards the lake. He hit Kirakai in the stomach and Kirakai winced a tad, before plunging Theo head first into the water.

It all happened so quickly. He wriggled and fought, yet the giant was too strong. He was running out of breath and swallowing water. It seemed as if his whole head had filled with water and he was choking frantically. The giant pulled him out of the water and he coughed and spluttered and it came out of his nose and throat and he gasped, "No!" as he was plunged back in again. He struggled and fought but he was too weak and he swallowed a large gulp that hurt his throat and stomach and he had the feeling he was about to black out when the giant pulled him out again.

"Never talk to me like that or I will send you to the bottom of this lake where you belong, understand?"

Theo coughed water out of his lungs and gasped for air, and said nothing.

"Did you hear me, puny?"

Theo spat on the floor, still upside down. He didn't want to lose.

The giant plunged him back into the water and held him down. Theo tried to conserve his energy, relaxing and hoping it would make the giant give up. He held his breath as calmly as he could for what felt like an eternity, and then his chest started jerking and he had to force himself not to breathe in the water, and he began to panic and fight again, expecting the giant to lift him out once more. He didn't.

Black, cold, wet rock surrounded Theo. The grave-like obsidian stone beneath his feet had lines carved into it in the shape of rings with patterns within those rings, suggesting at arcane and secret knowledge. Three daunting extrusions arose out of the platform, their sleek surfaces curved upwards to a point that bore down on Theo like ominous conductors of dark forces. Clouds blew past him with a ferocious wind that howled around the tower.

A greying witch with a startled expression pointed a crystal staff at Theo. "I knew there was something odd about you, from the moment I sensed you. It appears that irritating guardian of yours has finally given up."

"Where am I? What guardian?" Theo said.

"You are dying at the bottom of a lake, boy." The witch waved his staff and Theo saw water and blurriness, and he heard muffled screaming. "Your defences are so weak now. I will dissect your mind with ease." The witch advanced, laughing. Lightning tore past the tower and the witch's face lit and shadowed. It was an old, hard face.

Searing pain. Theo gasped. His mind was pried apart by something invisible, horribly painful, and sharp, as if one side of his brain was being torn from the other.

"Theo from Blackhill, what are you hiding from me?" the witch said.

"Stay away from me," Theo roared, and the witch appeared taken aback, as if he had been repelled by Theo's words. The pain in Theo's head intensified.

"Where did you learn the ways of the mind?" the witch said.

I don't know the ways of the mind, Theo thought.

"How is it that you can't know?" the witch said, cutting through Theo's thoughts like butter. "Is it that damned guardian of yours? Who is she?"

The pain was unbearable, and Theo was compelled to search his mind for information about a guardian, but there was none.

"Tell me of this dwarf and giant who defy the lore."

No! Theo wanted to stop the witch from entering and tearing his mind apart, but he had no idea how.

"The giant Toarer, he does not believe in the order of things. He will pay the price. He did what? The Dwarf. The dwarf can read? They plan to usurp. This is treachery!"

Theo was devastated that he had given the witch so much information. His pocket began glowing vigorously. He took the protection stone and thrust his closed fist towards the witch. The glow was blinding and it illuminated patterns and textures amongst their cloudy surroundings. The witch soared backwards and slammed against a rock. Groaned as his breath was knocked out of him. *What guardian?* Theo demanded.

The woman with the magic of sound. She sings from the aether. She protects you. What? How did you get in here? How did you coax me? The witch appeared dumbfounded as he staggered to his feet.

Who are you? Theo demanded, pushing the protection stone closer to the witch. Even as Theo held the advantage, the air around him chilled as the sinister essence of the tower seeped into his bones.

I am Rakuul Mordaker. What? How is this possible? The witch fell to his knees. *No! I am the great witch servant of the High King. You are a mere human. What is happening?* He raised his staff and slammed it on the ground.

Theo's feet were pulled from underneath him and his back slammed onto the ground, hard. He dropped the stone, and it bounded on the slick rock. The magical glow faded. The searing pain returned to his head. He dragged himself along the floor towards the protection stone, the flat surface wet from the condensation in the clouds.

"Block me no longer, mere human." Rakuul raised his staff and thudded it on the ground. It sent a wave of force through Theo that made him collapse. His chin hit the smooth stone beneath him.

"So much love and admiration for the girl. The girl who is at the mercy of the taskmaster Kirakai. And you do nothing to protect her? Yes, you are a coward. Worse than a coward. You are slime. A waste of life. Yes. You know it, don't you. You know your place, human," Rakuul said. He had plucked the thoughts and memories from Theo's mind.

Theo lay defeated. His body so exhausted he couldn't move, and the witch was prying his mind open more and more. *I can't do anything,* he thought. *I'm done.*

"You are done, kid. You are done indeed. There is no match for Rakuul Mordaker, and now you die, and your dissident accomplices with you."

Theo thought of Avira, her kindness and her brilliance, and of Toarer and his gentleness and his optimism, and of Pika and his impressive intelligence, and of Tico and his amazing ability to be direct when it was most needed. He saw their endearing faces looking down at him and it gave him a burst of strength. He snatched the protection stone and with his energy it burned so bright that he had to look away as he threw his fist towards the witch again.

The witch waved his staff, and a force collided with the light coming from the protection stone, dulling the stone's beams at the edges. Theo pressed forward against the force. The ferocity of the wind and lightning around the tower intensified. Theo kept pushing the light towards the witch, and the witch's force pushed him back. Theo struggled and struggled with all his might, pushed and pushed and slowly he made ground, slowly, surely, slowly, pushing with all his might.

The witch looked more and more incredulous, and he trembled as he said, "Your mere tricks will not bother me, human. This is not over." He hammered his staff against the rock, and a pulse pushed Theo's consciousness back to Blackhill.

He was beside the lake. Avira was crying and Pika was shaking him. He coughed and sputtered water from his mouth, nose, eyes, and stomach. "I'm okay, I'm alive," he said.

"Wait until Master Toarer hears about this," Pika shouted at Kirakai.

"I barely touched the rat," the giant grunted, walking off. There was a sulky tone in his voice. One Theo had never heard before. "Finish your work, those guest tents still need to go up. They had better look perfect," Kirakai mumbled, before he faded out of sight.

The servants talked amongst each other with outrage in their voices. It was the most discord Theo had ever seen them express.

He realised he was smiling. The smile disappeared as soon as he remembered the watcher. "A watcher got into my mind. He knows about us now. I'm sorry," he said.

"You almost died, Theo, and you had one of those fits again as we pulled you out of the water. Your mind is playing tricks on you," Pika said. "You're alive, that's all that matters."

Avira stroked his wet hair and his wet cheek. "I thought he was going to drown you. I felt so helpless," she said. "And then all of a sudden it was like he was shocked by something and he just let you go. Something scared him. We had to pull you out of the lake."

"I think it was the stone," Theo whispered. "It protected me from the watcher too." The trees rustled with the wind above. A few leaves fell. The atmosphere was calm and tranquil, devoid of howling wind, thunder, and lightning.

Avira appeared puzzled. She smiled and ran her hand down his cheek once more, and they shared a beautiful moment of connection. For once in his life, he didn't feel helpless. He felt as if he had bested a watcher and Kirakai in one battle, and it was overwhelmingly surreal, though he also wondered whether the watcher had been real at all. It had certainly felt real, like a lucid, yet otherworldly occurrence that he couldn't quite grasp, other than its significance. More significant than a nightmare, or a daydream, or a mere rambling of the imagination.

He fingered the protection stone in his pocket. There were cracks in the stone threads and the crystal, and he didn't feel any strength or protection coming from it.

CHAPTER 12

ASH

Ash couldn't sleep. No news of Serene was worse than knowing. *Where had she gone? Had the snarler got her? What would happen when they found her? Hanging or torture, to set an example*, she thought. Her mind raced to a hundred conclusions, and she could never settle on one. The uncertainty was driving her mad. She thought of ways they could save her once the snarler returned with her, but each idea was futile and impossible.

The snarler's horrid growls and grunts could be heard, and the taskmaster shouted, "Snarler's back with a bit of pretty prey." Ash shot out the door. Serene was in chains and barely conscious. Her clothes were covered in blood and so was the snarler's mouth. First light was creeping out of its slumber.

"Listen here, runts," the taskmaster shouted. "I want you all to see this, get out here now." The servants stirred and groaned, and came out of the house. Ash was dismayed. *What can I do? What can I do?* The snarler was like a big dog, but its head was bigger and rounder and its nose was giant and bulbous. Its body was stockier and more muscular than any dog Ash had ever seen. *I wish the taskmaster would die. I wish the taskmaster would die. I wish the snarler would die.* She hoped so desperately for it, and she put every ounce of her will into it. *This all started with the Prince, the poison in the apple, so why won't anything happen now? It couldn't have just been coincidence, it couldn't! I wish the taskmaster would die.*

The taskmaster threw the snarler a big piece of meat and said,

"Well done girl, well done."

The beast chewed and clawed at the meat, whining, grunting, and drooling.

"Nobody runs, because it disrupts the order of things, do you understand? We give you favourable employment given your runty weaknesses and lack of ability to function in our society, and you should be grateful for it, do you understand?" He took his wand and made a swirling motion as it pointed at the ground. The ground began falling away, creating a deep, muddy pit. He kicked Serene into the pit, and she screamed as she thudded onto the ground.

The taskmaster said, "Put a grate over it, you scabby rats." He spat into the pit. "Nobody's to feed or water her, do you understand? You will watch her deteriorate and die, and you will learn again that nobody runs."

Four servants carried a heavy metal grate and dropped it on top of the pit. The taskmaster flicked his wand and the chain attached to the snarler slid across the ground and wrapped around the grate, and the snarler was pulled away from the piece of meat it had been nursing. It grunted and growled and whined. The chain was pulled so tight to the grate that the snarler could either sit above Serene, or just next to the grate. Nobody would be getting past the snarler to help Serene.

"Get working, or get punished," the taskmaster roared.

Everyone was more subdued than usual that day. Even Nifty seemed to have given up. They trudged to the fields and did as they were told, creating riches for Lord Sully whilst grinding towards their miserable end.

At dusk, Ash watched everyone silently eat their slop. Her stomach felt uncomfortable and she worried about how she'd get through two weeks of work without supper. Nifty offered her a bit of his. She took a spoonful. It was extra cold, tangy, and gloopy.

"Help," Serene said, feebly and desperately. The sound struck Ash with a sharp sense of helplessness and hopelessness. "Help," she groaned again, crying, and puking violently. "It hurts."

Ash snatched Nifty's bowl. He frowned, but didn't question her as she left the house. She approached the snarler. It sensed her and perked up.

Its eyes were big and droopy, and its mouth looked somewhat dopey, until it opened and she could see all its horrible layers of sharp teeth, some big and long and some small and rough. "It's okay," she said. "Shh, shh, shh…" She trembled as she spoke, her legs shaking as she approached. She threw a clump of slop on the floor just to the right of the snarler and it leapt towards it. It caught some in the air and licked the rest from the ground.

Slowly, cautiously, she approached. The snarler was wholly distracted by the food and she felt she may have a chance. "Serene, I'm going to pour some food through the bars," she said. "It's all I can do for now."

Serene groaned.

Ash was shaking so much it was hard to hold the bowl. The snarler licked the floor and chomped its mouth trying to find more slop. Closer, she edged, shaking. Closer. Almost there.

Snap! The snarler shot at her and barked wildly. She jumped backwards, falling and spilling her food. It almost got her leg before its chain yanked it backwards and it recoiled awkwardly, the metal clanging and smashing and sounding horrible alongside the beast's howl.

Fury and fire raged in Ash. She wanted to tear the beast apart. But she couldn't, she was small and weak compared to it. She had no chance of helping Serene. The princess of Ul Nirin would die a slave in Eliniar, in a pit of mud and filth, guarded by a snarler.

Without water, injured, and weak, Serene should have gone within days. But she hadn't, and it made things much harder to bear. Ash hated it every time she heard her groan or call for help. It disturbed her and made the fire in her grow fiercer. She couldn't stop picturing the Princess injured, thirsty, hungry, and helpless. It plagued her that she couldn't do anything.

She had been sharing Nifty's supper. It was barely enough food for one, never mind two, but he had insisted. They were both weakening and becoming a shell of themselves. It made her feel even more sorry for the Princess.

Ash and Nifty were together in his hideout. The magic lantern burned warmly. The blankets around her were comforting. But she couldn't shake her thoughts about Serene. "How's it possible she's still alive with no food and water? I can't stand it anymore, we have to do something, or…"

"…You think she's gotta go…." Nifty finished her sentence, morbidly, quietly. "Truth is, I've been feeding her and giving her water in the dead of night. I can't stand the thought of her dying."

"How?" Ash asked, dumbfounded.

"Saving some of my slop, foraging, whatever I could. And, well that snarler ain't so bad after all, you just gotta approach it right. It's quite an affectionate little…well, big… thing, you know. All creatures are kind at heart, somewhere, deep down. That's what I believe, maybe even…"

"Don't you dare! There's nothing good in those witches," Ash snapped. She thought of Serene, thought of how much the witch princess seemed like one of them now, just a slave on a plantation in Eliniar. If she believed there was no good in Serene at all, she wouldn't be so sad about her suffering. *Ugh,* she thought, so conflicted.

"I can't bring myself to group 'em all in one basket, you know. They do that to us and that's how we got 'ere. Every creature is its own creature, with its own spirit and its own heart, and each deserves to be seen in its own right, you know?"

Ash melted. "You're amazing sometimes, Nifty," she said, hugging him.

Nifty received the hug shyly.

"But if you've been giving Serene your half of our food, you must be eating nothing?"

"I'm hungry, but it could be worse. I could be in a pit guarded by a snarler," he grimaced. "And it won't be forever, I'll get to eat more soon. Maybe I'll get a chance to nick a bit of meat from the house."

He stared at the wall longingly, weakly.

"We have to do something!" Ash said.

"I've been thinking and thinking about it, and I've got nothing. I tried to set the snarler free, but I couldn't break the chains, the magic's too strong. I've 'eard the taskmaster talking as well, he don't understand how she's lived so long, and he might just do it himself. I dunno what to do, but we gotta do it fast."

They sat in silence, thinking.

Nothing of significance came to them. They reluctantly left the hideout and walked back to the servants' house. The wind gusted harshly every now and then, causing the trees to growl and groan. The night sky was thick and cloudy. Thunder roared and rain began to fall. Lightning lit the sky for a moment, then darkness resumed.

The snarler was trying to pull free of its chains, turning and clawing at them with its sharp claws, chewing at the metal. Serene groaned and cried, "Let me out, I won't run again."

The fire in Ash was too much. "LET. HER. OUT," she screamed.

Nifty curled down with his hands over his ears, frozen on the spot. The ground shook and the storm calmed, seemingly at the same moment. He looked shocked and scared. As his eyes conversed with hers, his look subsided into confusion.

Something had grown in Ash as she had shouted. She had felt an energy inside of her, a fire, and it had attached to her words and come out of her with them. It had rumbled everything around her, and now the whole world seemed to stand still for her. "Let her out!" she screamed again.

The snarler panicked and tried to run. Its chain yanked it back violently.

"Let her out," Ash shouted again.

"Let her out," Nifty screamed, with impressive strength.

The servants congregated outside the house, first appearing confused and angered to have been woken. They stared at Nifty and Ash who shouted, "Let her out," in unison.

"Let her out. Let her out. Let her out," they shouted, and Ash could feel the fire raging inside of her and connecting to every word.

The snarler put its big paws over its face and tried to hide, whining.

One of the other servants tentatively joined in. "Let her out. Let her out."

Another joined. Then more joined, until they were all screaming, "Let her out, let her out." They marched towards the main house, screaming, and shouting, and the energy was unbelievable. Nifty was jumping and shouting at the top of his voice and his smile was undeniable. His thrill was one Ash had never seen in a servant.

The taskmaster met them on their path. He raised his wand, but the servants didn't stop shouting or marching.

"He can't kill us all," Ash screamed. "Lord Sully would have no workers. Keep going."

"Let her out. Let her out. Let her out."

"Stop," the taskmaster said, waving his wand and creating a barrier. The barrier stopped them in their tracks. They surged around it, and he panicked and roared and cast an even bigger barrier that contained the crowd. "Okay, okay, let's talk before you wake Lord Sully." He was putting so much energy into the barrier that his words were weak, and he was shaking.

The servants stopped and listened. The air felt warm and strange, as if the high spirits of the servants had affected it.

"She is an awkward worker, but she is clearly new to plantations," the taskmaster said. "You don't say a word of all this to Lord Sully, and you go back to normal tomorrow, right? Right!" he shouted, trying to be more authoritative. "I think she might have learnt her lesson. I will let her out, and if she stays in line, everything can go back to normal." The taskmaster was clearly panicked, but he held them in a magical barrier, he had the power, and he flicked his wand to flex that power. The barrier tightened and squeezed the crowd.

Ash could sense a realisation in the crowd that they had overstepped the mark. She could feel them thinking, *What are we doing, we have just flesh and words, and they have magic.*

The taskmaster lowered his wand having gained control of the situation, and he said, "Now get back inside."

The servants smiled and pat each other on the back, some hugged, and there was a distinctive sense of hope and wonder amongst them, though there was also hesitation and confusion.

Ash had never felt so alive. For a few moments, it was enough to distract her from the strange shift that seemed to have occurred in the land and the air when she had shouted. Nobody else seemed to have noticed.

Led by Ash and Nifty, the servants pulled Serene out of the pit and washed her. There was little life left in her. She was skin and bones, and her cuts from the night she had escaped hadn't healed well. She was light, though a dead weight and awkward to carry. Her soul had been sucked out of her.

Nifty gave her a tiny bit of food and water. "Can't give her too much, it'd shock the body," he said.

They laid her down and wrapped blankets around her. Ash wasn't sure whether to comfort her or not, but she nestled in close to Serene and put her arm around her. Serene was as stiff and still as a rock.

"I'm sorry," Ash said.

No response.

"We're going to get out of here, and we're going to make them pay. Every single one of them." Ash realised how conflicting her words must have been to Serene. Serene was the princess of Ul Nirin and with her brother dead, her mother mad, and her father ill, she was likely to take the throne one day. One day, she would be the queen of Ul Nirin. She would be duty-bound to lead the witches, not make them pay.

For days, they helped Serene rebuild her strength. They rubbed her skin with herb balms, fed her and gave her water. Eventually, she started looking better. Every time someone had tried to talk to her, she had said nothing. Every day, Ash had whispered to her, "We're going to get out of here, and we're going to make them pay." Serene wouldn't even look at her.

One day, when the morning bell rang, Serene got up promptly

and left the house without a word. She clearly wanted to be left alone, so Ash left her to it. Ash got her slop and sat on the floor next to Nifty, who talked a lot about random things that Ash didn't pay much attention to at all.

They walked into the fields together and found Serene with her basket almost full, working faster and more determined than she ever had before. Her hands were covered in dirt and blood. She didn't pay Ash or Nifty any attention.

We're going to get out of here, and we're going to make them pay, Ash thought. "Nifty," Ash said, quietly. "If I asked you to gather all the potion ingredients and implements you could without getting caught, and hide them in your home and not ask me what it was for, what would you say?"

"I'd say you're cruel for depriving me of my cheeky curiosity, but I've taken much bigger risks than that for myself so why shouldn't I take 'em for another? All I'd say is most of 'em will go foul and useless after a while so you'd better know what you're doing with 'em. And if you know what you're doing with 'em, my curiosity would be too much and I'd find it harder to say yes so I'll assume you don't know what you're doing and just wanna experiment. And if you just wanna experiment..." He stopped and gulped. "Stealing potion ingredients could get us killed if I was caught," he said, solemnly. He thought about it for a moment, and his eyes filled with pure sincerity. "I'll do it." Nifty screamed and fell to the ground and writhed, curling into a ball, shaking.

The taskmaster laughed. He was at the other end of the field, with his wand out. "Less chatting and more picking," he said.

Ash helped Nifty up and brushed dirt off his clothes.

Nifty grinned at her and said, "What don't kill me makes me stronger, don't he know that?"

"You're unbelievable," Ash said.

"I'm very happy today," Nifty said. "I've been thinking... I've got a home. You called it my home and I never really looked at it like that, but I guess that's 'coz I never got to show anyone before, and now I can't stop thinking, I've got a home. Not many humans in the Nine Lands can say that, can they? Maybe none at all. And even better, I got to share it..." He fell to the floor again. This time his screams were unbearably loud.

"Don't end up like your father, boy," the taskmaster roared.

When the magic had stopped, he lay still, with foam coming from his mouth.

Ash wiped the foam with the bottom of her robe and hugged him.

"That one knocked me sideways," he said, weakly. "Got a home though, 'aven't I?"

❧

That night when everyone was asleep, Ash woke Nifty gently and said, "Can we show Serene your home?"

"You wake her up and I'll see you there," Nifty said. "Let me go first else it'll look weird the three of us goin' off to the loos together."

Ash lay for a little while longer while Nifty moved swiftly and quietly. Once he had gone, she went over to Serene and lay with her for a bit. Serene was fast asleep. Ash shook her gently. Nothing. She shook her a little harder. Nothing. Whispered in her ear, "Serene?"

"I don't want to talk," Serene whispered.

"Please, I have something to show you. It's incredible. You need to see it. It's fit for a princess."

"I am a princess no longer," Serene said.

"You are. You're the future queen of Ul Nirin and we won't let anything get in the way of that. We're going to escape, and we're going to make them pay. You can come back and burn this whole place down."

"We are never getting out of here," Serene said. "Now leave me alone."

"No. You and your lot bossed me around all my damned life, and now I'm asking you to come with me to see something important and I need you to listen," Ash said. *We're going to escape, and we're going to make them all pay.*

After a moment, Ash felt Serene's body soften. She turned and looked Ash in the eye, briefly, but not so briefly that Ash didn't catch the shame and sorrow in Serene's eyes.

Serene followed Ash into the darkness, and down the hatch to a smiling Nifty who was boiling some water on a nifty-looking stove system with a chimney to take the smoke from the fire. Ash wondered where it was positioned to let the smoke out so as not to be discovered.

"Well, what do you think?" Ash said, brimming with excitement. Silence.

"'Ere," Nifty said, passing Serene a cup of tea.

She took it to her lips in a daze and sipped it.

"Look 'ere," Nifty said, opening a small sack. It was full of herbs of all sorts. "Got these today, I'll hang 'em and dry 'em for you, or did you want 'em fresh?"

Ash was excited to see all the herbs and she imagined a potion brewing ready to magic them out of there. She wished she understood the art of magic. She shrugged, unsure, looking to Serene for an answer. Serene took no notice and sipped her tea.

"I'll dry 'em so they last longer," Nifty said. "Shall I get you more?"

"As much as you could, please, Nifty, of as many varieties as you can," Ash said, feeling a well of anxiety and hope flooding her stomach. The three drank tea and nobody spoke. Once Nifty had finished his tea, Ash said, "Could Serene and I have a little time alone here, please?"

"Of course, you can," he said, and he left them alone.

"I can't believe it," Ash said, her spirits lifting again at the thought of their luck. "We can use this place to practise magic and get out of here. We'll make them pay."

"*We?*" Serene said, bitterly.

"I'll help in any way I can. We've got everything we need to get out of here."

"My magic is too weak, it is pointless."

"Serene, you're the princess of Ul Nirin. You're a powerful witch. We'll get out of here, don't doubt it."

"Do I look like a princess to you? I am no princess."

"I'm sorry for what happened to you, Serene. I'm really sorry.

It doesn't change who you are, though. You have the power to change everything."

"I just want to die," Serene said.

"Please don't say that. You'll get through this, I promise."

"You don't know how I feel, you don't know what I can get through," she said.

Ash snapped. "How dare you, Serene! I've been a slave all my damned life. What happened to you happens to all of us. We get beaten and starved and made to feel like we're nothing all the time. What you're feeling is so normal to us we learn to brush it off like it's just another part of nature's way, but it's not, and I'm sick of it, and we're going to make them pay."

Serene avoided Ash's gaze, looking embarrassed.

"If you need time, take all the time you want. If you need space, or sleep, or anything, anything at all, just tell me. But don't you *dare* give up on this. We're going to make it happen. We're going to! Do you understand me?" Ash said, her voice cracking with frustration.

❧

Day upon day passed and Serene showed no signs of perking up. She kept herself to herself most of the time and Ash left her to it. Serene would need time, Ash knew that. *Time heals all*, Ash often reminded herself. Yet the days were unbearably monotonous and full of oppression, and she dreaded what terrible thing may come next. She missed her mother's stories. She needed the wisdom and comfort they gave her. If it wasn't for Nifty's company, she would have felt horribly alone.

True to his word, Nifty stocked his home with ingredients and apparatus for potions and magic, and not once did he ask Ash what they were for. She was beginning to worry that it was all for nothing.

Ash and Nifty were in his home one night after lights out and he said, "I was wondering, and don't get me wrong, I hope I'm not overstepping the line 'ere asking this, 'coz I won't ask what you want it for... I just wanna ask, are you gonna use any of this stuff? I notice you 'aven't touched it yet."

"We'll use it, yes," Ash said.

"You and Serene, you mean?" Nifty said. "You know I wish I could ask how, and don't get me wrong, I'm enjoying all the sneaking about and being clever about it, it's giving me an excitement I need, it's just hard to keep it up without much information to go by. We all need to know our purpose, don't we? Is there anything you can tell me, Ash?"

"What if I told you that this thing you're doing is the seed of something that'll grow bigger than you could ever imagine?" Ash said.

"Well, you know that'd spark my curiosity even more and I'd struggle not to wanna know what you were talking about, and I assume you wouldn't wanna tell me anyway," Nifty said. "It's a wonderful thought though, so I'll keep it goin' and hope the purpose is as grand as you say."

"Thank you, Nifty," Ash said.

Nifty grinned and winked cheekily. "How well do you know her, anyway? Serene, I mean. What's your story together?"

"I've known her my whole life, as long as I can remember."

"I only ask because I wonder if she's alright. The other night I saw her sitting in the woods not too far from 'ere whispering to a stick. She talks to herself a lot and not really to anyone else, which I get, but a stick? I think she might be goin' a bit mad, and not my kind of mad. This looked a bit, you know, *proper mad.*"

"Uh," Ash stuttered. "Oh…no…that's… a method used by palace servants to reduce stress. She's been through a lot. Yes, the elder servants taught it to us." She couldn't be sure what Serene had been doing, but she suspected it might have to do with magic. She felt bad lying to Nifty, but she didn't want to compromise their chances. She had already given him more trust than she had wanted to in the first place.

"That's interesting, maybe you could teach me one day," Nifty said. "So, you *did* work in the palace? You weren't joking? Next, you're gonna tell me she actually *is* the princess of Ul Nirin," Nifty laughed.

"Don't be so silly, Nifty," Ash laughed with him. "Yes, we're from the palace."

"Yeah, of course. The Princess is dead. It must have been a different world up there," Nifty said. "Were you there with the fighting?"

"What makes you say that?"

"I was doing errands in the house and I overheard Lord Sully talking."

"We escaped during the fighting," Ash said. "What did you hear?"

"The rebels overpowered the palace guards and they killed King Ingamar and the Princess. Prince Gideori is paralysed from poison, said to be in an endless sleep. The rebels captured the Wild Queen and the city guards, along with the palace guards, and held the city for a few days before the emperor of Lor Kithin commanded the other regions to send reinforcements. They took the city back and the Wild Queen executed pretty much the whole lot of 'em."

"That's terrible," Ash said. *Mother wouldn't have got involved. She's got to be okay.* There was so much to process and take in, she couldn't fathom it all. *Gideori didn't die. The King is dead. The Wild Queen is in charge. What a mess. Executions.* Everyone she had known and grown up with was probably dead. And it was all her fault! She felt sick. Her heart thumped so hard, as if it were battering her insides. Her head felt distorted with thoughts and pressure. She felt lost. She would have to tell Serene, and she dreaded that.

"I wish the rebels'd held that city and taken refugees. That'd 'ave been a story for the ages," Nifty said. "I can speak honestly with you, can't I, Ash? It wouldn't leave this home?"

"Whatever you say won't leave this home." Ash's curiosity was sparked.

"Well, I know it's cruel to say but when I 'eard about the city being taken by slaves, I felt so *good*. I just felt like maybe there's proper hope, not just the hope that we'll all get through this and 'ave alright lives making the most of what we've got as slaves, but real hope that we might one day be free. The fact that many died didn't bother me, the hope was stronger, and I feel wrong about it."

"Oh, Nifty, sometimes I worry you're too nice for your own good.

There's nothing wrong with being that desperate for freedom. We all are." *He's happy enough here,* she thought. *Why put his life at risk forever. He's the happiest person I've ever met. We shouldn't take him with us. We can't take him with us.*

"Right," he said, conflicted in his views. "Either way they didn't hold the city for long so what hope of freedom 'ave we got at all? We really are puny compared to witches and giants, and I guess we just gotta keep making the most of what we got, even if it ain't much at all." He looked around his home and he smiled. "Could be a lot worse, couldn't it?"

"This is a lovely home you have, Nifty. You should be so proud of it," Ash said.

"Oh, I am, I really am," he grinned.

"You're not puny either, Nifty," she said. "If everyone was as strong as you are in spirit, it would only be a matter of time before we were all free."

The hatch began to open, and Ash and Nifty tensed with fright. Serene popped her head in and forced a smile before climbing in and closing the hatch behind her. A chilly draft sank into the room. Serene quietly curled up next to Ash in the pile of blankets.

"It won't be long before the morning bell," Ash said. "Maybe you should head back, and we'll follow a little bit after," Ash said to Nifty, hoping to talk to Serene alone for a moment.

"It's been a wonderful night," Nifty said, taking his last sip of tea and leaving.

There was silence for a while and Ash appreciated the warmth of Serene huddled next to her. She passed Serene her mug, which had a few sips of tea left in it, probably cold. Serene sat up and sipped it, looking at Ash with bright eyes. She looked much livelier than Ash had seen her in a long time.

Serene said, "Magic lore says that if humans practise magic only darkness and chaos will be found. They are too weak to control it."

"I know, that's about the only thing they *do* tell us about magic lore," Ash said.

"Since we left the city, there has only been darkness and chaos and none of that has been human doing, only witches."

"Ironic, isn't it?" Ash said.

"Well, I have come to the conclusion that darkness and chaos might be just what we need to get out of here," Serene said.

Ash's heart quickened. "You think maybe I could learn?"

"As far as I know, nobody has ever taught humans magic, we never questioned the lore. I don't think I am strong enough to protect us both, I may never be."

"You are, Serene, your magic skills are renowned across all of Ul Nirin."

"No," Serene said. "I can't fight. I barely ever practised combat magic, why would a princess ever need it?" Serene took a wand from her pocket and balanced it on her palm. "I am going to learn. All my life I have been told to be quiet, my questions were never *right* for a princess. Now I see it much more clearly. The giants and witches are merciless. It has nothing to do with race or blood. It is pure greed. The princess of Ul Nirin was a naïve coward who let things happen that should never have happened. I *am not* her."

The wand had slight curves at one end forming a handle about the size of a hand, and a straight end about the length of the bottom of her palm to the end of her middle finger. The handle was perfectly smooth, and the straight end was rougher.

"Her name is Chaos, and I made her for you," Serene said, handing it to Ash.

Ash felt a peculiar warmth and vibration as soon as she touched the wood. It felt good in her hand, like it was meant to be there. She was in awe, and excited. A rush of disbelief and apprehension ran through her. She had the feeling she stood on the precipice of profound transformation, and it both scared her and thrilled her.

"Chaos has a sister, made from the same wood and also enchanted with my essence, my blood," Serene said. "They say blood is a dangerous and powerful source of essence, just like fire. We will use them both." She revealed another wand. This one was completely straight, about three palms in length and it had rough notches all over it. "Her name is Darkness."

CHAPTER 13

EXILUK

Exiluk walked north to Avenia, to Blackhill, to find the dwarf and giant and their map with the rune spells that opened the cavern of Old Dwarven treasure. The thought of it all excited him greatly. He had never used his powers to hurt anyone before, never even for his own gain. He felt guilty and ashamed, yet something in him felt stronger and more vibrant than ever before, as if using his essence to incite the killing of the giant had sparked a fire in him. But amongst that fire was a deep confusion. He didn't know who he was anymore. He didn't know how to reconcile himself and he felt sick recalling clashes of blood, flesh, weapon, bone and spirit. *The axe. The woman's gasp.*

He passed through lands of light snow and cold, the landscape transforming as he pressed forwards. Gradually, the scenery shifted, revealing warmer lands of lush greenery. Fertile fields stretched far, the scent of blooming flowers danced through the air, and the sun cast long shadows as he walked and walked, until finally he reached the even warmer lands of Avenia.

Avenia was more developed than Okuden, where Exiluk had just come from. The buildings were smaller and less grand, but they still seemed like small castles compared to the buildings Exiluk had encountered in his extensive travels. It made sense for the buildings in a land of witches and giants to be grand, and he was thoroughly impressed by the feeling of wealth and power. It felt as if a thousand years of history and painstaking labour had gone into every structure. He thought about how many slaves must have been involved in the history of the Nine Lands and it made him feel rather uneasy. *How can I admire such grandeur and yet remain true to myself? What is becoming of me?* he thought.

A line of grubby, sweaty dwarves trudged ahead of him, linked by a chain at the ankle, each one carrying a pickaxe that looked blunt from overuse. A giant with a monstrous whip towered over them, telling them to keep up or they would get lashes. The giant's muscles were as chunky as boulders and his stride was powerful, long and effortlessly strong. He cracked the whip and it sounded like two shields clashing in battle, hard, heavy, and sharp. The dwarven slaves scurried and skipped forwards.

He passed isolated, massive buildings and settlements, farms and mines, and other signs of riches and industry. He saw in the distance a city formed of wide, towering buildings spread apart. It looked as if a dozen castles had been placed together to make a statement. The magnitude of it felt unrivalled. It seemed almost desolate, resembling mountains shaped by creatures of flesh and bone rather than benevolent Gods or elders, and not for virtuous purposes.

There was something sinister about such epic creations sitting on the earth, something sinister about their creators. The power oozing from the city and its megastructures also spoke of unparalleled strength. So much stone and so much energy must have been sunk into it. Blood and bone. And although he was most intrigued by it all, he continued his walking. *I stop at Blackhill*, he thought. *There lies my destiny.*

Exiluk eventually found himself overlooking Blackhill, which seemed to be comprised of three settlements. A walled manor sat atop a prominent hill for all to see, with well-kept manor grounds surrounding the hill; this settlement stood alone and away from the main road. Beyond the manor walls sprawled vast lands and numerous small dwellings, presumably for servants. Along the main road, there was Blackhill Pass, which mainly centred around Blackhill Inn and a few other dwellings, and in the distance was Blackhill city.

Exiluk was curious that in all his time in the land of witches and giants, contrary to his expectations, the presence of witches and giants was scarce compared to the multitude of slaves. Blackhill was no different. Weary slaves could be seen all about the few buildings and toiling the lands. Yet the presence of giants, those beings of immense power and wealth, was notably absent.

The slaves stopped and stared at him, and when they noticed him noticing them, they dropped their heads and carried on with what they were doing. They had likely never seen a keradin, and he appreciated that with their spirits so crushed, he meant little to them except, perhaps, as some amusement.

He wandered past the settlement. The imposing stature of the Blackhill Inn caught his eye. Unlike the weathered and rustic inns from other lands, this one stood tall and wide, built from sleek, grey stone. Its clean and modern appearance stood in stark contrast to the more charming and cosy nature of the inns in other lands. Travelling for so many years, through so many lands, Exiluk thought he had seen just about every type of inn there was, from rough and ready to elegantly decorated. He remembered singers and bands, drinks spilling, and people jumping and dancing. This inn was quiet, almost lifeless.

Past Blackhill Pass, the city loomed over him. The giant guard at the city gate inspected him curiously and cautiously, and after finding no weapons and plenty of treasure for trade, he let Exiluk through without further questioning. Exiluk wandered into a long hall with a market. Strange and seemingly random arrangements of stalls for smaller beings and larger stalls for giants filled the space.

Giants and slaves, and beings Exiluk assumed were witches because they looked like humans but they didn't have the telltale brand mark burned above the eyes, tended the stalls. Flashes of light and smoke of all colours danced in the air. Strange creatures in cages and baskets made strange noises. The market thrived with activity, bustle and chatter, and the aroma of the various foods for sale was tantalising, although they didn't mix too well with the smell of the spells the witches showed off to sell their spellwares.

It excited and intrigued Exiluk to see the open display of magic. Throughout his travels, magic had been veiled in secrecy, except for Whoff, where a diverse array of peculiar and wondrous magical practices had also been openly displayed. Exiluk had come to realise magic was present in various forms all over the world. *This must be what the sorcerers call cheap magic,* he thought, remembering a sliver of something he had heard once about true magic and cheap magic, also known as material magic.

He caught the eye of a giant who looked at him welcomingly, if not a bit cautiously, and so he went over and examined the giant's wares. The giant sold a marvellous assortment of mechanical puzzles made of wood, gemstones, and metals: lock puzzles that could only be opened with hidden mechanisms and secret combinations, disentanglement puzzles of wonderfully intricate shapes, interconnected rings that needed separating, beautiful cubes of irregularly shaped pieces that seemed impossible to reassemble once taken apart, and so on. Some were human size and others were so large they were clearly for giants. They talked about where Exiluk had come from, but not wanting to purchase anything, Exiluk moved on.

A couple of stalls on, Exiluk caught his breath. *I know that scimitar. Surely, it can't be. Skup?* In front of him was an array of swords, scabbards, daggers, knives and armour. Amongst the swords was Skup's scimitar, he recognised it for sure! "Where did you get this?" he asked the witch selling the wares.

"That's goblin steel," he said, taking the scimitar out of its worn and battered leather sheath, "infused with dragon blood."

Exiluk felt sick. "Where did you get it?" he said. At that moment, he realised clearly that for a while, he had managed to remove his bond with Skup from his mind. A memory of death threatened him. A memory of the spirit leaving the woman he had killed. Of blade and blood.

"Have you heard the legend of the pirate Skup?" the witch said.

"Did you meet him, was he here?" Exiluk could sense the desperation in his voice. He could feel a thread of energy gripping him, pulling him towards the scimitar. He resisted it. *We are not bonded by death and blade, surely. We can't be. Blood and blade are a crooked bond.* He so wanted to believe his thoughts, but he knew there was truth in the bond he sensed. He could feel it. His entire existence had changed course that day. He closed his eyes and focused on the blackness, resetting his mind.

"Of course he wasn't here, what would the legendary pirate be doing in Blackhill? No. This special blade came from the ports. Couldn't tell you who traded it there, though I assure you of its authenticity."

"I know it. How much do you want for it?" He needed the blade, it called to him. It told him that his path led back to Skup. It wasn't just some random, accidental killing. He hadn't killed for nothing. There was more to it than that. His mind raced frantically. *The pirate. The jewels of the aerie. The map. The cavern full of treasure. The pirate. The legend.* The magnitude of it all. The significance of his fate.

"You there," a giant interrupted. She wore official-looking clothing with an emblem picturing a giant on a throne overlooking vast hills drawn with basic shapes on her chest, and an emblem depicting a snake devouring the tail of a dragon on her shoulder.

Heartbeat rising, Exiluk assumed he had attracted trouble.

"I couldn't help but overhear you came from Anhera, and I would love to hear more about it. Would you care to join me for lunch?" it was a pleasant surprise to hear her say.

"Of course, it would be an honour to dine with such a decorated member of this place." He eyed her clothing again. "Though first, excuse me, I must buy this scimitar. It belonged to an old friend."

The seller laughed, "An old friend. The pirate king?"

Exiluk scowled at him, and he silenced.

"Give him the scimitar," the giant said.

The seller frowned and a sulk enveloped his face.

Exiluk held his hands out and the seller placed the blade on his palms, a reflection of light flickering in its grey and red-tinged steel. He felt its sturdiness. The weight at the handle and tip were well balanced. "Why?" he looked at the giant. "I can pay."

"That won't be necessary. Your eyes tell of a lust for the blade more intense than I have ever seen. I admire it. Perhaps you can tell me the tale of the blade in exchange for this gesture." The giant held out her hand. Exiluk shook what he could of it, his hand being much smaller. Her grip was painfully firm. "My name is Naara Darthik."

Exiluk couldn't believe his fate, remembering hearing the giant Toarer and the dwarf Pika talk about her as the woman that Toarer would marry. *That map is well within my reach, after all. Perhaps it is meant to be,* he thought. He considered what he knew about the Old Dwarven, the treasure, the map, everything, and he determined he must use such valuable information wisely.

Her house was one of the most magnificent buildings in the city. Its opulence excited Exiluk. Colossal gates opened onto meticulously manicured sprawling gardens. The entrance hall was vast, and its white and slightly smoky stone was polished to shining perfection. The stone that lined the floor, walls and ceiling had an interesting design and structure that Exiluk had never seen before. There were images in the stone that appeared to be there naturally, as if formed in the stone rather than painted on top. *It must have been crafted with magic,* he thought. The images were of flowers, plants, and patterns. Arched columns opened onto passageways that led to other rooms. A white staircase with elaborately carved handrails branched off to the right and left wings of the mansion, and a decadent waterfall of glistening water poured down into a marble pool on the landing and served as a centre piece.

Naara and Exiluk dined in the great hall, where Exiluk felt rather insignificant. "Tell me about your home," Naara said.

"There was once a time I thought it the most brilliant place in the world. It is a swamp at the edge of the forest of Darpirith and I saw it all as bursting with life and colour. Yet now I have seen the luxuries of the wider world I can't help but feel my return to the swamps would be glum and uninspiring."

The giant nodded and smiled, "I feel I understand. I yearn to see the wider world, and if it wasn't for my responsibilities in the High

King's palace guard, I feel I might have travelled as you did," she said. "Tell me, what do you think of the might of the Nine Lands? I have always wondered how we compare to other civilisations. It seems a curse we are surrounded by such unforgiving places. The treacherous sea to the east and south, the silent desert to the north, and the impenetrable forest to the west, often I feel we are trapped here, and this could be the sad peak of our might."

"There is much yet for me to see, but what I have seen so far has been most intriguing." Exiluk thought of the dark and foreboding palace in Okuden and the glittering cave of treasure beyond that, and he admired the ornate marble building he was in with all its intricacies. "Your architecture is amongst the most amazing I have seen, and I am sure the land of witches and giants is amongst the mightiest."

Naara's eyes lit up and Exiluk could feel the energy of her ego expanding. It was a strange energy that he had always been taught to avoid, one known to be an energy of darkness to his fellow keradin. Yet this energy that he absorbed from the giant's ego, which he had deliberately fed, didn't feel dark at all. It felt powerful and invigorating, even just a sliver of it.

"Perhaps you could tell me more about the great barrier of magic that controls the passing from Darpirith to the land of witches and giants?"

Naara laughed awkwardly. "Is that what they call us out there? The land of giants *and witches?* You know, we giants were here first, much before the witches started venturing south. It is said they came from the desert early in the second age, and great wars were fought between witches and giants, until we came to a truce and generously shared some of our lands for the greater prosperity of both civilisations. We shared *our* land, do you understand?"

"I do," Exiluk said. Her passion and anger excited him, subtly feeding his essence. "And where do humans and dwarves come into it all?"

"They were created by the First Giants, the god giants, to serve our might. We have always looked after those poor creatures, punies and wimples are the weakest and dumbest of sorts. Sometimes I wonder how cruel the First Giants might be to create such a feeble thing, and yet we see much feebler in the rest of nature, so I don't question it too much."

"How interesting," Exiluk said. "And what of all the humans and dwarves beyond the Nine Lands? Were they also created by the First Giants?"

"Of course they were. Before the barrier, some escaped and populated other parts of the world. The barrier is there as much to maintain control of what comes in from that ghastly forest as it is to control what goes out." Naara gulped some wine and cut a big piece of cheese. "You see, it is known that humans populate a large portion of the world, and if humans and dwarves were made by the First Giants to serve us, all they own belongs to the giants, wouldn't you agree?"

"Hmm," Exiluk said, understanding the logic and yet wondering if the giant realised the jump she had to make to get to her conclusion. Exiluk didn't believe in the First Giants as gods, just like he didn't believe in all those other weird and wonderful gods he had heard about around the world. "What would the witches have to say about it?"

"They are our allies, are they not? Whether we have the same theological beliefs or not doesn't deter from the fact that together we are an incredibly powerful force. They benefit from the First Giants' creations as much as we do, and they should be most grateful for it, don't you think?"

"I see," Exiluk said.

"Do you know how many witches it takes to maintain that barrier at one time?"

"I don't," Exiluk said, intrigued.

"Technically we have two barriers and several additional defence systems supported by magic. One hundred witches at any one time feed the magic that creates a physical barrier between us and the forest. A further hundred and fifty at one time maintain the barrier of magic that forms a dome around our lands, protecting us from any magical attack from air, sea, or land. We also have witches with the sight, and these watcher witches can see into the minds and intentions of any creature they cast their attention to. They are constantly scanning the minds of servants to find dissent." Her grin was arrogant, clearly impressed with herself, her power and control.

"That is impressive indeed," Exiluk said, feeling genuinely excited by that level of organisation and power. It was so material, so wasteful in relation to the keradin way, yet it was so *exhilarating*. He felt a fire warming in his core. "And who orchestrates all of this, is there a supreme ruler of the Nine Lands?" Exiluk asked, goading her slightly as he remembered what the giant and dwarf had said about her in the hut.

"You would have thought so, wouldn't you? It makes sense to centralise such efforts, yet there is the League of the Nine Lands, which is an alliance between the emperor of Lor Kithin and the High King of Midvale, and the independent kingdoms of Craddock and Okuden," she said, waving a servant over to clear their plates and top up their drinks. "It seems you have a keen interest in politics?"

"I am interested in everything," Exiluk said.

"I suppose you must be, having travelled so much," she said. "Do you have anywhere to be, or would you tell me more about the beyond? Not to forget our deal, I simply must hear about the blade."

"It would be my pleasure, so long as you can tell me more about the Nine Lands in return," Exiluk said.

The keradin and the giant sat and talked and drank for a long time. Naara was most interested in the forest beyond the barrier, and Exiluk could tell she was scoping out whether giants could pass through it. He didn't tell her he knew ways of getting through the forest safely, or the fact that most of the time keradin wandered through the forest without any real encounters of danger. He wanted her to feel she needed him, just in case he needed leverage later down the line, and so he teased some details and kept others to himself.

She told him all about the Nine Lands and its history, which he intuitively felt was slightly skewed towards the might and delight of giants, and yet it was a rich and intriguing history of war and peace and riches and ambition, and the story moved him.

She was most interested in learning about the keradin and their simple yet exotic way of life in the swamps, and she questioned the strength of every civilisation he had come across. She was overly dismissive of the strength of the humans beyond the barrier, seemingly unable to comprehend they could build wonders and survive without the giants. Her eyes lit up when he told her of the winged aerie with jewels in their skin.

The more they drank the more Exiluk realised he liked something about the giant's ambition, and he resonated with her desire to know the world beyond the barrier. He knew what it was like for her to have all her community try to convince her that they had everything they needed in the Nine Lands and thus no need to go further. He said, "If I had listened to them, I would still be in the swamps none the wiser."

"And now look at you, in league with mighty giants."

The thought stoked the fire inside of him. He was beginning to feel unstoppable.

He was delighted to hear about the elven band that played at important occasions in the Nine Lands, and he was even more delighted when she said, "They are playing at my wedding. It would be an honour to have you there, you are an exotic guest after all. I am sure everyone would be *so* interested to meet you."

The lore of the keradin respected the elven as higher beings from the aether. Parts of the keradin teachings were said to be derived from ancient elven lore. Never did Exiluk think he would get a chance to meet elven beings in the flesh.

The guest bedchamber in the Darthik's city house was sumptuous and Exiluk was grateful to have been considered an exotic guest, not a threat. He enjoyed exploring the city and its surrounding areas while he waited for the wedding.

It was a city of giants, and that meant it was formed mostly of colossal, ancient buildings of stone, each standing as wide as a castle and reaching imposing heights. The witches' buildings, though fewer in number, exuded grandeur that eclipsed those found beyond the Nine Lands, yet they remained dwarfed by the magnitude of the giants' dwellings.

The humble abodes of the servants' shacks and halls were tucked away amidst the dark, shadowed corners of the city. Throughout the city was the omnipresent force of the many servants ceaselessly engaged in cleaning, building, gathering, and running various errands.

No servants spoke to Exiluk, and it didn't take long for him to realise word had spread of Naara's exotic guest. The occasional giants and witches he encountered would acknowledge the matter, exchanging pleasant words with Exiluk before continuing along their own paths.

All the time he had been in Blackhill, he had felt a burning urge to find the dwarf and his map. He had gathered that the dwarf was likely to be at Blackhill Manor, where the giant Toarer lived, and Exiluk looked forward to the day of the wedding so he could be invited into the Goaner family's home.

The wedding was the focal point of the bustle of the city, and for days he heard servants gossip and aristocratic talk of the luxurious and extravagant imports of foods, clothing, jewels, plants, potions and powders, and decorations that would mark the most important wedding in a long time. *The mining of Avenia is marrying the military and ministry*, he heard this sentiment aplenty and he was glad to be a part of that history, whatever may come of it.

Something in his heart told him there was much excitement to come. He could feel the threads of his essence intertwining with his new path of destiny and it invigorated him. Getting off the goblin ship prematurely had clearly been the right decision. His thoughts became heavier remembering the bet of destiny he had made with the goblin. He shrugged it off, *I will probably never see that goblin again.*

CHAPTER 14

THEO

Blackhill Manor and its grounds were full of the bustle you would expect from one of the most talked about and lavish weddings of the time. Esteemed guests had been arriving from all over the Nine Lands.

Theo was mesmerised by an approaching caravan. Two massive animals with long tusks decorated in gold carried two giants wearing crowns and furs. The animals' trunks were long and dexterous, their legs, chunky and daunting, and what appeared to be an impenetrably tough hide was covered in thick, rough, finger length hairs ranging from dark grey to light brown. Behind them, more of these creatures pulled carts as other giants walked beside them. Human and dwarven slaves jogged to keep up behind them.

"You, Blondie, stop gawping at the Okudenians and help that band to their tent," Kirakai commanded. "Pika, help him with their things."

Three elves with instruments had arrived in the courtyard on fine horses. It was the first time Theo had ever seen elves, a moment he had long anticipated because of the buzz surrounding the famous elven band playing at the wedding. Resembling humans in many ways, their faces were sharper and more pronounced. They were distinguished by their pale skin, tall and elegant frames, glowing and silky silvery blonde hair, and silvery grey eyes with the slightest hint of blue.

Pika briskly strode past Theo and said, "Mamuphaunts, wow,"

presumably talking about the creatures the giants rode.

"Welcome to Blackhill Manor," Pika said.

The elves nodded at Pika. They looked at Theo with more scrutiny, talking to each other rhythmically in a language Theo assumed was Elven. Their whispers and gazes were heavy on him, as if there was more to it than appeared on the surface. It was almost as if the language sounded familiar. Familiar, yet distant, and he couldn't understand why. Pika eyed Theo with a curious frown. The elves refused when Pika gestured to take their bags. Pika signalled to another dwarf to take their horses to the stables.

They showed the elves to their tent. Theo appreciated that they had been happy to carry their own bags. That was most humble compared to the giants and witches, especially considering the elven band were so famous and respected across the Nine Lands.

"Sit," one said to Theo. He was a little rougher around the edges than the other two. The other two appeared somewhat perfect, in a strange way. *Because there's no such thing as perfect*, Theo told himself. This one's hair was a little frizzier and his skin was less youthful. There was slight yellowing and darkening around his eyes. He said, "Pass me a drink."

"Of course," Pika said.

"Not you, we don't give anyone orders," the elf said. "You can just relax here for a moment." He took a giant swig from a skin his fellow elf had passed him. The smell of alcohol cut through the air. The three elves, the dwarf, and the human sat quietly on the beds in the tent. The moment, the mood, was strange and surreal.

The tent was made of a greyish-green hemp canvas. A lamp cast a warm glow about them. The elven skin and hair shimmered subtly in the darkness. There was a washing bowl and a vase of water, and each bed had a vase of water next to it. No matter what Theo tried to focus on, he couldn't shake the feeling the elves were thinking or feeling something significant about him, but he couldn't grasp what was happening with any more clarity than that.

"I am Nilinriall," the drinking elf said with a deep, comforting voice. "This is Gwynnestri," he pointed to the female elf, "and this is Dillinir," pointing to the other male elf. "You two are?"

"Theo."

"Pika."

"In Avenia, there aren't many who look like you," he said to Theo, no doubt referring to his platinum blonde hair and pale skin. "Where are your parents from?"

"They say my mother served at Blackhill Inn, and she died when she had me."

Nilinriall's jaw tightened and a look swept through his eyes that Theo couldn't interpret. The elves talked in their own language with low voices. They hummed a harmony that made Theo feel melancholic and a peculiar sense of nostalgia he couldn't explain.

"The dwarf has an artefact of witch magic on him," Nilinriall said. "And you," he gestured to Theo, "have an artefact of a much deeper sorcery."

Pika grabbed his pocket and flushed red. Theo's heartbeat became unbearably heavy. They would be killed if the witches and giants discovered it.

"It does not concern us, yet we must urge caution. The more powerful witches can sense the essence," the elf said. "And whilst these witches' magic is weak compared to the old sorceries, there are some worthy of recognition here, we can sense it." Nilinriall was calm and his voice smooth until he gulped his drink contrastingly vigorously. "We can take care of your things for you while we are here, if you wish?"

"No!" Pika hissed. "Nobody's touching our things."

Theo was surprised to find himself trusting the elves unconditionally. If Pika had handed his orb over, Theo would have handed his stone to them too. Though it was broken, he still preferred to hold on to it. He was amused by the idea of a protection stone needing protection, and although he was nervous about the trouble they might get into, his nerves were much lighter than he expected them to be.

"Fine," the elf said, taking another swig of the harsh-smelling drink. "The witches here will be too intoxicated to sense it, I am sure," he laughed. The alcohol smelt fruity, like a strong wine. "How many years do you have, boy?"

"About seventeen," Theo said.

They talked in Elven some more, and afterwards Nilinriall said, "Thank you, we require privacy now." He appeared uncomfortable.

As Theo and Pika left the tent, Pika said, "That was odd."

"It was," Theo said.

"I suppose an encounter with the elves *would* be odd, wouldn't it. Apparently, they're not from our world, and those three are the only ones here. They've been here for centuries, so the lore tells."

"What're they doing in this world, then?" Theo asked.

"The scriptures of different cultures have different stories. Some say they're banished to our world for doing wrong in theirs. Others say they're here to save our world, and are heroes in theirs," Pika said.

"Why did they want to know how old I was?" Theo said.

"I'm really not sure," Pika said, a little disengaged. His hand was in his pocket, no doubt fingering the precious orb that could grant their freedom. "I wonder if we can ask the elves for help," he said.

A magnitudinous sound from a mamuphaunt stopped them in their tracks. Outside the courtyard, the mamuphaunts were being taken away to be cared for. They were bigger than any animal Theo had ever seen. Their steps were long and slow and powerful. Theo caught one's big golden eye and he experienced an inexplicable sadness.

"You two, go and serve some drinks," Kirakai said.

Large silver trays were being loaded with crystal vases and glasses of fine wines, beers, and lemonades. Theo was tired and thirsty and looking at the drinks made his mouth feel thick. Avira was waiting by one of the trays and he rushed to help her carry it. The metal was heavy. They walked together into the great hall where guests were standing and talking, waiting to be called to the site of the ceremony.

A stocky being with curved horns and lightning-blue eyes was talking with a group of witches. Theo had never seen someone like that, and he wondered where he was from and what he was doing there. Lord Minister Fimni Darthik approached the group and Theo offered him a drink.

"You came, Exiluk, I am so grateful," Lord Minister Darthik said, stooping down towards the horned man and the witches. They looked up at him with courteous smiles. Lord Minister Darthik's wedding clothes were sharply shaped and well fitted, creating an elegance unusual to giants, who often could never quite shake their bulky and brash demeanour.

"No, Lord Minister Darthik, I am *so* grateful for the invite. What a pleasure it is to meet such marvellous giants and witches. Never in my time did I think I would be conversing with the most important rulers of the Nine Lands." The horned being wore a dress robe more aligned with the high fashion of the witches. It was smooth and silky with elaborate trim.

"And never in my time did I think I would be introducing a keradin at my daughter's wedding," Lord Minister Darthik said. "And it is a pleasure to see you all again," he addressed the witches. "How is the herb trade treating you in Eliniar, Lord Sully?"

"Brilliantly, as always," Lord Sully said, and he chuckled arrogantly with the other witches. "I trust the ministry is treating you well?"

Lord Minister Darthik smiled and nodded. "And what of the wand craft, Lady Viola? I am sure all is well."

"Well indeed," Lady Viola replied. "There has been a particular uptick in demand for luxury wands this year, which has been a pleasant surprise. You can't always predict these things." Her jewels were so light and fine Theo wondered how they didn't break. Silver with white gems, all over her arms and neck. It was clear that everyone was trying to make a statement with what they were wearing.

"I am most happy for you," Lord Minister Darthik said.

"Perhaps not as happy as one could be when uniting the military, mining, and ministry of Avenia all through marriage," a witch man said, grinning in jest. His skin was dark, and he dressed exotically. His robe was black with gold embroidered trim. His jewels were chunky and gold, around his neck, waist, wrists, and fingers. He wore a mask that cast patterns around one eye.

"Love can be mysterious, Dar Koras, wouldn't you agree? Isn't it wonderful that marriage can serve our society *and* love," Lord Minister Darthik said. He glared at Theo and Avira, likely having noticed they had been lingering.

"The tray's so heavy," Avira muttered.

Theo guided Avira towards a group of giants without drinks in their hands. The giants reached for the drinks taking no notice of the people carrying them. Theo did his best to eavesdrop on Lord Minister Darthik's conversation.

"Did the troubles with the workers in Ul Nirin affect you much, Dar Koras?" Lord Sully said.

"That is not something we discuss so openly in the north, Lord Sully. I feel you know that," Dar Koras said, glaring at the chubby lord.

What troubles? Theo thought.

"My utmost apologies, I would never mean to offend you or the northern empire. We are *one* Nine Land after all," Lord Sully said, with a slightly facetious tone. "A blow to the north is a blow to us all," he said.

An awkward silence ensued until Lord Minister Darthik said, "All is under control up there, no need to worry yourself, Lord Sully." More silence ensued. A lady witch approached Lord Sully and took his hand—his wife, presumably—and led him to speak to some others.

Drumming sounded from outside, and the long howl of a battle horn. "Oh marvellous, someone rather important is about to arrive," Lord Minister Darthik said, heading to the courtyard. Witches and giants followed in excitement.

Theo and Avira found an inconspicuous spot from which to watch the arrival. A giant played a drum and another played a horn while an extremely well-presented giant wearing the crest of the High King of Midvale walked up the courtyard. The giant playing the horn pulled it from his lips and said, "Prince Keroak, first son of the High King."

"What an honour to have the King's own flesh and blood at our humble estate," Master Goaner said. Though Lord Goaner was the master of Blackhill Manor, Theo seldom saw him. He was a strong, well-groomed giant who took pride in his vast wealth of mines and other production in Avenia.

Lord Minister Darthik joined them. "Prince Keroak," he bowed, and they shook hands.

"An honour to be here," the Prince said. He appeared calm, with a hint of a jovial mood, and lacking in the self-importance Theo expected of such a giant. "We have another guest joining us, by command of the King," he said, his tone less jovial now.

Lord Minister Darthik and Master Goaner appeared uneasy, but they smiled and nodded at the Prince. A puff of smoke appeared in the courtyard. A witch appeared in the smoke. The smoke dissipated into the air. Rakuul Mordaker! Theo's heartbeat raced and he flushed with sweat. He *had* fought a watcher. He *had* been on top of the tower with Rakuul Mordaker.

"Advisor of Magic to the High King," said the giant who had announced the Prince. There were murmurs in the crowd.

Theo tugged Avira. "We have to go to the kitchen," he said. "That's the watcher I fought," he whispered, as they slipped away.

"I don't understand it, Theo. How could you fight a witch while drowning in a lake?"

"I wish I understood. I really do," he said. "The watcher knows about us. What're we supposed to do?"

"We have to leave," Avira said. "I think we have a bit of time. If they wanted to make a scene they would have brought guards. He's probably just here to sniff around, but we have to be careful. We have to tell Toarer and Pika and we have to use the orb as soon as we can."

A beautiful harmony of bells rang, and the guests began filtering towards the site by the lake. There was an air of excitement and intrigue in their chatter. Servants were not permitted to witness such a special ceremony. Instead, they would be adding the finishing touches to the great hall for the feast.

There were tables for giants and tables for witches, and where it would be improper to separate them, such as the table for royalty, the witches' seats were built up so they could sit at the table at the correct height. Theo had heard the giants complaining about having to adjust their homes for witch guests on several occasions.

The tables were lined with rich cloth embroidered in silver thread. There were perfectly placed plates and silverware engraved with intricate swirls around the edges; fresh flowers in stone vases; and tall, thin, taper candles in diamond-grey. In the centre of the tables were beautiful clusters of the firefly baubles. The fireflies flitted around the baubles, and despite daylight coming through the windows, they glowed magnificently.

"It *is* beautiful, don't you think?" Avira said. She arranged the flowers in a vase, inhaled deeply, sighed, and put them on the table. "Imagine having a wedding like this."

"Yes..." Theo said, feeling sad that Avira would never have such a wedding.

He noticed an unusual feeling in himself. He noticed he wasn't clinging on to a strong sense of impending doom like he usually would. Yet he knew Rakuul Mordaker was after him, and knowing a watcher was so close to finding him would usually cripple him. There were his thoughts about Avira. He was unsure if she would ever want to marry someone like him, and humans were forbidden to marry in the Nine Lands because giants and witches sought to extinguish any semblance of hope or unity. He didn't have a single coin to his name to pay for anything, never mind a lavish wedding like this one. Yet it didn't feel impossible.

He watched as she arranged flowers in a vase. They were stunning. She had an eye for that kind of thing. He wondered what weddings were like beyond the Nine Lands, and he felt a sliver of hope for him and Avira. Though the thought of escaping still burdened him. He felt so torn, and yet he knew deep down that they had to go.

If we escaped beyond the barrier, things would be so different, Theo thought. *But they'd catch us, and torture us, and kill us. It's pointless hoping. Pointless dreaming. You'll never go, so why even think about it?*

He was so conflicted.

Pika entered the great hall through the kitchen and Theo found a quiet moment to tell him all about Rakuul; that he really had fought him, and that he was there now.

"Are you absolutely sure?" Pika said, scratching his head.

"Yes, absolutely," Theo said.

"We leave tonight then, during the distraction of the wedding. I'll tell Toarer. And I bet the elves are our best hope," Pika paused, deep thought etched heavily between his brows. "Yes, that's it. Theo, you have to talk to the elf, make him help us, please. He seemed... intrigued by you, open to you, I can't explain it, but I feel you felt it too.

"We have to leave tonight! Be ready."

CHAPTER 15

ASH

Two thin wands pointed at a feather in Nifty's home. The lamp glowed orange and there were soft shadows on the walls and surfaces. A milky white potion with a blue tint simmered in a pot, with a harsh, concentrated scent, unlike anything Ash had experienced before.

"My father always said magic is more complex than any being could ever grasp, and that each piece of magic is an expression of just the smallest piece of the universe, like one grain of sand in all the sand in the world," Serene said. "The more we learn, the more we realise how much we don't know."

Ash wanted to tell Serene that her father was dead and that her brother was still alive. But she couldn't bring herself to do it. "He's wise, isn't he?" she said instead, trying to hide her shudder at the memory of the stinky and cruel old man he had become.

"He lost it with age," Serene said. She moved her wand gently from side to side and the feather lifted from the floor and floated in mid-air, and she said, "In all things, there is the essence, and we harness the magic with our will. I am willing the feather to rise. Air magic, essence, and my will are combined with the feather's essence. My wand is amplifying my will. It helps me channel my essence." She lowered her wand. The feather dropped.

"You make it look so simple," Ash said. "When your father spoke of the complexity of it all, was he talking about all the possible combinations?"

"I think so," Serene said. "There is fire, water, air, earth, and essence, and each thing contains some or all of those things, and the way they are harnessed can manifest in infinitely different ways. Father said the strongest mages are not from the Nine Lands but from other worlds, ones who experiment fearlessly with all sorts of magic."

"How can we learn *that* type of magic?" Ash said.

"We can't. We would destroy ourselves learning it without a tutor, and there are none who would teach us. None in the Nine Lands know true sorcery. Father said that was a good thing. The power corrupts you beyond comprehension," Serene said. "Will the feather to rise. Focus on the energy in your centre and feel it flowing through the wand to the feather. That energy you feel is your essence, and the more attention you pay to it, the stronger it will become."

Ash felt a murmur of energy in her centre and tried to follow it into her wand. But she couldn't feel it beyond her centre and no matter how much she willed the feather to move, it wouldn't. She moved the wand side to side, gently, like Serene had. The feather didn't move. She intensified her will, *I wish the feather would move.* Nothing. *Move, you damned thing!* Nothing. "There's no magic in me," she said.

"It's fine, not even witches get it the first time. It takes practice. To be truthful, I was worried about what would happen. I thought you might summon a shadow of chaos or something, like the lore says will happen when a human gets hold of a wand."

"I wish I had summoned something. I feel useless."

"Not a shadow of chaos, not your first time!" Serene said, sternly. "We need to be so careful. But don't worry, the magic will come. There is magic in everything."

The potion sang, bubbled, and popped and drew their attention. "Look, it is as blue as the ocean on a summer's day. And now look, a few stirs and it is as thick as cream. That means it is ready, and we take it off the heat."

"I've never seen the ocean," Ash said. The potion was a delightful colour between turquoise and bright blue, and its scent was much milder now.

"One day, I will take you there," Serene said. She sipped the potion. "It is right. Excellent. This will strengthen our focus. And focusing on our essence will strengthen our essence. So long as we use the focus correctly." She moved the big wooden spoon towards Ash's mouth. "Potions take the essence from the things we put into them, and that essence interacts with our essence when we ingest them. Father said there are countless types of potion and each has benefits and disadvantages. Knowing the consequences is the difference between wisdom and ignorance."

Ash sipped the potion. The bitterness caught her off guard and she grimaced. The taste didn't match the appearance or scent. Her senses sharpened instantly. Her mind felt perfectly clear and everything about her seemed crisper. She took her wand and focused on the energy in her centre. That energy felt much more powerful. "What's the consequence of this one?"

"This is an extremely mild one, it merely focuses the senses. Most of the herbs can help you accomplish that without magic at all. You might feel tired afterwards, and if you used it all day every day you might deplete yourself severely. Father said that we don't need potions like this, but they can help us realise how sharp we can be, and then we should try to manifest that sharpness without any potions at all." Serene took a big gulp of it. "Father wasn't enslaved on a plantation, though." She smiled, and gave Ash some more.

Ash felt anger surrounding the energy in her centre, her essence. An irritation of fire and agitation, and she didn't like it at all. It worried her, like an unknown shadow lurking, one she couldn't understand. "I feel agitated, but it's not like I've felt before. It's more shadowed," she said.

Serene frowned. "Maybe I gave you too much. Try to channel it through your wand."

The feather lay still and lifeless as she gently moved her wand side to side. Her energy grew, she could feel it inside her. The feather didn't move. *Move, you damned thing!* "Rrrrrgh!" she roared, and shook her wand aggressively. She wanted it to move so badly. She wanted to gain some control. "This is such a waste of time," Ash said.

"Don't be upset, it takes practice," Serene said. She poured the potion into vials and hid them under a floorboard. "We had better get some sleep."

Ash couldn't sleep. All she could think about was magic. She had wanted to conjure magic so badly and the thought that she had failed made her angry. That anger weighed down on her all night.

≈✦≈

The next day was sunny and they worked the serpentsmane fields. One of the serpent-like heads dodged Ash's hand as she tried to grab it. It hissed at her and retaliated, jabbing a spiky prickle into her hand, drawing a tiny speck of blood. She grunted and grabbed it at its base, near the bulb where all the snaky vines came from. Ripped it from its bulb. It screeched as if steam whistled from it, just for a moment, and then it flopped dead. She threw it into the basket.

Ash couldn't stop thinking about magic. She had held a wand. She had felt her energy. And yet she hadn't been able to conjure any magic. Every time she thought about it, she wanted to scream. It made her feel as if there was no hope after all. But she knew she wouldn't give up, no matter what it took. They would escape, she would save her mother, and they would make them all pay.

In each moment she remembered to do so, she made a conscious effort to focus on her essence. It was just a slight something in the centre of her body. An energy, a feeling, a knowledge of something that wasn't physical like her body, but it wasn't just her imagination either. It was there, and it was calling for her. There was something so energising about focusing on it. Something so moreish. The more attention she paid to it, the stronger her awareness of it became. She wished she could take her wand out and practise a spell. Every time she realised how desperate she was to practise magic again, time seemed to slow, and the slowness agitated her.

"Ah, you cheeky little thing," Nifty said. He had just been pricked by a serpentsmane head. His hand danced with the head, dodging and attacking each other until he got pricked again. He put his finger in his mouth. "Oh, 'ello Ash," he said, and then he whispered very quietly, "I'm at the house later. I might try swipe something nice from the kitchens. You and Serene can meet me in our home, and we can eat it together if you like."

"No. We need privacy again," Ash snapped. She had spoken the words involuntarily.

"Oh, again? Alright then, you gotta do what you gotta do," he said. "I'll save some and maybe we can eat together tomorrow night."

She could tell he was disappointed and she felt terrible for it. She knew she could simply backtrack and agree to his invitation, yet the words wouldn't come out of her. All she could think about was practising magic. "Maybe," she said.

Nifty pointed surreptitiously. Lord and Lady Sully were observing the workers and conversing with the taskmaster. The taskmaster dished out punishment more often than usual and with even less reason than usual. "Work, you damned pigs," he shouted. He must have been trying to impress the Sullys.

A popping noise and a sinister giggle froze the workers. Malfin, the young son of the Sullys', was zapping the workers with spells at random, giggling with each bit of pain and discomfort he caused.

"Please tell him to stop that," Nifty shouted. "How're we meant to work in the midst of a high chance of being turned into a toad?"

Lady Sully said, "That is some excellent witchcraft, dear boy. There is no need to waste your magic on this lot, is there?"

"Don't spoil my fun," the kid said, with an evil look in his eye, and he waved his wand at Nifty. "Mortificus."

Nifty doubled over, appearing pale and weak. He tensed, twisted, and writhed in pain. Red whip marks appeared on his skin, and tears appeared in his clothes.

"Stop that!" Ash said, shielding Nifty with her body. The spell hit her. She felt sick, and weak, as if she hadn't eaten in months, and so dehydrated and disoriented. Pain, as if she was being whipped. Her flesh stung as if salt had been poured into the cuts.

"Thank you," Nifty said, weakly, as a red line appeared on his face and cut his lip.

The kid had used a lash of magic to tear Nifty's face. *Enough!* Ash felt something erupt in her, so intense and blinding, as if she was on the verge of insanity. A rage she couldn't control. A fire. She screamed. Birds flew from the trees. The world froze. Everyone stared as if she was possessed.

An ominous silence ensued, with thick tension in the air. The vastness of the land now felt daunting, as if a shadow had crept over it.

The kid had fallen and was scrambling backwards, being nipped by serpentsmane heads. He scraped himself up and ran to his mother crying. She hugged him and comforted him. "My poor boy," she said. "How dare the swine shout at you like that. She should be executed."

"I only just bought her, Lavinia, let me get my money's worth. She only screamed in pain, we can't blame her entirely for that."

"Well, she should be less aggressive about it," Lady Sully said. "Rorxis, make sure she learns her lesson."

"Certainly," the taskmaster grinned. "Get back to work, now!" He whipped a few slaves at random, a sinister satisfaction showing on his face.

Malfin glared at Ash vehemently. The other slaves pretended to work while they observed, stiffened. The Sullys' eyes pierced through her, yet underneath it appeared as if they were confused and shaken and doing their best to hide it. Ash knew her scream had been more powerful than just a scream, and the look on Malfin's face confirmed it. Lord and Lady Sully and the taskmaster had their suspicions too, that was obvious. Nobody would look Ash in the eye. Not a single person, not Serene, not Nifty. Ash felt tired and strange. Her body was heavy and her head was cloudy.

Nobody spoke to Ash. Not even the taskmaster. She kept herself to herself until everyone was asleep, and despite being extremely tired, she dragged herself off the floor and headed to the hideout.

The dark sky glistened with stars and the moon cast a soft, pale light over everything. The walk was beautifully quiet and peaceful, with only the soft tread of her footsteps and the tooting of an owl.

Serene caught up with her. "I don't think you should practise magic today," she said, hushed.

"You've ignored me all day, I'll practise alone," Ash said.

"How did you do it? When you screamed."

"Do what? I screamed, it was loud. What's the big deal?" Ash didn't believe what she was saying.

"I have never seen someone scream darkness into existence. I felt cold, as if a shadow was sweeping over everything around us. It wasn't like the magic I am used to. It was something else, something deeper. How could a human do something even a well-trained witch could not do, and by accident? I am not sure what to make of it."

"There was no darkness, nothing happened."

"We felt it, Ash. Everyone did, you could see it on their faces. They didn't know what it was, not the servants, anyway. The witches did, though. They knew something *odd* had happened. Even the serpentsmane was shaken."

"I didn't mean to. I couldn't help it," Ash said.

"Yes. That is the problem," Serene said.

They had reached the hatch. Ash looked around to make sure nobody was watching them. No signs of anyone.

"Please, Ash, just sleep tonight," Serene said.

Ash ignored her and climbed down the hatch. She lifted the floorboard that concealed their wands and potions. She placed a feather on the floor. Serene watched, curiously, cautiously. Ash handed Serene her wand. "We're going to get out of here. That's all that matters," she said. "We need a teleorb, don't we?"

Serene hesitated, and then she sighed and said, "That would be the easiest to use, and the hardest to get. They are usually locked away with the more expensive wares, and it is likely they will notice it gone. Some witches can teleport with their own magic, though very few. My father could when he was at his strongest." She looked sad. "I wonder how he is."

I haven't told her yet, Ash thought, anxious. *I've got to tell her. I... just... can't. But I've got to. Have to.* She took a deep breath. *One, two, three,* "Serene, I know what happened in Ul Nirin. Your father was killed in the riots. The Wild Q... I mean, your mother, has taken the throne. Your brother hasn't risen since he was poisoned, but he's not dead."

Serene was stiff as stone.

"I'm sorry," Ash said.

"It is fine," Serene said, her lips trembling. She downed half a potion and gave the rest to Ash. Picked up her wand. "There are certain words that can connect us to the forces we are trying to manipulate. Some witches find incantations more effective than will alone. Though, the words themselves are not magic, they simply invoke the will in a more focused manner." She waved her wand. "Levium," she said, and the feather rose swiftly, and floated from side to side as it descended back to the floor. "You try, and make sure you focus on the essence."

Ash downed the potion and felt instantly focused. She put her attention on the energy in her centre and she waved her wand. "Levium," she said.

The feather lay still, lifeless, angering Ash. She tensed her whole body, so tight it felt she might break her wand. She waved her wand aggressively. "Levium," she shouted, forcing the energy from her core towards the feather. It rose in an instant, fast, defying its feathery nature. It burst into flames, then dropped to the floor, a shrivelled black mess.

Serene was horrified, stiffer than before. "That is enough for today. Let us get some rest."

"What?" Ash said, satisfied that she had conjured magic. She felt a vivid lucidity that she hadn't experienced before. It was much more intense than the feeling of focus the potion gave her. She felt strong and energised and powerful.

Serene scooped up the feather's remains and gave them to Ash. "Bury these and thank the bird for its essence." She seemed panicked and confused. "I have rushed you. We have to be more careful. I have to teach you to relax and connect better before conjuring. I have been a careless teacher."

"It was only a feather," Ash said.

"A feather is of earth and air. You conjured fire from a different source," Serene said. "That is rather *peculiar*. It is not supposed to happen."

"Maybe the lore is right, maybe humans really shouldn't do magic." She couldn't quite understand what the problem was, but she could read in Serene that there was a problem, and it unsettled her.

"I am not so sure this has anything to do with your humanness, Ash. If the lore was right, it would have taken you decades to be able to conjure anything at all." Serene snatched Ash's wand and put it under the floorboard alongside hers.

"Why did you bother making a wand for me then! How do you think it feels to get things so wrong all the time." Ash stormed off.

Ash couldn't sleep that night. She couldn't stop thinking about the magic. The way the feather had risen, the way it had burst into flames. She had conjured magic! Real magic. Flames. She couldn't believe it. She pictured flames flowing from her wand and creating a giant, deadly barrier between her and the taskmaster and other witches trying to stop her from escaping. Every time she tried to relax and sleep, her mind just brought her back to the magic, the flames. Every time she thought about it, she felt energised, like a power was growing inside of her.

The workers' bell rang and Ash felt heavy and drained. She didn't want to get up. Nifty peered over her and said, "You alright, Ash?"

"I'm not well today," she said. "I feel a bit sick."

"Don't worry, I'll help you out today," he said, offering her his hand. He pulled her up. He was much stronger than he appeared.

Serene ignored Ash that day.

As they worked the fields, Nifty swapped several baskets with Ash. She was extremely grateful because her body was tired and weak. She couldn't stop thinking about the magic she had conjured. It had become an obsession. She relished the next opportunity to practise. She wanted nothing more than to go back to the hideout and make more magic. It called her. Whispered to her. Lured her.

She picked some red bimbleberries and placed them in her basket. The Sully kid, Malfin, was lurking in the distance, standing by a tree at the edge of the field and staring at her. She averted his gaze and kept picking. Every time she looked up, he was still there. Scrawny and bony and unpleasant to look at. Now he glared at Nifty.

Ash wondered what Malfin was thinking. She could see that whatever it was, it wasn't pleasant. She wondered how such a young, privileged kid could be such a brute. He had the whole Nine Lands on a platter and he still felt the need to torment servants. She wondered what kind of a witch he would end up; what kind of a master he would be to the slaves he was so malevolent towards. She was mostly angry at him, and scared, but there was a small feeling of pity in there too. He was just a kid.

Nifty moved swiftly from bush to bush, his hands picking and placing with impressive nimbleness, and smiling and greeting those he passed, despite mostly being ignored. He stopped by Serene and they talked under low voices. When he left her, he was smiling and said, "Looking forward to it."

No! Ash thought. She was worried they had arranged to hang out in the hideout later. She wanted to practise magic and the thought of having to wait was unbearable. She picked at the bimbleberries quickly, carelessly, as she sped up to catch up with Serene. "What were you and Nifty talking about?"

"He invited us to eat at his home," Serene whispered. "I accepted, of course."

"We can't. We need to practise," Ash spat in a harsh whisper.

"*You* need to rest," Serene said. "I need to ask Nifty for something, anyway. We can't escape without it."

CHAPTER 16

EXILUK

Up close, Blackhill Manor was as beautiful and as impressive as he had heard it would be. A building of perfectly carved stone, polished to perfection, stood at least three levels high. There were windows made of small pieces of glass and crystal in a variety of colours, their shapes placed in a way to form various images such as giants, animals, towers, and flowers. He had never seen windows of such detail before. The colourful crystal pieces caught the light with various intensities, beaming as if illuminated by magic.

The grounds were a delight of flowers and plants arranged in the most elegant of ways, with each colour and form masterfully complementing its surroundings. It was all so vibrant, so extravagant, so wonderful. A sweet and heady fragrance welcomed him to the manor.

He reached the courtyard, and a dwarf named Tico greeted him and showed him to the great hall where trays of a variety of drinks and foods were held for him to choose from, and everything he tasted was delicious. Beings looked at him with pleasant and curious smiles, and some averted their gazes, likely out of fear of staring too long.

Pika! He was thrilled to see the dwarf. The dwarf meant the map, and the map meant treasures, and the treasures meant unfathomable power. He realised his train of thought and shook his head. He was torn between his excitement and shame that he had actually thought of unfathomable power. *In reality, nobody wants unfathomable power,* he thought. *Nobody.* Yet the feeling was so alluring. So powerful.

The dwarf was carrying a tray of small parcels of gourmet food: a white seafood wrapped in a light-purple grass with white and blue petals, and a drizzle of a glowing silver sauce. Exiluk wanted to sneak off and try to find the map, the commotion and busyness of the wedding would provide as good an opportunity to seek it as any. But there were too many eyes on him at present.

A witch approached him and made small talk, clearly curious about Exiluk, who was evidently an outsider. Considering that outsiders rarely entered the Nine Lands and insiders seldom ventured out, the witch was most interested in discovering where Exiluk was from and how he had ended up at a wedding of giants.

"Do you believe in fate? Or destiny, as some call it?" Exiluk asked the witch.

"Loosely, to an extent, I suppose," she said, seeming intrigued and caught off guard by the question.

"We keradin believe there is nothing but fate, nothing but destiny, and my destiny is to be here, right now, and one may perceive it to be a coincidence or a linking of the threads of the universe to my own threads, I guess that is a matter of two opinions of the same outcome, and perhaps the outcome is the only thing that is important."

"Threads?" the witch said. Her hair was copper with peach streaks.

A rare colour, Exiluk noted. "You understand the concept of the essence, perhaps known here as the aether or spirit?"

"Indeed," she said. "Where magic derives its power."

"The keradin call the connections between one source of essence to another a thread, and there are those who can actively see and connect their threads to others, like the legendary sorcerers and elders. They are the ones to control destiny itself, and there are those who are completely oblivious to it all, like most of us," he said, attempting to avoid alluding to his powers.

"You might be *impressed* to know there are strong witches in the Nine Lands who can sense the essence in others, and you might be talking with one right now. If I hadn't already had too many drinks, I might have looked deep into your soul."

The witch did indeed have more strength than most around them, Exiluk could mildly sense it. He remembered that he had neglected his practice and already what he had recovered of his skill had waned. He resented himself for that because he might need his powers to find the map, or at least stay out of trouble finding the map.

"I *am* impressed, perhaps a time after the wedding you could teach me about the ways of the witches of the Nine Lands," Exiluk said.

"Perhaps," she said. "I am from Lor Kithin, an empire far from here in the north. I am an envoy of the emperor, believe it or not. If you ever venture that far, ask which palace the emperor currently occupies and come to ask for Inmira."

"I am most grateful, Inmira," Exiluk said.

The witch and the keradin parted to make conversation with others. Exiluk met all manner of witches and giants: moguls of trades spanning from herblore to robe making, magic craft, slavery, surveillance, artistry, and everything in between; lords and ladies of distant lands; politicians and more. The Nine Lands were the wealthiest he had encountered, and seeing exhausted human and dwarven slaves sweating and shaking on the brink of collapse, he wondered how much suffering had gone into it all. It didn't disgust him as much as he thought it should. His attraction to the power around him was overwhelming and he couldn't completely understand why.

There were no chances to slip off and search for the map before the ceremony. Before he knew it, the bells were ringing and he and all the guests were being ushered through to the garden grounds, down a levelled path of massive stone slabs and to a site overlooking a gorgeous lake where they were seated. Two giants radiating with elegance and energy, literally glowing, stood on a platform by the lake. Naara and Toarer.

All watched in silence and anticipation as Naara took a stunning dagger from its sheath, a short sword to a smaller creature, and cut a line in her hand that trickled with blood. Both giants appeared somewhat stern and cold, a mood Exiluk had seldom seen between two souls about to be wedded. It wasn't the first time he had seen a reluctant marriage, and he assumed it wouldn't be his last. *Just the way of the world,* he thought. And he caught that thought. *It is not the way of the world, it is the way of those who have lost their way. It is not the keradin way.*

Toarer cut his hand with the fine dagger, and he made a tiny incision in his lip, wincing a little at the inevitable sting, and he slit a tiny slit in Naara's lip and she didn't even flinch a little, and their eyes were locked upon each other's the whole time. They put their hands together and kissed, and they were bound by blood and intention.

The crowd cheered and clapped and the sound was thunderous. Witches sent flames and sparks of all colours, and illusions of birds and bees and baby dragons into the trees and sky, and the whole place was an explosion of merriment. Exiluk thought he could sense a slight undertone of curiosity and uncertainty for the future ahead. The future where the mining, military, and ministry of Avenia were married. *Perhaps I am overthinking it,* he thought, smiling at the magic and celebration around him.

Awkward speeches were made by the head table, and elegant and delicious foods were served abundantly while the elven band sang and played. Exiluk hadn't heard anything so mesmerising and moving in his life, and he often found himself struggling to focus on what those around him were saying because he was so enchanted.

"Trouble's brewing, you know," a gossiping witch said. She looked Exiluk in the eye but he didn't pay her much attention. "The fighting in the north, the murder in the south, never in my life have I heard of a murder."

Exiluk perked up at the words, remembering the thick blood seeping from the giant and colouring the snow. "A murder in the south?"

"Some are saying it was a koar wolf," the witch whispered slyly, revelling in the gossip. "Yet others have said the body was half buried and the injuries were from weapons. What koar wolf half buries its kills? Nobody's seen a koar wolf in these parts before either."

"Right," Exiluk said, uncomfortable. "It could have been another animal."

"Which?" the witch said.

"I don't know these parts, though I have seen animals with horns as long as swords and mace-like tails that look just like weapons."

"Beyond the barrier, no doubt, but we're a tame land compared," the witch said. "Between me and you, it was bound to happen eventually." She looked about her to make sure nobody else was listening. "Those southern giants have never been able to completely let go of their primitive ways. They were rolling around in their muddy caves until witches brought some order to this land. They would be nothing without us, you know. And now look. Giants marrying in ultimate *luxury*." She sipped from her intricately engraved crystal glass and then put a finger to her lips. "Don't tell anyone, would you?"

"Your words are safe with me," Exiluk said, and he meant it because he had no time or desire to gossip, and it was at that point he reminded himself of the map. The witches and giants of the wedding were becoming more intoxicated and more sociable, and some were beginning to dance and move and mingle. Food was being cleared from the tables and trays of potions and powders were being served, and things got a lot looser a lot quicker than Exiluk had ever expected them to. After some mandatory mingling, he slipped away and began his search for the map.

Blackhill Manor was an expanse of many expansive rooms. Exiluk was impressed by it, though it meant that finding Toarer's room would be a challenge. He slipped from room to room and remained slight and vigilant, ready to hide should he encounter anyone. He found it exhilarating, almost as if getting closer to the map, or even just the thought of getting closer to the map, energised him. The treasure was as rightfully his as it was theirs. *The Old Dwarven abandoned it long ago,* he thought.

Whispering. Shadows. He merged into darkness and listened.

The whispers were deep and heavy: of giants, not witches. "The witches of the north are losing their grip, Baldarak," one said. "I trust we can count on your support when the time comes. For how long have we put up with the witches in *our great* lands? How many generations did our ancestors have to suffer the humiliation of living alongside this twisted evil? Now we may send them back to the arid desert where they belong."

"I am merely a businessman." Exiluk recognised Lord Goaner's voice. "Though I do recognise how *profitable* times like these could be, I am not sure even *my* conscience could handle having a hand in breaking so many centuries of peace."

"You can't change the inevitable, Baldarak, now is the time for choosing sides. Who knows when it will be too late?"

"I hope you are wrong, Idar. Things are good for giants and witches, just look at our power, there is no need for change."

"*They could be even better*, just as the First Giants intended," the giant hissed. "Never forget that, or you will soon be as soft as your son."

There was a scuffle and a thud. "Be *extremely* careful, Idar, I will not be insulted and neither will my son. He has always done his duty to his family and I am proud of him for that."

Through erratic breathing and a tight throat, the other giant said, "I spoke irrationally, I apologise." The squirming ceased. "Things are changing, Baldarak, and we will be much better off facing it together."

"That may be so, but *never* forget how powerful my family became today. I could take the Nine Lands in the palm of my hand if I wanted, and the rest of the world with it. Do you understand me?"

"I do," the giant said, and they slipped away.

Exiluk remained in position for a while. He was daydreaming, something he had never done before, for keradins had no need for wishful thinking or daydreaming. But Exiluk was imagining himself as a person of consequence, someone with power. He had just listened to a lord grab a king by the scruff, and he was astounded. He knew of mystical and mental power, but never worldly power, and its promise of status, control and influence was new and thrilling to him. He saw himself regal and commanding, issuing mandates that echoed across many lands. A mere gesture from him shifting fortunes, forming alliances and reshaping policies. And all the while amassing immense fortune.

A nearby noise brought Exiluk to his senses and he hurried himself to search for the map, feeling unusually exhilarated. It was obvious which room was the good giant's because it was the simplest, the most modest, and now that Exiluk had finally found it, he was hopeful. He carefully and quietly searched every little part of it, but he found no map. *That is fine,* he thought. *The dwarf has likely hidden it in the servants' quarters.*

He went up the ladder into the servants' quarters, as quietly and sneakily as he could, and he was pleased to find nobody around. It smelt musty and mouldy, and there was nothing to distinguish where the dwarf slept. He silently and quickly searched everywhere he could and to his disappointment, it soon became evident the map wasn't there.

Someone was coming up the ladder, quickly, lightly. There was nowhere to hide. His heart beat hard. He harnessed a thread of his mind's essence and waited, calming himself.

A small figure entered the room and froze. "This isn't your room," the kid said, staring at Exiluk in wide-eyed wonder.

"Hello," Exiluk said. "You are right, it is not my room. I got lost, and I am a bit embarrassed about it. Be a good boy and don't tell anyone I got lost, would you?"

"Yep," the boy said. "I'll show you back to the great hall. I'm Squeak."

"Thank you Squeak. Do you know the dwarf Pika by any chance?"

"Yep," Squeak said. The kid had a lot of energy about him.

"He is my friend, and we are playing a game of hiding things, do you want to play?"

"Yep!" squealed Squeak. "I love games what's he hidden I bet he's buried it that's what I would do, wouldn't you?" Squeak ran around in small circles, his words tumbling out over each other in his excitement.

"That is such a good idea, Squeak. Where do you think Pika would hide things?"

"By one of the trees with names, I reckon. Then it wouldn't get lost in the ground, because most of the ground all looks the same, doesn't it."

"And do you know which ones have names and what their names are?"

"Yes I do, there's Garamite, Steelmane, and Lorevine, and they're the oldest and strongest trees in the wood. They're as old as the First Giants, and that's really, really old!"

"You are a very smart kid, Squeak," Exiluk said. "Please don't tell Pika you helped me win this game, or he might not let you play the second round with us."

Squeak grinned and gestured that their secret was safe with him. They reached the party where giants and witches were scattered about dancing and dabbling debaucherously, and the elven music warmed the air and sent waves of delight through Exiluk. Exiluk turned, but the kid had disappeared. His eyes searched, but the dwarf Pika was nowhere to be seen.

One of the elves was sitting at the end of a long table and drinking heavily. A servant who was with him stormed off, angry about something. *Intriguing,* Exiluk thought. He took the opportunity to meet the drunken elf and sat next to him.

"I don't feel like company," the elf said.

"I only wanted to say hello and compliment you on your music. The elven are highly regarded in my culture."

"There would be no respect for me, look at me, keradin." The elf was swaying, and his breath stank. His skin was reddish and blotchy. "And don't for a moment think that I can't sense you, keradin. Now drink with me, and we can talk a little about our unexpected paths." He pushed a glass full of golden-brown ale towards Exiluk.

The elf drank a lot and Exiluk drank a little while they talked. It was hard for Exiluk to get much sense out of the elf's words, and he mostly gathered that they had come from the aether under the orders of the High Elven and they had lost their way.

Especially Nilinriall.

While they talked, they sparred and grappled with the threads of their essences. Nilinriall would reach out and try to connect with and read Exiluk's essence, and Exiluk would push the probing threads of energy away while trying to coax information out of the elf's inner being. The sparring frustrated Exiluk. There was a time he would have been able to completely unwind a drunken being, and he could sense there was a time the elf could have done the same to him with ease. It felt like they were two has-been warriors scrapping over spilled drink.

A fear gnawed at Exiluk as he observed Nilinriall, once noble, now lost to drunkenness. He dreaded succumbing to a similar fate, fearing a loss of his keradin essence and powers. He recognised himself in Nilinriall, and if an elf could lose his way, would not worse be in store for him, a mere keradin? He couldn't help being awed by Nilinriall, whose enduring strength and powers were still so formidable in spite of his downfall.

Then the keradin landed an unexpected blow. He found a particular memory and the elf winced and lashed out as Exiluk's thread touched it and absorbed it. *A servant, your son,* Exiluk thought. He sensed deep despair in the elf, and confusion, guilt and self-loathing, and it all happened in a flash, and just as he was grasping at the faintest image of the boy, it all disappeared, almost as if it hadn't happened at all. Yet, he knew it had. And he knew it was significant.

Get out! The elf expelled him. It shook Exiluk to his core. "There is no going back, keradin, have you figured that out yet?" The elf spat his words as he stood. "The path we have chosen is too far from the Way."

Exiluk saw the look on her face as the axe impaled her flesh. He saw the giant's dismay as his comrades turned on him. Exiluk fought back tears of distress. He felt the darkness darkening and thickening inside of him even more, darkness surrounded by fire, and he threw the sadness away with anger. The anger was energising. The power was balancing. He felt better. *Enjoy the party,* he told himself. *Yes, see what unfolds ahead. Do not dwell on the past.*

As the elf headed towards his band, he turned and said, "Don't think I can't sense you, keradin," and he swayed as he said it and he almost fell. He rejoined his band and caught the harmony of the girl elf as she sang. His voice was sublime and tinged with a sadness that made it all the more poignant.

Time passed and Exiluk observed. The giants and witches were smiling and dancing and swaying and sniffing and drinking. They had become much more juvenile over time, and it was intriguing to see. Witches and giants would come and talk to him, no doubt curious about the exotic guest Naara had invited. He entertained them and conversed politely, all the while thinking about the map, the treasure, and the elf with a half-human son. *What would it mean for the Nine Lands to know an elf could breed with a human?* he thought.

The giant groom was talking and dancing with some guests and his new wife. He seemed more lucid than the others. He was smiling gently as he moved awkwardly. The dwarf Pika caught his eye and approached him cautiously with a drink in a mighty-fine beaker made of silver and gems. The giant crouched down rather cumbersomely to the dwarf's level and the dwarf whispered something in his ear. He handed the giant the drink.

They edged off to the side of the room and spoke privately. Both were anxious and agitated and Exiluk tried to thread towards them, but their agitation and determination towards whatever they were talking about created a barrier that was difficult for Exiluk to pierce. He sensed only fear, uncertainty, and doubt, and he was desperate to know if their conversation was about the map or the treasure or the fate of the Nine Lands. The giant Toarer discretely put his hand on the dwarf's shoulder and their faces flooded with sadness.

CHAPTER 17

THEO

We leave tonight. Pika's words haunted Theo. He despised the urgency. He felt so unready. *It's absurd though, we can't leave so abruptly. How could it happen? I just can't see it*, he thought. Though he felt a profound sense of fear and excitement as if it was going to happen. *But how could it?*

The bells rang again, this time more upbeat and celebratory, and the guests began filtering into the courtyard. The wedded couple were seated at the head table in the great hall along with their immediate family.

Theo wondered how Toarer felt. He seemed happy enough, smiling and talking to others at the table. The ceremonial cut on his lip rendered his smiling a bit awkward. His right hand bore the silken red ribbon that covered the other ceremonial wedding cut. Naara looked stern and cold, as she always did. Possibly even a little angry. Theo wondered how Toarer would put up with someone like that, and he worried that she would drain the happiness out of him.

"Prince Keroak of Midvale and Advisor of Magic, Rakuul Mordaker," a giant herald bellowed from the doorway. The Prince and Rakuul entered the great hall and Theo slipped as deeply into the corner as he could. Rakuul kept his eyes on the head table. Theo was thankful for that, for now. There was no way he could avoid the watcher for long. He couldn't hide from his duties, either. Kirakai would try to kill him again.

"King Idar and Queen Revar of Okuden," the giant herald called.

The giant King and Queen entered the great hall and took their seats near the head of the table. Their furs were fancy, doused with jewels and a dark, hide-lined trim with patterns embroidered in silver.

"King Valoris and Queen Enamil of Ter Noris," the herald said. The royal witches entered the great hall looking tiny in comparison to the giants. Their appearance made up for their size: magnificent silky robes, and long magical staffs detailed with carvings of wolves and giant cats with gems as eyes.

"The royalty of Ul Nirin send their deepest apologies and greatest wishes to the wedded, for exceptional circumstances have rendered them unable to join us on this fine occasion," the herald said.

The giants and witches muttered and murmured to each other. Theo's heartbeat quickened. Lord Sully's conversation about the troubles in the north had been cut short earlier. The royals of Ul Nirin hadn't even sent representatives. The exceptional circumstances affecting Ul Nirin must be a grave threat to the Nine Lands. He wondered what it could be, but his mind drew a blank.

What could be out there? We can't really be leaving, can we? All I know is Blackhill, all I know is Avenia. He felt an overwhelming anxiety, as if the weight of the world was crushing him. *What if it's worse than here? Actually, nothing's worse than here.* Theo's thoughts ran away with him and he found it hard to concentrate.

The herald proceeded to announce a long list of honoured guests before the rest of the party were permitted to sit. The honoured guests included the king and queen of Izmoran, who were witches dressed much like the royalty of Ter Noris. *Izmoran borders Ter Noris and Ul Nirin,* Theo thought to himself. Toarer had told him about the geography of the Nine Lands many times before, and he deliberately and methodically ran through his knowledge of the Nine Lands to try take his mind off the panic of escaping. *Those three lands make up the region Lor Kithin,* and *Lor Kithin is predominantly a land of witches, most of whom don't like the alliance between witches and giants. The emperor of Lor Kithin is too important for this wedding.*

So is the High King of Midvale. Which lands are of Midvale? Avenia, of course, and... Eliniar, which sits in the middle of the Nine Lands.

He eyed the Lord Minister of Eliniar, a giant who sat next to the king and queen of Okuden, awkwardly trying to make conversation with them. And he looked at Prince Keroak and Rakuul Mordaker, glad he was behind and far from them. *Eliniar and Avenia are powerful lands with giant and witch ministries. The High King recognises the strength of giants and witches combined and prides in their alliances. Ah, and Urwald, which has no ministry and is said to be even more primitive than Okuden.* A tribal chiefess from Urwald picked at her food. She appeared reluctant to be there.

The giants of Craddock never venture to Midvale, Theo remembered Toarer saying. *That's eight lands, what of the final one? Garaduk.* The Lady Mayoress of Garaduk was a witch, and her fashion was significantly simpler than the witches of the north. Her robe was thicker and less silky, and she wore plain gold earrings and necklace.

For a while, Theo was able to immerse himself in the wedding and forget about their impending escape. As he watched them all, waiting to fill drinks and plates while he starved, he noticed a strange ceremonial demeanour in almost all the giants and witches there. He could sense that they were merely pretending to be happy to be in the company of other leaders of the Nine Lands. Underneath it all, he could sense mounting tension like the fraught atmosphere before a storm.

A bell rang, loud and sharp. Quiet flooded the room. All but a murmur remained. Master Goaner stood and welcomed the guests to his home, especially his new family. "I am most delighted for the future, for the wedded, for our family, and all of the Nine Lands. No matter the troubles one land faces," he said, throwing a look at the northern witches, "we are one land, and our strength is your strength."

They all cheered and drank. Theo smiled, recognising the dig that Master Goaner had made towards the northern lands. He could see on some faces that he wasn't the only one who had picked up on

Master Goaner's sentiment.

Lord Minister Fimni Darthik stood. "Thank you all for coming to my daughter's wedding, it is an honour to have you all here. It goes without saying how strong and ambitious and impressive Naara is, and I trust that Toarer's kind heart and generous nature will impress upon her and together they will be magnificent."

There was an awkwardness for a moment while everyone reflected on what Lord Minister Darthik had said. It was almost as if he had been hinting that he wanted his daughter to be more kind-hearted. Theo thought he sensed it in the Lord Minister's tone, and he suspected others had too. Larani Darthik scowled at her husband. Theo wondered how long the tensions at the heart of House Darthik had been brewing.

Lord Minister Darthik held up his glass and said, "To Toarer and Naara."

"Toarer and Naara," everyone said, and they raised their drinks and drank. The servants rushed to top the guests' drinks up. Theo took the opportunity to refill Lord Sully's crystal glass with purple-red wine. He hoped Lord Sully would gossip about the troubles in the north, as he had seemed so keen to talk about them earlier. Theo topped up the glass of the witch next to Lord Sully and stepped back out of sight, lingering as close as he could without being improper. At least he was far from Prince Keroak and Rakuul Mordaker.

Larani Darthik stood. "I would also like to say a few words about my daughter and my new son." She appeared as elegant as a giant could be. Her dress had been made by the most famous dressmaker in Anhera, the fabric from a plant so rare it took centuries of harvesting, and Larani was most proud of this status symbol. She brushed her dress down, ensuring everyone took note of its immaculate, silky-satin finish. "Naara, never let anyone interfere with your ambition. You are so wonderful you could rule the world one day, and I wish you all the fortune your drive brings you. To Naara." She raised her glass and drank.

Everyone followed.

"Toarer," she said, "you are indeed kind hearted, and some

admire your, uh," she paused, "*progressiveness*." She paused again. "Opposites attract, do they not? And I am sure that is what made you both fall in love and I am sure it is what will fuel your marriage for eternity. Your union can bring a great balance and stability to our families, and quite likely the whole of Avenia, perhaps the Nine Lands entirely... maybe even beyond. Thank you, Toarer, for taking my daughter's hand and promising to support her, no matter what." There was something awfully snide and sinister in her tone.

Toarer reddened. He forced a nod and a smile.

If everyone knows this wedding is about power, not love, why do they bother pretending? Theo thought. And thinking of love, he looked at Avira and smiled. His heart swelled. *She is so pretty!*

"Thank you, Larani. Those were... *kind*... words," Master Goaner said. "It is an honour to have you all in my home, this occasion will go down in history. Drink until you can't possibly drink anymore, eat until you are so full you cannot walk, and enjoy celebrating this beautiful and historic union." He raised his crystal cup, and everyone cheered. "I am so proud of you both, we all know a commitment like this takes sacrifice and you deserve much praise for your bravery and determination." Master Goaner looked momentarily awkward, perhaps realising he had said too much. "May your love and the fruits of your union echo in eternity."

Chatter ignited, the elf played an energetic tune on her harp, drinks flowed, and food was devoured. Everything appeared delicious and extravagant. Theo's stomach rumbled with hunger. He couldn't wait to steal some scraps.

"... the rebellion in the north," Lord Sully said to the witch next to him.

His wife hit him on the shoulder.

Theo focused on their conversation.

"What!?"

"Do you have to gossip so incessantly?" Lady Sully hissed. Her determination to stop her husband talking about it seemed to go beyond a negativity towards gossip.

"It is not gossip, it is fact. Everyone is talking about it. Rightfully so, too. Never in the history of the Nine Lands has a city been captured by servants. They held Ul Nirin for three days. Can you believe it! Three days."

Theo felt a sickly gloominess. He wondered how many of those servants had been tortured and executed. Probably all of them. But he also felt hope. *A rebellion!*

"Tell him to shut up if you wish, Lady Rivika," Lady Sully sighed.

The witch said, "If the most successful rebellion in history lasted three days, I am sure its news won't last much longer."

Theo topped up their wine, listening intently. He could hear looseness forming in their tongues, and he pushed the wine on them as much as he could.

"Oh, I beg to differ. They killed King Ingamar and Princess Serene. Prince Gideori will not wake, and the Wild Queen will probably drive Ul Nirin into ruin," Lord Sully chuckled.

"I have heard that the Princess's body was never found," Lady Rivika said in a low voice.

Lady Sully blushed deep red, struck with horror. "The emperor will not allow Ul Nirin to go to ruin, you are just stirring ideas Edward," Lady Sully said. "Now let us move on to a more palatable topic of conversation."

"Perhaps, but you have to admit, this isn't just something they can brush under the carpet. Ul Nirin has shown cracks that may affect the whole of Lor Kithin."

"Ed!" Lady Sully said, through clenched teeth. "You really are insufferable sometimes. Just drop it."

Theo topped up their drinks. The guests had begun to move about the room, chatting and swaying with the music, drinking and laughing and enjoying themselves. Theo's stomach hurt just looking at the scraps.

Rakuul Mordaker had remained seated, talking to those seated around him. Theo feared that Rakuul would soon rise from his seat, and he didn't want to be in the great hall when the watcher started moving around. He gathered some plates that had some food left on them and took them back to the kitchen, making sure to stay out of Rakuul's sight.

Little Squeak had his mouth full and his cheeks covered in cake scraps. His eyes were wide and excited.

"Make sure you clean yourself up before you go back out there, Squeak," Theo said, tucking into some grapes and cold meats.

Squeak nodded, his mouth too full to speak.

"Oi, Theo, once the tables are cleared, they want the party potions and powders out on trays, make sure there's no delay," the kitchen master said.

The witches had all sorts of concoctions to make a party more exciting. The potions were being carefully poured into beautiful vials of all sorts of crystal with cork stoppers, and the powders were wrapped in leaves from rare plants.

Someone thrust a tray into Theo's hand and he wondered how long he could linger in the kitchen before someone noticed he didn't want to go into the great hall. He knew he couldn't hide forever, so he edged into the great hall and lingered in the corner as far from the main congregations of guests as possible.

A witch spotted him and his tray of goodies and she headed over like a moth to flame. The witch took a vial of pale turquoise liquid from the tray and popped the cork open. Poured it down her throat. Her eyes lit up and she smiled. "You've got to love a bit of lively potion, don't you?" she said, rhetorically.

Two of the elves began singing in harmony while the other continued to play the harp. The sound felt as if it was coming from right next to Theo, yet the band wasn't in the great hall. The witch who had just taken the potion left the great hall towards the gardens. He saw Rakuul at the far end of the great hall and it set his heart racing. *Best to slip into the gardens,* he thought.

The music was delightful and the guests were dancing and smiling. The witches' dances were choreographed, and they were teaching the giants some of the moves. The giants were clunky and ungraceful. A witch moved mesmerizingly around the elven band, his robes flowing around him in swirls. The shining patterns on the trim of the robe created swirls of light that lingered in the air just a little longer than his movements.

Fireflies flittered in their little glass balls on thin chains. They twinkled like stars, lighting the wedding site up in a dreamlike and enchanting glow. Everyone was so well dressed in the finest fabrics, with elegant embroideries and a beautiful range of colours, and so smiley, it was truly a magnificent thing to experience. Theo realised he was completely disregarding all the suffering they had gone through to make it all happen. *These tyrants don't deserve the celebration. We do,* he thought. He hoped Toarer was able to find at least a little delight in the evening.

Theo noticed Nilinriall staring at him, and it made him uneasy. The elf was singing in harmonies with the other two, and their voices were so enchanting and powerful that the sounds loosened his tension and put him at ease. Nilinriall's voice came from the heart, deep, powerful, and emotional. They made curious eye contact for as long as Theo could bear it. He looked away.

Kirakai giggled. The sound caught Theo off guard. Never had he heard Kirakai sound happy, and somewhat vulnerable. "I can't feel anything," he said.

A witch lady who had been dancing with Kirakai grabbed his hand and led him to Theo. "Maybe it's because you're so big," she said. She took a leaf wrap from the tray and opened it. "Whizzle powder," she said. "Try a few of these." She handed Kirakai some wraps.

He opened them eagerly and put them to his giant nostrils and sniffed the multicoloured powder. Much of it fell all about his face and dropped onto the floor, and he laughed.

"You," Kirakai said. "Go get us some more."

"Give it a chance to work on you," the witch said. "Come on, I will teach you more dances." They galumphed back to the dancing. Kirakai was heavy, clumsy and giggly.

Theo was left perplexed to see Kirakai like that. He had genuinely thought the only happiness Kirakai was capable of was in the presence of suffering. Cracking the whip. Drawing blood. Causing terror.

The marvellous aesthetic of the primed gardens mesmerised him: the firefly lanterns, the warm glow of the torches, and the vibrant and elegant decorations. He admired the sumptuous fabrics of the guests' outfits; the fancy dancing of the witches; the crack, pop, and fizzle of show-magic, and then he slipped around the back of the house towards the kitchens so he didn't have to go through the great hall.

The gardens away from the wedding site were dark, and peaceful, the sounds of the wedding merrily blurring into one energetic noise. The peace hit Theo powerfully, as if it was something he was experiencing for the first time. He had been so wrapped up in fear of Rakuul, so torn in his thoughts about leaving the Nine Lands and how many unknowns he was being exposed to, and so rushed because of the wedding, he hadn't realised how exhausted he was. He was out of breath, and his breath was the most frantic thing around him. Once that calmed, everything felt rather blissful, except for the exhaustion he couldn't shake.

An owl hooted from somewhere nearby. A cloud moved softly and revealed a dense patch of bright stars. The muffled sounds of laughter and chatter warmed him. *Maybe this is a taste of things to come beyond the Nine Lands*, he thought.

He could have sworn he saw a shadow slip from one statue to another in the corner of his eye. He put his hand in his pocket and the protection stone reminded him of his courage, as new to him as it may be. The protection stone was damaged, sure, *yet he had defeated Rakuul Mordaker with it.* He could have cowered and given up, but instead he had stood up to the formidable witch.

He heard voices and froze. Concealed himself behind a wall of the house. He peered around the corner to see Master Goaner and Lord Minister Darthik arguing. Their silhouettes loomed tall.

"I heard you and Toarer have been spending an unusual amount of time in your library," Master Goaner hissed.

"What has that got to do with anything?" Lord Minister Darthik said.

"That is for you to tell me, isn't it?" Master Goaner said. "If you tell me what is going on, I can help. Neither of us wants trouble from the High King and I fear we are on the precipice. Why else would the watcher Mordaker be here?" Despite such a hushed voice, his tone was harsh, as if each syllable was a punch thrown.

"Are you accusing me and your son of treason? Preposterous!"

"*Nothing* is out of the question right now," Master Goaner said. "Look, Lord Minister, I *want* to help. We are family now, after all, and the last thing I want is my family name tarnished by the radical views my son may have." His voice was calmer now. "So, please, if there is *anything* I can do to help, just tell me. Anything. For you, for my son, for the Nine Lands."

A cold silence cut through the air and the darkness weighed heavily around them.

"I have nothing to tell you," Lord Minister Darthik said.

"What is Rakuul here for then?" Master Goaner muttered, as the giants headed Theo's way.

Theo crouched in the corner in the darkness and held his breath. They strode past him, their footsteps heavy. When they were long gone into the wedding party, he took a deep breath, inhaling the last moments of peace and tranquillity before continuing his detour around the house and into the kitchen. Servants dashed between stations, some rushing in with empty trays ready to be filled, while others dashed out with drinks and powders and potions. He was back in the bustle.

"The elf man wants to talk to you in the great hall," Pika said, opening a barrel of beer. "Don't worry, the witch is in the gardens." Lavish gleaming crystal was filled with golden liquid from a rustic wooden barrel. "Theo, please, make it happen if you can."

Theo knew exactly what Pika meant, and he knew he should do his best. He didn't know where to start, or how. He edged into the great hall, worried Rakuul might be around, and with it emptier now, it would be easier for Rakuul to spot him. No sight of the watcher witch.

"Boy," Nilinriall called. He was sitting at a table on his own with three drinks in front of him. The great hall was looking somewhat dishevelled with empty glasses and spilled drinks, drapery in disarray, floral arrangements askew, and candles burning low, though the effect was still charming. Giants and witches were loud and unrestrained. Nilinriall took a big glug from one of his drinks and waved Theo over, gesturing for him to sit with a drunken, swaying lack of control.

"Can I serve you?" Theo said, instinctively.

"We don't take servants. I told you. I just want to talk," Nilinriall said. "I bet you thought you would never see a drunk elf. It helps me cope with this disgusting place," he grinned. "We are not supposed to drink this dirt." He took a humongous gulp and said, "Have you ever wished your purpose was clear here?" and the elf gasped at his own words. "Oh, I am so sorry. Of course, you haven't, a servant's purpose is somewhat non-negotiable." He drank some more. "We were sent here by the High Elven some centuries ago to 'Spread the elven sound and bring its essence to that beyond the aether.' What kind of a quest is that? When does it end? And to be sent to this miserable world, what did we do to disgrace the High Elven?" He stared deeply into Theo's eyes, as if he expected an answer.

Theo felt stiff and said nothing. "I have to go serve, I'll get into trouble," he said, getting up.

Nilinriall grabbed his arm and pulled him back down. He said, "Look, everyone is far too intoxicated to notice what you are doing right now. Sit and talk." He drank more. "The orb the dwarf had..." he paused, seemingly deep in thought.

Theo flushed with heat. *What if someone heard? It would be the end.*

Nilinriall remained silent, staring blankly into the space in front of him. He said, "The keradin, he's got an interest in the dwarf. I have noticed it. I don't like him. Be careful of him. And the High King's Advisor of Magic, his threads search for your mind. I have been guiding them away from you. What does he want with you?"

Despite the concept being abstract, Theo felt he vaguely understood what Nilinriall meant. He appreciated the warning. "He got into my mind when I almost drowned. I fought him on his tower, I sort of won."

"That is magnificent," Nilinriall said, his face lit with so much pride it confused Theo. The pride waned, giving way to worry. "You are in grave danger. You ought to use the orb as soon as you can. If it were me, I would fake my own death. Burn a building you are supposed to be in or something like that. Whatever you do, *do not* make a scene escaping, don't let them know you have escaped. They are a proud and crooked bunch, these witches and giants, and they will hunt you for the sake of their pride, and probably for the fun of it."

The words chilled Theo. "Please, don't talk about it, especially here," he said.

"I want to help you," the elf said, drinking some more. He looked somewhat worn, haggard. "We have sung at various occasions..." He stopped, losing his trail of thought again. "In Avenia, I mean." He looked around to see if anyone was nearby. "I am going to tell you something only the band knows about me.

"There was a servant woman at the Blackhill Inn and I liked her an awful lot, and I disgraced myself by falling in love. The elven don't give in to love, not in the way I did, and I am telling you this because I think I could be your father. You have an elven essence in you." Nilinriall laughed and sighed. "I can't believe I just... said that."

The elf was being ridiculous. Theo was too shocked for words. He just about managed to force something through his lips, "You've had too much to drink."

"No!" The elf slammed his drink on the table, golden-brown liquid splashed on the wood. "I mean... Yes. Always. But I am sober enough to know what I am talking about. You are my half-elven half-human bastard, and you are the first of your kind, and I will never be allowed to return to the aether. I will be singing in this forsaken place for the next two hundred years until I die." He flopped forward and his forehead splashed in his spilled ale. He lifted himself up. He held Theo's shoulder desperately, tightly, madness in his eyes. "So let me help you, for my sake, for my conscience."

"Let me go." Theo wriggled out of his grip.

"You are the butterfly! We saw you. We saved you in the dream realm. You have the power to interact with the other realms, and with the aether. We *see* you," Nilinriall said, and his words chilled Theo to the core.

Darted towards safety.

The cellar. Door unlocked.

Orange light below.

Avira's voice. Familiarity.

Deep breath.

Comfort.

"Theo, you found the real party," Pika said, slightly sarcastically. Pika, Tico, and Avira were sitting on the musty floor playing a game of cards. They had drinks and food.

"We're discussing our escape," Tico said, excitedly.

The mention of escape hit Theo with so many emotions, as it had all evening. The darkness of the cellar, its musty smell and the flickering of the lantern made him feel uneasy. The shadows on Pika and Tico's faces, though not Avira's—even in the dingy cellar, she shone.

"What's wrong?" Avira said. "You look shaken up."

"Nothing," Theo said, straightening himself up. "You stole Master Goaner's cards?" he said, changing the subject. They were hardened sheets of hide, cut into small rectangles with pigments tattooed into them forming patterns and shapes.

Avira smiled at him and it eased him.

"These are much too small for a giant's hands," Pika said, holding one up to Theo. It had three leaves drawn on it. "Remember, I won the orb in a card game. Toarer gave me these and taught me to play, just for fun. He had heard about a card game played every full moon behind closed doors at the Blackhill Inn, and it so happened that a slave smuggler was supposed to be attending one of the games. Toarer suggested I go and acquaint with her and negotiate our freedom."

The thought of the Blackhill Inn made Theo feel lightheaded. He thought of his mother, who died because of him, and the drunken elf, so ludicrous and mad. His music, so moving. *Urgh. What does it mean if I'm half-elven? Don't even entertain the idea. It's madness.* So many questions. He thought about the fits, the shadows, the butterflies in his dream, the glowing protection stone, fighting with Rakuul Mordaker, the singing woman who had supposedly protected him from Rakuul, and he wanted to ask the elf about it all. *But the elf is mad!* he thought.

"What did she say?" asked Tico, impatiently.

Pika said, "Well, she didn't turn up. I was devastated. Until I won the orb, of course." He took it out of his pocket and showed them again.

Theo was mesmerised by the mysterious grey mist swirling inside, whispering to him, pulling his attention towards it.

"What did the elf man say, Theo? Can he help?" Pika said.

Theo swallowed a gulp of anxiety and before he talked himself out of it, he said, "It's complicated... He'll help."

"You talked to them about it?" Avira said, curious and confused.

"It's nothing, don't worry about it, he'll help, that's all that matters," Theo said. "Meet me at the lake at first light, and we'll go." The cellar was almost empty, cleared out by the wedding. The lantern light weakly touched the stone walls. Theo's pulse skyrocketed at the commitment he had just made. He wasn't even sure that he could keep it. And he intensely disliked the thought of going back to Nilinriall to ask for his help.

"See, I knew we'd be able to do it, I knew it," Pika said.

"Do you think the elf can protect us from the orbing going wrong?" Tico said.

"Their magic is said to be much more powerful than the witches. With their help we'll be fine. We've got nothing to worry about," Pika said.

Theo could tell Pika was holding back some reservations.

"Except for what we're going to do on our first day of freedom, of course," Pika grinned.

"Oh, stop that. You're making me too hopeful," Avira said.

"Freedom!" she sighed.

Theo didn't like it. If they were able to orb out of there without any trouble at all, it would be too good to be true. *And everyone knows what happens when something is too good to be true*, he thought. *Nothing is worse than living under Kirakai's whip, though.* The smiles and excitement on his companions' faces warmed him. The fear of falling into imminent and irreparable danger tore at him. He shook his head and pulled himself back to the conversation.

"What should we take with us?" Tico was saying.

"Only what we can carry, and only essentials. I'll sneak some food from the kitchen once it all quietens down."

"Get a knife as well," said Avira.

Tico said, "And a map. We should get a map of the Nine Lands..."

Theo felt his eyes roll back and the sound of their voices fading.

He felt Avira's soft hand on his and she squeezed it gently. "Take a break and play one game with us, it's easy, we'll show you." She was clearly trying to ease his tension and he felt touched and grateful.

Pika handed him three cards. "There are many games we can play with a pack like this, we'll start with something nice and simple. You'll see you have one swordsman, one archer, and one mage. After the count of three, we'll each throw one card down at the same time. Sword slashes archer, magic beats sword, and arrow beats mage. I'll face you, Tico faces Avira, and winners will play each other afterwards."

The hide was stiff, the figures depicted in impressive detail. Theo held his cards close so nobody could see as he chose the archer. He didn't really care about the game in that moment, all he could think about was the elf man, and it tormented him.

"One, two," Pika said. "Three."

Four cards hit the floor.

Theo's arrow had been slashed by Pika's sword. Avira's magic had beaten Tico's sword.

"One, two, three." Two cards hit the floor. Two mages.

"One, two, three."

"Yay," Avira said. She had thrown the mage again, and Pika had thrown a sword.

"We'd better go, we'll get into trouble," Theo said.

"A couple more games, please," Avira said. "Have you seen them up there? Their heads are in the stars, they won't notice we're gone. And I don't want Kirakai to find me, or Lord Sully, he's so weird and creepy."

"Fine," Theo said. He desperately wanted to tell them what the elf man had said, yet it was so ludicrous he felt embarrassed talking about it. It felt like a thick shadow was seeping through his insides. It was heavy, but powerful. He couldn't work out if it was anxiety or excitement he felt. They played cards for some time until it got a little boring and they had finished their food and drinks.

"Right, I'm going to tell Toarer," Pika said, as they left the cellar and reluctantly went back to serve their masters.

The debauchery had escalated. Giants and witches were half naked, chasing each other around, giggling and laughing and dancing. "What have you had tonight?" a witch asked the giant dancing vigorously next to her. "All of them," the giant guffawed.

The elvensong was louder and so moving. Nilinriall's voice, powerful and enchanting, lifted the hairs on Theo's skin. *He's not my father. He's a mad, drunken elf. A coward.*

Yes, coward. It was as if the elf had spoken close to his ear.

Theo looked around him, unsure. Avira was behind him. "Did you say something?" he said.

"No," she shrugged. "I'm going to help in the kitchen, and hide from Kirakai." She slipped away.

The music drew Theo towards it. He found himself watching over the gardens from the stairs, mesmerised by the band. The danger of Rakuul was somewhere in his mind and yet it didn't bother him in that moment. The music was too powerful.

When Nilinriall sang, his drunkenness and vulnerability completely disappeared. He stood mighty and invincible. His voice so impressive it could command a kingdom. *I'm a coward, yes, and a disgrace. I'm sorry.* His eyes had found Theo's.

Theo knew that he wasn't imagining things. Nilinriall could

communicate through his mind. Perhaps it was something all elves could do. *You can hear my thoughts,* Theo thought.

Yes, but only when you want me to. You have to be open to threadsong. You are extremely closed, most are. When you called me a coward, you must have really wanted me to hear that. Funny. Nilinriall continued singing beautifully as he spoke to Theo's mind. *Empty your mind, boy. I have to show you something. Just look at the darkness between your eyes when you close them. Focus on nothing else.*

Theo's heart and mind were conflicted. He wanted to tell the elf to leave him alone, to stop with his absurdities, but he also experienced a strange sensation urging him on, telling him to go with it.

Theo closed his eyes. Focused on the darkness. He found himself looking out the window of a room on to a dirt street with a few large buildings scattered around it. He recognised Blackhill Pass. Two hands wrapped around him and kissed him on the cheek. He pulled away from the woman and stood back so he could see all of her. She had a servants mark above her eye. She was blonde and short. He felt a deep connection to her. He felt uneasy and he opened his eyes. The vision disappeared, and his awareness returned to the wedding party.

You know who that is, don't you? Nilinriall said.

Theo suspected it was his mother, especially considering the strong bond-like emotion he had just felt. He refused to believe it. *Don't play with my mind like that again, you have no right,* he said.

I thought you would like to meet her.

I said don't!

"No, no! Let me go," Avira shrieked.

"Oh, come on, it's only a bit of fun," Kirakai said.

Theo's heart fell into his stomach as he followed Avira's voice. Kirakai was carrying Avira over his shoulder. The guests were too oblivious and intoxicated to notice or care, and the servants watched in horror. Pika chased after them and Kirakai batted him away like a fly. The dwarf hit the wall with a terrible thud.

"Let me go!" Avira screamed.

"We will only have a dance," Kirakai said, tugging at her clothes. He had lost his mind.

Theo felt horrible, watching, doing nothing. *But what can I do? Quick, think of something. Think Theo, think!* Kirakai's rock-solid muscles and towering frame sent doubt through him. *He's a giant!*

Don't overthink it. Don't be like your father. You are not a coward, Nilinriall said.

Without a thought, Theo took a flaming torch from the wall and cut Kirakai off. "Stop. Now." He waved the torch in Kirakai's face, the flames swaying with it.

"How dare you threaten a giant," Kirakai said. He batted the torch out of Theo's hand and it landed on the table. A wave of fire flooded across it, following a flammable liquid that had spilled on it. "Get out of my way before I have you all hanged," he said.

Watching the flame spread across the table, Theo saw a giant's meat knife near him. He took it and plunged it into the side of Kirakai's leg, rage overpowering his reason. Kirakai's skin and muscle were so thick the knife barely went in a third. The giant laughed.

"Put her down," Toarer's voice commanded.

The flames danced over the table. A crowd gathered around. The music stopped. The keradin smiled at Theo.

"I am not listening to a sympathiser, you should be hanged with them," Kirakai said.

"Your tongue is loose, giant," Naara said. "You will not speak of my husband in that way."

"The boy stabbed my leg. You all saw it. He has to be hanged."

"I said, put her down." Toarer marched over to Kirakai and took Avira from him. "She is my property, not yours, Kirakai. You work for us, nothing more."

"The taskmaster is right, the boy must be hanged," Naara said.

"I will not allow it," Toarer said, putting Avira down next to Theo.

Everyone gasped. Whispers of *sympathiser* filled the air. All eyes were on Toarer.

Avira hugged Theo tightly. "We have to go, now."

Theo hated to admit it. They had no choice, they had to go. He wasn't ready, but he realised perhaps he would never be. Tico was with Pika, and Theo called them over with a gesture of his eyes, discretely, desperately. *Show me a place beyond the barrier*, Theo said to the elf. *Quickly.*

"That boy's life is mine. He committed the crime against me. I will forgive it, just give me the girl to dance with," Kirakai said, moving towards them, swaying with intoxication.

Toarer stepped in front of Kirakai and held him back. Kirakai was angry and strong, and Toarer was losing the scuffle, bit by bit.

"When I say so, activate the orb," Theo said, as quietly as he could. Rakuul was grinning at him, edging closer to them. The keradin eyed Pika intensely, also grinning.

Pika nodded, his face stricken with uncertainty. A witch had drawn his wand and was threatening the giants to stop fighting, or he would stop them himself. He was extremely drunk and clearly didn't know what was going on. Another witch drew her wand and told the other witch not to interfere. A giant picked the first witch up and threw him into the crowd. A brawl began.

Theo closed his eyes and let the elf into his mind. An image of a woodland shack was printed in him so vividly he could smell the sweet, slightly earthy, pine-scented air, and feel a breeze. He sensed the solidity of the tree trunks and their rough barks, and the cushioned, mossy earth with a few prickles beneath his feet. He saw a tree with long branches extended over the roof of the vine and moss covered shack. He quickly wrapped his arms around Pika, Avira, and Tico, and said, "Now."

The orb smashed on the floor and its mist wrapped around them. Theo held onto the image of the shack in the woods as strongly as possible. He heard Kirakai grunt and roar and Toarer squirm and gasp. His mind began racing, as if his thoughts and experiences were being dragged through him at high speed. *Focus, Theo!*

Something heavy and dark hit Theo's heart, an inexplicable force, powerful and harrowing. The sounds of the brawl disappeared into a heavy whooshing and a feeling of being dragged violently through the air. He felt sick, all the while holding on to Avira, Pika and Tico as tightly as he could as he pictured the place—its calmness, the abundance of nature, the fallen leaves, the bushes, and the greenery. Nothing else, just the place, for all their safety. And then there was only darkness.

CHAPTER 18

ASH

Hot, roasted meat with a moist pink centre. Steaming yellow potato, crispy on the outside. Cheese. The little spread that Nifty had stolen to share with Ash and Serene was sublime. Ash's mouth watered. Herbs, meaty, buttery, it was just incredible. They devoured it without talking. Ash put a warm piece of red meat in her mouth, the herbs tantalising her tastebuds and the rich flesh making her smile. Yet despite how good it was to eat such sumptuous food, she felt irritated. She wanted to make more magic.

"Thank you so much, Nifty," Serene said.

His grin was endearing as always as he licked his fingers and lips. "That's gotta be the best meal I've ever had," he said. "Well worth the risk. Little treats like that can really make life worth living, don't you think?"

Serene wiped tears from her cheeks.

"What's the matter? Did I upset you?" Nifty said.

"Of course not, Nifty. You reminded me of how fortunate we can be and how easy it is to take it for granted, that's all."

"Yep, there's always something to be grateful for," he said. "Look." Nifty handed each of them a little sweet dessert. It was fruity and creamy, and delicious.

"Wow," Serene said. "You are too good to us, Nifty."

"Yeah, uh... but this time I feel selfish 'coz I've got a motive. It's hard for me to do this but I couldn't forgive myself if I didn't." He looked at the floor nervously. "I wanna'd to respect your privacy as you asked, but it wouldn't take a huge jump in the imagination to assume you know something about magic and you're gonna use it to escape. And if that's the case, I wanna go with you. Please. I can help."

"We asked you to stay out of it," Ash said. Her heart felt heavy, and she felt sick, yet she couldn't change her mind. *He can't come with us. It's dangerous for us, and dangerous for him. He's happy anyway.*

"Could Ash and I have a few moments to talk?" Serene said.

Nifty looked sad and subdued as he climbed out of his home. A gust whooshed through the entrance as the hatch opened. He closed the hatch behind him. Silence and stillness followed. Ash and Serene continued the silence for a few moments, thinking.

"We need him, Ash," Serene said. "I need a spell scroll, instructions for the potion. I can't proceed without it. And we will need rare ingredients, only Nifty can get those for us. We should say yes."

"It's too dangerous. We can't take him. I wish we could. I really do," Ash said. "But you're right. We do need him. We're going to have to tell him that he can come. We're going to have to lie to him."

"Ash! That is appalling. No. I am not going to do that. We can't. Nifty is the kindest person we know. He saved my life! We can't betray him like that."

"Do you want to get out of here or not? If we take him, it's one more person to put at risk. He's happy here. We don't even know what things are like in Ul Nirin."

Serene was silent for a long time, her eyes pleading with Ash. But Ash stood resolute. "Well, I vow to come back and save him," Serene said, and slowly, with sadness in her eyes, she nodded.

"As long as I get to my mother and I get out of the Nine Lands, I don't care, Princess, you do whatever you want." Ash felt horrible saying it, but she was so close to freedom she couldn't bear to ruin it.

They called Nifty back in.

Ash said, "We'll take you with us, but we need your help."

Nifty's grin was bigger than ever before. His eyes misted over and he seemed choked up. "I'll help in every way I can," he said. "What a blessing it's been you two arriving. This has been the best part of my life so far and it just seems to keep getting better. When you screamed in that field and we all got stunned I knew you had magic in you, Ash. I don't know how it is or why it is, and I probably wouldn't understand it anyway, it's not something I'll try understanding now. I'm happy as it is. Right, what do we need?"

"We need a spell scroll for a teleportation potion, there will be one in the house."

"I'll make it happen. But... uh... how'm I meant to know which one that is? I can't read."

Serene took a knife and scraped a rune sign into the floor. The sign was a combination of curved lines, straight lines, and circles. The circles were impressively round. "It will have this sign on it."

"Wow," Nifty said. "Dare I ask how you know how to do that? I shouldn't, should I?"

"I would rather you didn't," Serene said.

"In which case I won't, no matter how massive the implications of what I've just seen are, and the magic I felt in the field against that evil child who was torturing me. That *was* magic, wasn't it?"

Ash and Serene stayed silent.

Nifty winked, "Well, I guess there's some things we'll know and some things we'll never know, and I've just gotta be happy with both. That's okay with me, especially 'coz we're getting out of 'ere. We'll finally be free and that's more amazing than anything I expected in all my life. Thank you, girls. Really, thank you so much."

Ash and Serene looked at each other with disappointment in their eyes—disappointment in themselves, disappointment in each other, and disappointment that they would have to leave Nifty behind. Ash knew they would be feeding him to the wolves, and yet there was no other way.

～≈～

The three were in the hideout. Nifty had been quick to steal the spell scroll and the ingredients needed to brew the potion. He was sitting wide-eyed and unusually still, intently watching Serene, while Ash restlessly fidgeted and fingered her wand, desperate to use it. Desperate to practise more magic. She mustered all the patience she possibly could while Serene brewed the potion.

"I've been struggling to get it right," Serene said. "It has been so frustrating, but I think I am finally getting somewhere. Look," she said.

The potion was a thin, silvery-white, light liquid giving off a thick, murky mist. "All I need to do is drop one final ingredient in here and it will be ready to go." She transferred the liquid and smoke into a vial, dropped a pinch of a powder into it, and stoppered it. Specks of light appeared and disappeared within the mist, like miniature lightning.

"Wow," Nifty gasped. He seemed enthralled.

"I wish we could test it on the kid and send him to some dark corner of the world," Ash said.

"'Ave you noticed him always lurking about and following us in the fields since the incident?" Nifty said.

"Yes, and I don't like it at all."

"Me neither," Nifty said. "How about this?" He coaxed a spider onto his hand from a corner of the room. It was small, and not unpleasant. He let it run from his hand into a cup, and it stood still.

Serene poured some of the potion into the cup, waved her wand in the sign of the rune, and whispered something Ash didn't catch. The spider disappeared. It reappeared where Nifty had taken it from the wall. It was on its fine web, curled into a ball, showing only tiny signs of life in small movements.

"It don't look very happy," Nifty said, cautiously.

"It's confused. But it worked. The potion worked!" Serene said. They all looked at each other excitedly, too excited to speak, too busy trying to process the fact that it could really happen now. They could actually escape. Serene broke the weighted silence. "It's best you quickly sneak this back to where it came from," she said, and gave the spell scroll to Nifty.

"Brilliant. When do we go? Where're we goin'?" Nifty said.

"We need to work a few things out," Ash said.

"Right, of course. Just let me know how else I can help."

The spider stretched itself out into its natural form. It walked along its web. Ash was excited and nervous, and sad about Nifty. Every time her conscience toyed with the idea of taking him with them, something in her vehemently repelled the thought.

"Ash, I have been thinking," Serene said. "Your magic is powerful, though you struggle to control it. It could take you years to learn. Maybe we need to embrace the chaos more. I have been teaching you magic sourced in air, water, and earth because that's what I have been taught. But maybe you need to practise chaos and fire."

"Pardon my interruption," Nifty said. "Fire and chaos don't sound massively safe. And I get that you gotta do what you gotta do, but please don't get yourselves hurt."

"Yes, we will be safe. But we can't do it in here, we will need you to keep a lookout please, Nifty," Serene said.

They left the hideout and Nifty walked through the woods and towards the path to keep a lookout. Ash was wild with excitement. An owl hooted. Insects chirped and clicked. The trees rustled in the breeze, their leaves shaded with darkness and creating patterns against the night sky. Grey clouds moved gently, washed and highlighted with the shining of the moon.

Serene placed a small branch ahead of Ash. She said quietly, "Fire magic comes from rage and anger. I know signs and incantations from memory, but I never practised them, only learnt the theory. Here's a basic one to conjure normal fire. Woodfire." Serene drew a shape in the dirt with her wand. "Make that shape in the air repeatedly, until you can see its form, and concentrate your will on it. Then focus it on the branch. Channel your anger, and feel it coming out of you into the magic."

Ash made the sign with her wand. Nothing appeared in the air. She felt a hint of anger in her and she seized it and focused on it. She fed her anger. She recalled the horror of being tortured in the dungeons in Ul Nirin. She thought about Serene in a pit of filth, bleeding and starving. She pictured the red cuts the magic whip had torn into Nifty's face. His face! Anger welled up inside of her so violently that the wand left a red trail in the air. She felt and focused on the hurt in missing her mother so much.

"Good!" Serene cried, though Ash thought she looked a bit apprehensive.

The sign lingered for a moment and Ash waved her wand towards the branch. The branch caught alight. Her heart raced. A ring of fire dashed from it. Hot with thick smoke. They backed away, panicked, and Ash fell. She scrambled backwards as the fire chased her.

"Aqirus," Serene said. A flood of water appeared and pushed against the fire. The fire held strong for a while until it conceded and disappeared underneath the water. The water splashed and seeped into the ground.

"What happened?" Nifty said, rushing over. "Are you alright?"

"It's unbelievable," Serene said. Her face was pale and dry. Some of the trees around her looked more lifeless than before, drooping and weaker. Concern was deeply etched on Nifty's kind face.

Ash felt so tired, as if standing up would be too much. Serene helped her to her feet and her body felt like stone: cold and heavy. "I don't know if it's right or fair to put you through this," she said. "I will hide this." She took Ash's wand and concealed it with hers inside her clothing.

Nifty threw leaves and kicked dirt over the large, burned trail that had been left by the fire, and they hurried back. Ash was too exhausted to speak. Her mind was a whirl of thoughts and heavy tension.

Serene supported her as they snuck back into the servants' house and huddled under a blanket. Despite the heavy blur of exhaustion, she felt tension amongst the servants. *Did someone just say something about us sneaking off?* She thought she had overheard something. Some glared at her. Though her eyelids were heavy and she wasn't seeing straight, she could have sworn they were glares. They had pushed things too far, sneaking off while others were awake. They had been so stupid. So drawn to the magic and the thought of escaping that nothing else had mattered.

So much fire, Ash thought. *Wild, powerful fire.* She relived the conjuring of the spell, the wildness of the fire, the exhilaration and fear, the curiosity and confusion, and despite being so drained that she could barely stay awake, she longed to do it all again.

The blanket made her feel safe. Cosy, even. She pulled the blanket over her eyes. She needed to rinse her hands and face, but she really didn't want to. She was too tired. So she relaxed with Nifty and Serene around her, and pulled the blanket over even more, tucking it around her face as she let her eyes fall into blackness. Her thoughts were disjointed and she vaguely worried about the servants and their suspicions. But it didn't really affect her. She felt as if her concerns and dreams and thoughts were beyond the petty worries of the servants. She was a conjurer of chaos. A queen of fire. The thought made her smile as she drifted into the dream world.

Serene had convinced Ash not to go to the hideout. She had said that Ash needed rest and she reminded her that the servants had seen them sneaking off at night. They couldn't risk going again, not for a while. Nifty had been told to help out at the house, and so Ash and Serene ate their slop in a corner of the servants' house with a blanket over their knees, as they often did.

"We will leave soon," Serene whispered. "I think it is best if I take us to the palace. Once my mother learns what has happened, she will send the palace guard here right away and we will get revenge on Lord Sully. It's unprecedented. They will have to favour you and Nifty for what you've done for me. We could come back and save Nifty."

"This isn't just about you, Serene. I want to leave the Nine Lands, not gain your mother's favour. I'm going to get my mother and find a way out of here. I don't want to be hunted down, I don't want anybody to know I'm alive."

"Have you got any better ideas? We can't sail, we can't cross Darpirith, the silent desert would consume us, and we can't port beyond the barrier. I will hide you and your mother somewhere safe and find a way to get you out of the Nine Lands."

"Fine," Ash whispered.

They sat in the servants' house for a long time. It was well into the evening and Nifty hadn't returned. Ash began to worry. "He'll come back," she whispered to Serene. As she whispered them, she realised something in her didn't feel right, as if she didn't believe her own words. The servants were preparing to sleep.

Time passed. Snoring, sleepy breathing, and tossing and turning were the only sounds of the night. "They probably just made him stay a bit later to get more work done. He'll be back any moment," Ash whispered. There was zero belief in her words. She knew something was wrong. She could feel it.

"Should we go to the house?" Serene said.

"And do what? It's too risky," Ash said. "He'll be back by morning. What does it matter anyway? We have to leave without him."

Serene gripped Ash's arm tightly. "I wish we didn't have to."

"Me too," Ash said. They lay down to sleep and kept each other warm.

❦

The bell rang. Ash woke in a sweat. Fragmented memories of her dreams invaded her thoughts as quickly as her heart beat against her chest. Fat Lord Sully. Wildfire. Nifty crying out. A mouse turning into an old man. Nifty bleeding, his nails ripped off. Tears ran down her face as she tried to pull herself together.

Nifty was nowhere to be seen.

She hadn't considered, to its full extent, what would happen to him once they disappeared, and she realised she had been naïve. Everyone knew Nifty was their friend. They would be leaving him to a cruel fate. The Sullys wouldn't let things just go back to normal for the servants after they escaped.

The taskmaster barged into the room. Ash's heart sank. She could tell by the smirk on his face that something was terribly wrong. The taskmaster said, "One of you has been caught stealing. There will be no work first thing. We've got a trial and execution to witness." He laughed.

The servants groaned. Nifty's name was whispered here and there.

Serene turned white. Ash kept whispering that it would be okay, Nifty would be okay, repeating it like a mantra, but unable to convince either of them. Nobody washed, nobody ate, they simply dressed—drooping, hesitant, dismayed. This wasn't the first time they had witnessed a trial and execution, that was for sure. Ash hated the sorrow. She hated their apathy. Hated that there was no fight in them. Hated that even though they had made the taskmaster free Serene, they had learnt nothing from it, and had gone back to their old, weakened spirits within days.

Serene furtively slipped Ash's wand into her hand, and Ash slipped it up her sleeve as they followed the taskmaster and other servants out of the servants' house, a heavy sorrow in the air. The mood was glum, and all that could be heard were sorry footsteps, trudging over lifeless ground. The trees surrounding the path seemed to tower over them, shaking their heads at them, telling them they had done wrong, they had messed up, and now they were going to pay the price. Everything else lay heavy, cold and still. The earth itself: solid, still, heavy.

Secretly having her wand on her gave Ash an unfamiliar and unnerving sense of power. She felt a shadow of darkness forming around the pain in her heart. But the darkness wasn't a mood, and it wasn't heavy. Instead, it pulsed an energy into her pain. She began to feel frantic. She didn't want to see Nifty suffer. She couldn't see him executed. She couldn't handle it, and she feared what she might do. She feared what she couldn't control.

Nifty was on the gallows with a rope around his neck. He was battered, bruised, and cut, and his clothes were stained with dirt and blood. His hands were tied behind his back. He looked resolute and surprisingly calm. Ash wished she knew what was going through his incredible mind. An executioner witch stood on the gallows. Lord Sully stood before the crowd.

The crowd was hushed and solemn. Some stood stoically while others fidgeted nervously. Most looked as if they wanted to be sick. It was clear how much of a positive and warming impact Nifty had had on every servant there. Though they had often ignored him and seemed fed up with his cheer, the depth of his positivity and kindness had touched them deeply, and the severity of the situation was weighing down on them now. Ash could see it in their faces, and she could feel it all around her.

Clouds momentarily parted to reveal a cold sun, and closed again darkening the mood even more. Ash's heart beat painfully.

"The servant known as Nifty has been witnessed tampering with the property of witches, a crime punishable by death," Lord Sully said. "Tell them, boy, what did you see?"

Malfin took Lord Sully's side. "Him, that one, he had the scroll. I saw him with it in the house."

The crowd gasped, knowing it was enough to seal Nifty's fate.

"Have you anything to say, servant?" Lord Sully said.

A drizzle of rain spattered down on them from thick grey clouds. Nifty held his head up high and strong. "I'm a servant. I can't read. The scroll'd fallen from the shelf, and I was putting it back, that's all. I'm sure the child is mistaken with his accusations."

Chatter from the crowd, and they said, *He's innocent. Let him be. Let him be.*

"Could you be mistaken, young Malfin?" Lord Sully said.

"No. In the night, yesterday. I saw him. He took it from the shelf."

"That's a lie!" Ash shouted, anger and hatred emboldening her. The taskmaster waved his wand and Ash was hit by something invisible and hard and she flew back into the crowd, stunned.

They pulled her to her feet and brushed her off. The rain fell harder. Lord Sully nodded to the executioner, who flicked his wand and a part of the gallows floor disappeared. Nifty dropped. The crowd cried out.

"Levium," Serene countered. Nifty rose in the air.

For a moment time stood still and the air was charged with shock, confusion, outrage, disbelief, and fury. They stared at Serene, baffled as to how she could have cast magic.

Then chaos.

Lord Sully's eyes blazed and the executioner sneered as they and the taskmaster chanted dark incantations and sent shadows twisting and snaking towards Serene. Swiftly and artfully, Serene traced protective patterns and deflected the spells. The crowd scattered, their cries loud and frenzied. Ash felt panic, she wanted to run. Nifty dropped again and Serene only just lifted him in time before the rope could snap his neck.

Dance, don't run. The words of the old man in the dungeon rang through Ash's mind and she found herself conjuring the fire sign. It seemed to light a fire in her and she threw the sign at the Sullys, the pain in her turning to a cold fury. A flaming ring enveloped the Sullys. Fumbling, astonished and afraid, the executioner and taskmaster conjured water to defend them. The fire was too strong, it roared towards the taskmaster and executioner and closed in on Lord Sully. The wood of the gallows caught alight. They began to scream. The witches fought harder, fighting for their lives, working together to push the fire back.

Serene cut Nifty's rope with a spell as she fought against the crowd to reach him. He fell awkwardly.

Anger raged in Ash. She wanted to burn the witches! Rain streamed down her face as she conjured more fire. It surged from her wand in a magnificent fashion, and slowly and surely consumed the barriers the witches were struggling behind. Fire, so much fire, roaring and surging around the barriers like a dragon.

"Let's go!" Serene said, helping Nifty to his feet and helping him hobble away through the howling and terrified crowd.

Ash's anger only grew and she covered the Sullys with more fire. It raged from her wand and destroyed everything in its path. The water barriers became weaker and weaker while the fire grew and grew, until she couldn't see anything except fire in front of her. She caught up with Serene and Nifty. She put her arm around him and they moved faster along the path and through the woods. They retrieved the vial of porting potion and in a hurry, Serene smashed it on the ground.

The mist enveloped them. Rushing, swirling, being dragged. Lights flickering. A sickly, nauseous feeling that intensified as the rushing of movement increased. Blackness. Nothingness.

Ash found herself on the Princess's bed. Nifty had been sick and was coughing violently. Serene wiped his mouth with a cloth. "You saved me," he said.

All three were silent. In shock. Relieved. Taking it all in.

"I thought I was gonna die, like, really die. I knew they wouldn't believe me, there was nothing I could do, and I'd accepted that. I mean, what else can you do when you know you're gonna die, except think of all the good things you've had and are grateful for. So that's what I was doing when the floor fell away and I felt the rope squeeze my neck, and then you saved me." Nifty's voice was filled with deep awe and reverence. "You're my best friends and now I owe my life to you. More than my life."

"Oh Nifty, you owe us nothing," Princess Serene said. "We wouldn't be here, safe, without you."

"We're safe," Ash mused, faintly. She felt sick and her head ached.

Nifty dragged himself into a seated position, shaking and weak. "Woah, where're we?" He looked around the room slowly, in awe. "I've never seen such a nice room."

"The Palace of Ul Nirin." Ash watched his wide eyes circling the room and taking in the deep blue curtains, the silken bedspread with its embroidered curved and intertwining lines and patterns, and the furniture and walls also with those patterns here and there, the blues, greens, golds, oranges, and charcoals. The vibrant and exotic atmosphere of the witches of Ul Nirin must have been rather peculiar to Nifty.

"Incredible," Nifty said. "Damn incredible." And then Ash saw it dawn on him. "So you *are* a princess," he said, looking at Serene in wonder.

Serene winked at him. "I'm going to find my mother and set everything right," she said, standing up slowly.

"Not yet," Ash said. "We need to rest, and we need to make a plan." She gestured for Serene to lie next to her, and the Princess nestled next to her without any fuss. They both sighed and smiled at each other, looking haggard and exhausted. Ash, finding humour in the situation, broke into a broad grin, and they burst into laughter together.

The enormity of recent events overwhelmed her mind—riots, fleeing the city, labouring in the plantations, all that fire, so much fire! The thought of fire put excitement and dread in her. She sighed once more, a tense exhale laden with anxiety. What had happened had been so significant there would be no going back, she knew that much. Thoughts of the future and what it may hold flooded her mind.

Serene held her hand and said, "It's all going to be okay. We did it. We escaped."

They lay quietly, and Ash found herself in a bit of a daze, the weight and shock of everything pressing down on her heavily. The more she tried to relax, the heavier she felt. Heavier, more exhausted. She was sinking, swirling...

The door burst open and Varamin rushed in with three guards. "Take them away," he said, startling them all.

"Wait, Varamin, it's me, it's Princess Serene!"

"You have a servants brand above your eye," he scoffed. "You don't look like the Princess, and you don't speak like the Princess."

"You saw me Varamin, you saw me during the riots before I was captured. I was branded. You must remember."

"Imposter, I am not falling for that," Varamin said. The three guards with him appeared less sure.

"How do you think I could have ported in here? Only royal blood and certain guards can get past the protection spells."

The three guards nodded to each other.

"That will be for us to figure out. The Princess is dead, and no imposter is going to meddle with the palace on my watch."

"Take me to my mother then, the Queen will know her own daughter."

"The Queen is ill in the mind and body now, everybody knows that. I am her guardian, and I am bound to protect her from threats like you lot." Varamin grabbed Serene.

"What do you mean, ill in the mind?" Serene asked, panic

marking her face as she tried to break free of his grip.

"The Queen is very sick, she fights for her life each day, it's common knowledge." He shook the wriggling Princess.

Serene stiffened and went white. Ash felt tired and bewildered. She tried to muster the feeling of fire but she was too exhausted. She fingered her wand, but Serene shook her head subtly, sternly. Ash frowned but hid her wand.

"You saw me Varamin, you saw they had branded me," Serene pleaded. "You gave me the orb. You're the one person who knows I could have escaped instead of being killed. Don't do this."

"Don't listen to her," he told his guards. "It is clearly rehearsed. This girl is an imposter. Now get them."

The guards yanked them, and roughly tied their hands.

THE END

BOOK 2 COMING SOON

For updates, follow @jkfsandham and @the.elderworld

www.elderworld.io

Please review this novel all over the internet, and tell your friends about it

ABOUT THE AUTHOR

@jkfsandham

J. K. F. Sandham is South African born, raised in England, and resides in Wales. Half his blood is Indian. He lives in Cardiff where he studied English literature, philosophy, and creative writing. He loves all things fantasy and holds the conviction there is more magic in the real world than meets the eye. His writing intends to inspire readers to overcome their adversities and open their minds to new opportunities, whilst entertaining them and immersing them in enchanting fantasy worlds.

J. K. F. also writes gritty British crime as Jameel Sandham

ACKNOWLEDGEMENTS

To everyone who has picked up this book, whether you loved it or hated it, thank you! Your attention is one of the most valuable things in the world, and it means a lot to me that you spent some of it here.

Mum, you helped me shape this book significantly, as well as my love for books and my ability to write. Though, most importantly, you demonstrated what it is to overcome immense adversity. Thank you.

Liz, thank you for all your support, especially when the imposter syndrome kicked in and I questioned whether anybody would like the book at all.

Ashley, you made this book possible in many ways, and you deserve twice the praise for the book cover. I love it!

To Nikki, when I was naïve enough to think I could write the next Lord of the Rings and make enough money from it to never need a job, you were nonetheless unconditionally supportive of that dream, and much of this novel started there. Thank you. Can you believe that was fifteen years ago!

To Byralsy, Kim and all my mum's friends who purchased my handwritten and illustrated stories about dragons for 20p when I was six years old, thank you for your early support and encouragement.

Everyone in the Stag Alliance community, thank you for your support. Onwards, we march!

I extend my heartfelt thanks to everyone who has played a role in shaping this project. Thank you to my beta readers, and to all who in real life and on social media gave me much needed encouragement, ideas, inspiration and lessons about the craft. While it's impossible to name each of you individually, I hope I expressed my appreciation effectively at the time.

Everything is connected—like the threads of one's essence, after all—so in some way everyone and everything has contributed to this book. Thank you!

In partnership with

We're changing the way communities
interact and create online.

Join our community to learn more about
A Tale of the Nine Lands. Meet the author,
team, and community behind the project,
and shape the Elderworld with us.

Printed in Dunstable, United Kingdom

74950133R00127